Dorothy Simpson

DEAD AND GONE

An Inspector Luke Thanet Novel

SCRIBNER

NEW YORK LONDON SYDNEY SINGAPORE

SCRIBNER
1230 Avenue of the Americas
New York, NY 10020

First published in Great Britain in 1999 by
Little, Brown and Company
First Scribner edition 2000

SCRIBNER and design are trademarks of
Macmillan Library Reference USA, Inc., used under
license by Simon & Schuster, the publisher of this work.

Manufactured in the United States of America

1 3 5 7 9 10 8 6 4 2

Library of Congress Cataloging-in-Publication Data
Simpson, Dorothy, 1933–
Dead and gone : an inspector Luke Thanet
novel / Dorothy Simpson. —1st U. S. ed.
p.   cm.
I. Title.
PR6069.I422D36   2000
823'.914—dc21   99-39091
CIP

ISBN 0-684-86336-7

To Charlotte, James and Elliot

And he said, That which cometh out of the man, that defileth the man. For from within, out of the heart of men, proceed evil thoughts, adulteries, fornications, murders, Thefts, covetousness, wickedness, deceit, lasciviousness, an evil eye, blasphemy, pride, foolishness: All these evil things come from within, and defile the man.

Mark 7. 20–23.

ONE

Thanet and Joan were getting ready for bed when the telephone rang. It was just after midnight. Their eyes met. *Alexander?*

Joan was nearest and she snatched up the receiver. 'Hullo?' The tension showed in every line of her body, in the intensity of her concentration. Then she relaxed. 'It's Pater,' she said, handing Thanet the phone.

The Station Officer.

Thanet found that he had been holding his breath. 'What's the problem?' he snapped. Anxiety was making him short-tempered these days.

'Woman gone missing, sir.'

'When was this?'

'Couple of hours ago.'

'Only a couple of hours? So why all the fuss? She probably had a row with her old man and walked out to cool off.' Literally and metaphorically, thought Thanet. It was high summer, school holidays and the middle of a heatwave, a prime time – along with Christmas – for domestic disputes to escalate.

'Her "old man" is Mr Mintar, sir. Mr Ralph Mintar.'

The rising inflection in Pater's voice indicated that he expected Thanet to know who he was talking about. As indeed he did.

'The QC?'

'The same.'

'Ah.' Thanet had come across Mintar in court from time to time. The barrister was hardly the type to lose his head in a crisis. If he had reported his wife missing he must have good reason for concern. 'I see. So what's the story?'

1

'Apparently she disappeared in the middle of entertaining friends. After they finished eating they all decided to go for a swim and everyone went off to change. Only she didn't come back. It was a while before anyone noticed she wasn't there and they've been looking for her ever since.'

'And no apparent reason for her to walk out?'

'Not so far as PC Chambers could gather. And he's pretty much on the ball, as you know.'

'Quite. Well, I'd better get out there. The Super been informed?'

Superintendent Draco liked to keep his finger on the pulse of what was happening on his patch.

'He's away for the weekend, sir.'

'Of course. I forgot.' That was a relief, anyway. Draco had a nasty habit of dogging Thanet's footsteps at the start of any remotely interesting investigation. 'Contact Lineham and lay on some reinforcements, will you? What's the address?'

'Windmill Court, Paxton, sir.'

Thanet scribbled the directions down. It was all too easy to get lost in a maze of country lanes in the dark.

'Sorry, love,' he said to Joan, who was in bed by now.

She shrugged. 'Can't be helped.' But her pretended insouciance did not deceive him. She would have liked him to be with her in case there was any more news.

They were both desperately worried about their daughter Bridget, who was thirty-two weeks pregnant with her first baby and had suddenly developed toxaemia. Although Lineham's wife Louise had had similar problems when their first child was born, until a few days ago Thanet and Joan hadn't known precisely what the prognosis was, but Alexander, her husband, was keeping them up to date on what was happening and they had learned fast: Bridget's blood pressure was alarmingly high and there was protein in her urine. She was therefore in danger of pre-eclampsia – fits – and the baby's oxygen supply was threatened. She had been taken into hospital for monitoring.

Thanet finished knotting his tie and went to sit on the bed, took Joan's hands in his. 'If you need me, just ring and I'll get back as soon as I can.'

She shook her head. 'I don't suppose we'll hear anything more tonight.'

'All the same . . .'

'I know.'

He kissed her and left.

Outside it was still very warm, well over twenty degrees, and Thanet took off his jacket and slung it on to the passenger seat before getting into the car. Then he wound down the window to get a breath of fresh air as he drove. At this time of night there was very little traffic about and once he plunged into the country lanes his seemed to be the only vehicle on the road.

In an attempt to damp down his worries about Bridget he tried to focus on Ralph Mintar. What did he know about him? Not a lot, it seemed. As a member of the South-Eastern Circuit Mintar was a familiar figure in courtrooms all over Kent and Sussex – less so, of course, since taking silk a few years ago. QCs travel further afield, sometimes having to stay away from home for weeks or even months at a time. Still, he didn't suppose Mintar had changed much. Always looking as though he had just had a wash and brush-up, the QC was a dapper, well-groomed figure, reticent and self-contained. He belonged to what Thanet always thought of as the softly softly school of advocacy, leading witnesses gently on from one apparently innocuous point to another until they suddenly found that they had fenced themselves in and there was no way out but the direction in which counsel had wanted them to go.

Thanet knew that in a high percentage of cases of domestic murder it is the husband who has perpetrated the crime. If the worst had happened and Mrs Mintar had come to a sticky end, Mintar would be a formidable suspect to deal with. Thanet felt the first stirrings of excitement. He hoped, of course, that she would be found alive and well, but if she wasn't, well, he had always relished a challenge.

He braked sharply to avoid a rabbit which had appeared from nowhere to scuttle across the road in front of him and had then stopped dead, transfixed by his headlights. He put the car into bottom gear and began to edge forward. *Go on, go on,* he muttered. *Move!* At last, just as he was about to brake again, it turned and dashed off into the undergrowth at the side of the lane.

He was on a slight rise here and ahead of him he could

now see some scattered lights. That must be Paxton. Street lighting would be sparse, as it always was in the villages, and he guessed that there would be few people still up – though more than usual, perhaps, as it was a Saturday night. He was right. Apart from the occasional glow from an upstairs window, Paxton appeared to be sunk in slumber. The village consisted of one long, straggling street with a pub at each end, one of them opposite the church. There was also a Post Office cum general shop, increasingly a rarity nowadays as the supermarkets killed off their smaller rivals.

Thanet had memorised Pater's directions: Turn left at the far end of the village into Miller's Lane. Take the first right then the second left and it's on the right, a hundred yards past the windmill.

There was the dark bulk of the windmill now, its sails a stark silhouette against the night sky and this, no doubt about it, was Windmill Court, lit up like a cruise liner. Thanet swung in between the tall wrought-iron gates and halfway up the drive pulled up for a moment to admire it. The mill owner must have been a prosperous man for he had built himself a fine dwelling. Classic in proportions and as symmetrical as a child's drawing, it looked for all the world like an elegant doll's house awaiting inspection. One half expected the front to swing open, revealing exquisitely furnished miniature rooms. As Thanet studied it someone came to peer out of one of the downstairs windows. There were no cars parked at the front so he decided to follow the drive which curved off around the left side of the house. Here, in front of a long low building which had probably once been stables, were several parked cars, one of them a patrol car. Lineham's Ford Escort was not among them, he noted. As he got out a uniformed constable hurried forward to greet him.

'Ah, Chambers,' said Thanet. 'No one else here yet?'

'No, sir. Just the two of us until now. Simmonds is inside.'

'They'll be along shortly. I gather you were first on the scene. Fill me in, will you?'

There wasn't much more to tell at this stage and as Thanet listened he looked around, taking in his surroundings. The cars were parked on a gravelled area which flanked a well-illuminated

L-shaped courtyard with an ornamental well in the middle. One side of the L was a single storey extension. A granny annexe, perhaps? Someone was a keen gardener: carefully trained climbers clothed the walls, and there were numerous tubs and urns of bedding plants. A faint fragrance hung in the still, warm air.

A door opened, casting a swathe of light across the paving stones, and PC Simmonds emerged, peering into the relative darkness where Thanet and Chambers were standing. There was a woman behind him.

Thanet moved to meet them and Simmonds introduced him. 'And this is Mrs Mintar senior, sir.'

'You took your time getting here,' she said. 'And I don't know what good you think just one more policeman is going to do.'

'Reinforcements will be along shortly, ma'am,' said Thanet. He was about to suggest that they go inside when, as if to prove him right, vehicles could be heard approaching and a few moments later two more police cars arrived, followed by Lineham's Escort. They'd supplied him with eight officers. Good. That would suffice for now. There was only a limited amount that they could do in the dark. If necessary they'd draft in more tomorrow.

'Excuse me for a moment, Mrs Mintar.' Thanet went to meet Lineham, pleased that the sergeant had arrived. They had worked together for so long now that he felt incomplete beginning an investigation without him.

'What's the story, sir?' said Lineham.

'I've only just got here; you probably know as much as I do at the moment. I'm about to interview the mother-in-law. Get this lot organised to do a search of the grounds, then join me.'

Thanet accompanied Mrs Mintar into the house. She led him through a well-appointed kitchen and square hall into a spacious drawing room. It was, as might be expected in a household such as this, an elegant room, furnished with well-polished antiques, luxuriously soft sofas and curtains with elaborate headings. French windows stood wide open to admit the marginally cooler night air and moths were fluttering around the lamps. Thanet crossed the room to glance outside: a broad terrace surrounded by a low brick wall with a gap opposite leading to a shallow flight of steps. Beyond, the shimmer of water. A swimming pool, by the look of it.

Mrs Mintar did not sit down. Instead, she went to the window at the front of the house and stood looking out, as if she expected her missing daughter-in-law to come strolling up the drive. 'Everyone has gone off again to look for Virginia.' There was impatience rather than anxiety in her tone. 'My son will be here shortly, I expect.'

'Everyone?'

She turned to face him and he saw her properly for the first time. She was older than he had first thought, he realised, well into her seventies. He should have known she would be as Mintar must be in his fifties. He had been misled by her slim, wiry figure, the vigour with which she moved and her hair, which was a deep chestnut brown without a trace of grey and was cut in a cropped, modern style. She was wearing cinnamon-coloured linen trousers and a loose long-sleeved silk tunic in the same colour. Around her neck was a leather thong from which depended an intricately carved wooden pendant. The effect was stylish, somewhat unconventional, and not exactly what Thanet would have expected of Mintar's mother. What would he have expected, if he'd thought about it? What was it that Joan called that flowery print material? Liberty lawn, that was it. Yes, made up into a dress with a high neck and full skirt. No, Mrs Mintar senior definitely wasn't the Liberty lawn type.

She sighed. 'Oh God, I suppose I'm the one who'll have to give you all the dreary details, as there's no one else here.' She turned to peer out of the window again. 'Where on earth has Ralph got to? He surely should be back by now.'

Still no word of concern about her daughter-in-law, Thanet noted. 'Meanwhile . . .' he said. Then, 'Won't you sit down, Mrs Mintar? I need as much information as you can give me.'

With one last glance down the drive she perched reluctantly on the very edge of a nearby chair. 'If I must.'

Thanet sat down facing her. 'If you could begin by telling me who "everyone" is?'

She sighed again and ticked the names off on her fingers as she spoke – long, elegant fingers with short workmanlike nails. 'My son Ralph; Virginia's sister Jane and her boyfriend Arnold something-or-other, they're down for the weekend; Howard and Marilyn Squires, our next-door neighbours, they were here for dinner too; and my granddaughter Rachel and her—'

As if on cue hurried footsteps could be heard on the terrace and a young couple erupted into the room, the girl towing the man behind her.

'Gran! Have they found her?' she said, dropping his hand and rushing across to her grandmother. Thanet might just as well have been invisible.

She was in her late teens, Thanet guessed, with the type of middle-class good looks which feature in the *Harpers & Queen* portrait: regular features and long, straight, blonde hair which shone white-gold in the lamplight. She was wearing an abbreviated bright pink cotton sundress which revealed a perfectly even golden tan.

The man hung back, acknowledging Thanet with a nod. He was considerably older than the girl – in his late twenties, Thanet guessed – and had the type of good looks Thanet always associated with male models: clean-cut, chiselled features and immmaculately cut hair as fair as Rachel's. He was wearing slightly baggy dark green chinos, a pale mauve long-sleeved silk shirt – brand new, by the look of the tell-tale creases down each side of the front – canvas deck shoes and white socks. Irrationally and instinctively Thanet felt a twinge of . . . what? Dislike? Mistrust? He wasn't sure. He only knew that he was glad Bridget had never brought home anyone like this. *Oh God, Bridget . . . Please let her be all right . . .* With an effort he dragged his attention back to the matter in hand.

Mrs Mintar shook her head. 'Not yet.'

Lineham slipped unobtrusively into the room. *All organised.*

'And you've called the police!' said Rachel. 'We saw the cars. Oh, Gran . . .' The girl dropped to her knees beside the old woman and buried her head in her lap. 'I can't bear it. It's Caro, all over again.'

Thanet's eyebrows went up and he gave Mrs Mintar a questioning glance. But her attention was focused on Rachel. 'Now don't talk like that, darling,' she said, stroking the girl's head. 'That simply isn't true. Your mother's only been gone a couple of hours. She'll be back soon, you'll see.'

7

Rachel looked up. 'But where can she *be*? Why should she just disappear like that? Where can she have *gone*?'

'Miss Mintar?' said Thanet gently.

She swung around to look at them. 'You're policemen.'

'Yes. Detective Inspector Thanet, Sturrenden CID. And this is Detective—'

She jumped up. 'A Detective Inspector! I knew it! She really has disappeared, hasn't she? Oh, Matt . . .' She whirled and ran to the man, who opened his arms to her. 'What if they never find her? Oh God, oh God, oh God, I can't bear it. It *is* Caro all over again. It is, it is, it is.' And she burst into tears, burying her face in his chest.

'What does she mean?' Thanet asked her grandmother softly. 'Who is Caro?'

Mrs Mintar shook her head irritably. 'Her sister,' she said in a low voice. 'Caroline eloped, four years ago. The circumstances are entirely different. Rachel was very upset at the time; she and Caroline were very close. All this is bound to bring it back to her.'

Headlights flashed briefly across the window. Another car was coming up the drive. Mrs Mintar hurried across to peer out. 'That may be Ralph now.'

'Dad?' said Rachel, twisting out of her boyfriend's arms. 'Perhaps he's found her!' And she dashed out.

Mrs Mintar shrugged and pulled a face. 'I'm not sure it was him.' She returned to her chair. 'We'll soon find out, no doubt.'

Thanet glanced at the man called Matt. 'And you are . . . ?'

'Matthew Agon. Rachel's fiancé.'

This last was said with a hint of defiance and a sidelong glance at old Mrs Mintar.

Her lips tightened but otherwise she declined to give Agon the satisfaction of reacting.

The first hint of family disapproval? Thanet wondered. Scarcely surprising, considering his own reaction to the man. 'You and Miss Mintar have been searching the garden, I suppose?'

'Yes. Pointless, really, we'd all hunted there for ages before splitting up.' Agon crossed to an armchair and sat down. 'Anyway, Rachel wanted to have another look so we did. Mr Mintar

8

and Mr Squires both went off by car, in different directions, with Mrs Mintar's sister and her boyfriend.'

A Londoner, thought Thanet. East End, by the sound of it. And, he guessed, not really at home in this setting, although he was doing his best to appear at ease.

'Are the gardens very large?' Thanet asked the old woman.

She lifted her shoulders slightly. 'A couple of acres or so, I suppose.'

The door opened and Rachel came back in, followed by Mintar and a woman, their faces betraying their lack of success. For the first time Thanet saw the barrister less than immaculate: his hair was slightly dishevelled and the sweatshirt which he had pulled on over his open-necked shirt was inside out. The woman must be Mrs Mintar's sister – Jane, was it? She was in her early forties, he guessed, and looked both prosperous and self-possessed. Her face was too wide, nose too prominent and eyes too small for beauty, but she had taken considerable trouble over her appearance: her shoulder-length brown hair had been cut by an expert hand and she was carefully made up. She had done her best to disguise her broad shoulders, wide hips and heavy pendulous breasts with an ankle-length straight black skirt and a silk tunic top similar in style to old Mrs Mintar's in a black and white print.

'Ah,' said Mintar. 'Inspector . . . Thanet, isn't it?'

'Yes, sir. And this is Detective-Sergeant Lineham. You've had no luck, I gather?'

Mintar shook his head. 'No sign of her. Oh, sorry, this is my sister-in-law.'

She gave a brief smile of acknowledgement and said, 'Jane Simons.'

Mintar crossed to a side table where bottles, decanters and glasses stood on a silver tray, and poured himself a shot of whisky. He held up the bottle. 'Anyone?' There was no response.

Rachel had gone to perch on the arm of the chair in which her boyfriend was sitting and Thanet thought he saw a twinge of distaste cross Mintar's face as his eye fell upon them.

Mintar drank the whisky in a single gulp and poured himself another, but he put the glass down without drinking any more and, gripping the edge with both hands, leaned heavily on the table, his bowed head and hunched back eloquent of his despair. His sister-in-law, who had seated herself nearby, rose swiftly and went to put an arm around his shoulders. 'I'm sure she'll turn up, Ralph,' she said. 'There must be some perfectly reasonable explanation for her disappearance.'

'What, for example?' He twisted to face her, needing, Thanet guessed, to find a focus for his frustration. Time to intervene.

'I think it would be more constructive if you could give me some idea of what happened here this evening,' he said.

Mintar made a visible effort to pull himself together. 'Very well.' Leaving the second glass of whisky where it was, he crossed to stand in front of the fireplace with his hands clasped together behind him, dominating the room. 'Briefly,' he said, 'we had a supper party here tonight. Afterwards, most people decided to go for a swim.'

Headlights again flashed across the front window. 'That'll be Howard,' said Mintar. He hurried out, followed by Jane Simons and Rachel.

Thanet and Lineham exchanged glances. *We're never going to get anywhere at this rate.*

Suddenly the room seemed full of people as they all came back in together. Mintar shook his head despondently. 'No joy.' He introduced the two new arrivals, both in their mid-forties: Howard Squires and Arnold Prime. They were a complete contrast to each other, the next-door neighbour being shorter and more compact of build, moving with an easy grace, Jane Simons's boyfriend well over six feet, loose limbed and gangling.

Thanet tried again. 'Mr Mintar was just giving me some idea of what happened here this evening. If you would all sit down . . . ?'

All but Mintar complied. He returned to stand before the fireplace, as if establishing his authority in the room.

'So,' said Thanet to Mintar when they were settled, 'if you would go on with what you were saying, sir . . .' Looking around, he could not prevent an inward smile: the room was beginning to resemble the denouement of an Agatha Christie mystery, the difference being that here they were at the beginning of a case, not the end, and were not even sure yet whether any crime had been committed. Though the cast

10

was not quite complete, he realised: Mrs Squires wasn't here. He wondered why.

Mintar nodded. 'Right. Well, I was just explaining that after supper everyone except me decided to go swimming—'

'And me,' said Mrs Mintar.

'Sorry, before you go on, sir, may I just ask if there'd been any kind of . . . disagreement, during supper? Any arguments, quarrels, even?'

Headshakes all around.

Thanet saw with some concern that Rachel's hands were starting to shake. After her earlier outburst she had been very quiet and he thought she had settled down.

Mintar hadn't noticed and he gave a barely suppressed sigh of impatience. 'Everyone except myself – and Mother' – he corrected himself with a glance in her direction – 'decided to go swimming. I had some work to do and was glad of the chance to excuse myself. I went straight to my study and stayed there. At around a quarter to eleven Rachel came to ask me if I'd seen her mother. She told me they hadn't realised at first that Ginny wasn't around. They'd looked in all the obvious places, she said, but—'

'We couldn't find her!' Rachel burst out. 'We'd looked everywhere! And then Dad came out, and we looked all over again. We looked and we looked, but she was gone! She'd just . . . disappeared!' The shaking was more obvious now.

Her father took a few steps towards her but she didn't notice, turning her head into Matthew Agon's chest as she started to weep.

Howard Squires jumped up. 'I'll get something,' he said, and hurried out.

Thanet was interested to note a flash of pure dislike in Mrs Mintar's eyes as she watched him go.

'Howard is our family doctor,' Mintar explained.

It was pointless to continue, Thanet decided. If Virginia Mintar really had disappeared, normal procedure would in any case be to interview everyone separately. He just seemed to have been pushed into this somewhat fruitless situation by circumstances. 'I think we'll leave this for the moment, sir. Miss Mintar is obviously very distressed and I suggest she be taken to her room. We'll go and see how the men are getting on outside and then, with your permission, we'll do a preliminary search of the house.'

Mintar hesitated, then gave a weary nod and waved a hand. 'Whatever you think necessary.'

Outside in the hall Lineham rolled his eyes. 'Whew! What a crew!'

'That's one way of putting it. We'll go back out via the kitchen.'

'A lot of undercurrents, didn't you think, sir? The prospective son-in-law doesn't exactly seem to be the flavour of the month, does he, and as for the old lady . . . She's a real acid drop, isn't she? Didn't seem to care tuppence that her daughter-in-law has apparently vanished into thin air, so she can't have been on particularly good terms with her. And did you see the way she looked at Dr Squires as he went out?'

'He's obviously done something to upset her.'

'I'll say! And I can tell you this, I wouldn't fancy her for an enemy myself.'

'What are you saying, Mike?'

The sergeant shrugged. 'Just that if young Mrs Mintar turns out to have had a nasty accident her mother-in-law would certainly go on my list.'

'Let's not jump the gun. We've no idea yet what's happened to her.'

'Difficult to think of an innocent explanation, though, isn't it?'

'Mmm.'

'Of course, just because they all agreed there hadn't been a quarrel doesn't mean that there wasn't one, does it?' They had reached the kitchen and Lineham waved a hand. 'I mean, say she came in here to tidy up a bit before changing and someone followed her . . .'

'True.' Thanet looked around. Dishes were stacked in little piles on the work surfaces near the sink and the dishwasher stood open. He stooped to look inside. Someone had loaded in the dinner plates, knives, forks and a couple of pudding dishes, but had left the task unfinished. Five more of the latter stood on the draining board nearby. 'I wonder if it was Mrs Mintar

12

who stacked the dishwasher. If so, it looks as though she was interrupted.'

Lineham picked up a champagne bottle which stood amidst a cluster of appropriate glasses and held it up to the light. 'Empty,' he said. 'Some kind of celebration?'

There was a tap on the window: PC Chambers was outside with several of the men.

Thanet and Lineham went out into the courtyard. 'Any luck?'

'Not so far, sir. It's difficult in the dark – lots of shrub borders and a small spinney at the far end of the garden.'

'I'm sure it must be. If no one finds anything and there's still no news of her by morning we'll put a lot more men on to it.'

But the initial search was concluded without success and after a brief search inside the house Thanet decided to call it a day. 'We'll be back first thing tomorrow,' he assured Mintar. 'Meanwhile, let's hope she turns up.'

She did, but not in the way Thanet had hoped. Next morning he was shaving when the phone call came.

'Bad news?' said Joan, as he put down the receiver.

'Mrs Mintar's body has been found. In a well in the garden.'

TWO

Lineham came hurrying across as Thanet's car drew up in the courtyard.

'You must have put your foot down, Mike.'

Lineham grinned. 'I was up and dressed and having my breakfast when I heard.'

The sergeant had always been an early riser.

'The SOCOs will be here soon,' he went on. 'I didn't see much point in taping off the whole courtyard, in view of all the people who were tramping through it last night, so I've just isolated the area around the well. I hope that's OK?'

'Fine.'

'And I've called the fire brigade. The gardener says the well's about sixty feet deep.'

'Good.' Kent no longer had an Underwater Search Unit and it wouldn't be worth calling on West Sussex for this. The fire brigade was used to cooperating with the police. Thanet glanced at a middle-aged man leaning against the wall near the door to the annexe. 'That him?'

'Yes. He found the body. And I said to notify Doc Mallard that we'd need him later. There's no point in him coming just yet. It'll take a while to get her out.'

'Quite.'

'Uh-oh, here comes Mr Mintar. Better brace yourself, sir. He's on the warpath, demanding to know why the well wasn't searched last night.'

That makes two of us, thought Thanet. How could he have overlooked something so obvious? All the way over in the car

14

he had been trying to answer that question, and the only explanation he could come up with was that he hadn't realised it was the genuine article, had thought it a purely ornamental feature. Even so . . . *Never take anything for granted,* he thought. *How often have I tried to din that into my team?*

'Here he comes.'

Mintar came charging across the courtyard, obviously seeking a focus for his anger. He had dressed in a hurry. One side of his shirt collar was tucked inside and he was wearing no socks. He was unshaven and seemed to have aged ten years overnight: every line on his face seemed to sag and his skin looked parched, as though all the youth and vigour had been irretrievably sucked out of it. Not so his eyes, which burned with fierce emotion.

'Thanet!' he said. 'About time too! I hope you're going to come up with a reason for your disgraceful negligence! Why the hell wasn't the well investigated last night? It's such an obvious place to look.'

In that case, why did you all overlook it too? But Thanet knew Mintar was right. The well should have been checked and that was that.

'You do realise that if my wife had been found then she might still be alive?'

Thanet trusted that this would prove not to be the case. Leaving aside any culpability on his part, Mrs Mintar was dead and nothing could bring her back. He hoped for her sake that death had come swiftly and mercifully.

'I assure you that I'm as concerned as you are to find out what went wrong.'

'I should hope so! In any case, you can rest assured that I shall be taking the matter up with your superiors.'

There was no point in making excuses. 'I can only apologise.'

But Mintar was not to be mollified. 'Easy enough to say that, isn't it? Words cost nothing. But they certainly won't bring her back.'

'I really am deeply sorry about your wife.'

'Yes, well, just think how you'd be feeling if it was your wife down there.' Mintar glanced at the well and perhaps it was the image which his words conjured up that unmanned him for suddenly his anger seemed to evaporate and he stopped, swallowed hard, his mouth trembling. 'You can't begin to imagine—' He turned abruptly away and blundered towards the kitchen door.

Lineham made as if to follow but Thanet stopped him. 'It wouldn't do any good at the moment. He needs to be alone for a while. Let's have a word with the gardener. What's his name?'

'Digby.'

'Going to be another scorcher, don't you think?' said Lineham as they walked across the courtyard.

Thanet agreed. Already, even so early in the morning, he could feel the heat of the sun's rays penetrating his lightweight jacket. He glanced at the cloudless sky, screwing up his eyes at the white-hot haze which surrounded the incandescent sun. He blinked to clear his vision, seeing dazzling silver discs within his eyelids.

Digby didn't look a very prepossessing character, he thought as they drew nearer. The gardener continued to lean against the wall, arms folded, watching them with a sardonic expression. He had a long lugubrious face with drooping jowls and soft pouches beneath the eyes. For one who worked out of doors his skin was surprisingly pasty, the colour of moist putty, and his wispy hair had been carefully combed across his scalp in an attempt to diguise the fact that there was little of it.

Thanet longed to bark, sergeant-major fashion, 'Stand up straight when we're talking to you!' Instead he said mildly, 'Tell us what happened this morning.'

'I've told him once already,' said Digby, jerking his head at Lineham. The man managed to make the word 'him' sound like an insult.

Well educated, Thanet thought, with just a trace of Kentish accent.

'I'd like to hear it for myself. In detail, please.'

Digby sighed and shrugged. 'Suit yourself. I was crossing the courtyard when I noticed that watering can standing beside the well. It struck me as odd. Mrs Mintar was always very fussy about not leaving tools and stuff lying around. Fanatical, you might say.' He glanced around. 'This courtyard was her pride and joy and she liked to keep it shipshape.'

Thanet looked as well. He had noticed last night that a great deal of hard work and loving care had been expended on the courtyard. Mrs Mintar had obviously been very fond of flowers. Climbing roses and clematis intermingled on the house walls; there were hanging baskets overflowing with colourful annuals and an abundance of terracotta pots and tubs. 'She looked after all of this herself?'

Digby nodded. 'Except for watering the camellias, yes.' He pointed out the four big evergreen shrubs planted in wooden half barrels on either side of both kitchen and annexe doors. 'I do them, during the week, anyway. Mrs Mintar did them at weekends.'

'Why didn't she always do those?'

'It's a heavier job. We use water from the well for them.'

'Ah.' Thanet was beginning to see where this was leading.

'Why?' said Lineham.

'Lovely soft water, isn't it. Tap water around here is very hard and camellias don't like it.'

'Go on,' said Thanet.

'Well, when I picked up the can I realised it was half full. Now that was even more peculiar. I mean to say, who'd leave a can half full of water, in a heat wave? But then I thought, perhaps they'd had people around last night, and she hadn't quite finished watering when they arrived, forgot to complete the job later. And sure enough, when I checked, I found that two of the camellias were bone dry. So I thought I might as well finish the job off.'

'Very conscientious of you,' said Lineham.

Digby scowled. 'It's important to keep camellias well watered in July and August, that's when the flower buds for the following year are forming. Anyway, I used up the water in the can first then went to draw more from the well. That was when I noticed the chain wasn't across and the padlock wasn't locked – the key was still in it.'

Apparently Mrs Mintar had been fussy about safety as far as the well was concerned, dating back to when the children were small. She had therefore had a removable cover made and this was always secured by a padlock and chain.

'Let's be clear about this. You're saying the cover was on the well but that it wasn't secured in any way?'

17

'Yes. Anyway, I took the lid off, the bucket went down, hit bottom, as I thought, and came up empty. I knew the water was getting low, she'd been worried in case it wouldn't last the season, but not that low. So I looked down.' He shrugged. 'That was when I saw her.'

'Let's take a look,' Thanet said to Lineham. And to Digby, 'Wait here, please.'

Normally he dreaded that first sight of a corpse but this time he approached the well without the usual churning in his gut. She would, after all, be sixty feet down. The bad moments would come later, when the body was brought to the surface.

The well was in the centre of the courtyard and in mitigation of his negligence last night Thanet could see why he had mentally dismissed it as purely ornamental, for ornamental it certainly was. Surrounded by a low wall of dressed stone, it was spanned by a decorative wrought-iron arch. The bucket suspended from the roller at the centre of the arch, however, should have alerted him to the fact that it might still be in use.

In the distance vehicles could be heard approaching.

'Sounds like the fire engine,' said Lineham. He had equipped himself with a torch and he switched it on as they ducked under the tape.

Thanet's over-sensitive back muscles protested as, careful not to touch the coping, they leaned over and peered down into the darkness. Far, far down the torch beam picked out a splash of brilliant colour and a paler crescent which could be the side of her face. Yes, it was. As Thanet's eyes adjusted to the dimmer light he began to make out the shape of a half-submerged crumpled body more clearly. 'Not much doubt about it, I'm afraid, is there,' he said, straightening up.

'Notice that, sir?' Lineham nodded at a smear of what looked like blood on the inner edge of the coping. 'Bashed her head as she went over, perhaps?'

'Quite possibly.'

They stood back and he and Lineham studied the well cover which was leaning against the low wall. It was made of varnished lightweight wood with a semicircular metal handle at each side to facilitate removal. When in position it rested on a narrow ledge fashioned around the inner rim of the wall.

'How did you say it's secured?' said Lineham to Digby, who was watching them with the same sardonic twist to his mouth.

'There's a chain over on the far side permanently attached to the wall. When the cover's put back on you just run the chain through the two handles and padlock it to that staple, on this side.'

The padlock was hooked through the staple, hanging open, key still in the lock. 'Simple but effective,' said Thanet. 'Where is that key normally kept? Somewhere handy, I imagine, if both you and Mrs Mintar had to have easy access to it.'

'On a bit of wire hooked over the rim of the bucket.'

The courtyard was suddenly full of noise and bustle as Scenes-of-Crime Officers, firemen and ambulancemen arrived simultaneously. Samples of blood were taken from the smear on the coping and then the well cover was carefully removed and stored in one of the SOCOs' cardboard boxes.

'D'you think we'll be likely to get any useful prints off it?' Thanet asked the SOCO sergeant.

The man shrugged. 'We might. Fortunately it's not rough wood, the surface is smooth and it's been varnished. When did the victim go missing?'

'Last night,' said Lineham. 'Around ten, we think.'

'In that case you might be in luck. If it had rained between then and now . . .'

'They'd have been washed off.'

'In effect, yes. It's the salts in sweat that create the prints and as rain would interact with them, either there wouldn't be any prints left or not enough to be useful.'

'Why are you taking the well cover away?'

Thanet hadn't noticed Mintar come up behind them.

'To test it for fingerprints, sir.'

'Why can't that be done on the spot? We can't have the well left uncovered, it's too dangerous.'

Thanet and Lineham looked at the SOCO sergeant, who said, 'It's best done in the lab, sir.'

'Why?'

'Because it'll be done by the superglue method.'

'What's that?'

'We put the article in a cubicle and suspend it from a wooden pole, rather like hanging washing out to dry. Then a small "boat" – a round metal tray two to three inches in diameter – with superglue in it is placed below it and heated. The fumes rise and attach themselves to the article and in fifteen to twenty minutes the fingerprints will show.'

'A pointless exercise in this case, if you ask me,' said Mintar. 'It'll be covered with prints.'

'You never know, sir,' said Lineham. 'In any case, we can't afford to miss the chance of getting a useful result.'

'I'm afraid we'll have to take the prints of everyone who was here last night,' said Thanet. 'And of Digby, of course.' How could he put this tactfully? 'Look, sir, I'm sorry, I should have said so earlier, but I'd be grateful if you would make it clear to the family that this courtyard is temporarily out of bounds.'

Mintar gave a bitter laugh. 'That includes me, I suppose. Very well.' He turned away. 'But if that lid is going to be missing for any length of time,' he said over his shoulder, 'just make sure you supply us with a temporary cover. We don't want any more accidents.'

'Just as a matter of interest,' said Lineham to the SOCO sergeant, 'how on earth did anyone discover you could use superglue like that?'

The sergeant grinned. 'Pure chance. Some characters working in a photographic department broke a plastic tray. They wanted to use it, so they stuck it together with superglue. The room was hot and when they came in next day they found the whole room plastered with visible fingerprints.'

The firemen's chief approached. 'We're ready to start the lifting operation now, Inspector.'

As there was very little water in the well they had decided a wet suit would not be necessary. Thanet and Lineham watched as a fireman in protective clothing and waders was fastened into a cradle and lowered down into the well at the end of a rope, carrying a sling in which to raise the body.

It was a lengthy operation and Mallard arrived well before they were finished. 'It's Mrs Mintar down there, I gather,' he said after they had greeted each other.

'Yes. D'you know her personally?'

'I've met her once or twice, but only casually. What's the story?'

Thanet told him the little they knew. 'We haven't started interviewing yet. I wanted to see her brought up first.'

'How's Bridget?' The little doctor was a longstanding family friend and had watched Thanet's children grow up. Childless himself, he had always taken a keen interest in their welfare and especially in Bridget since his second marriage to Helen Fields the cookery writer. Bridget was also a professional cook and she and Helen had spent a lot of time together, concocting and testing new recipes.

Thanet grimaced. 'Not good, I'm afraid.'

'You must be worried stiff. Which hospital is she in?'

'The West Middlesex.'

'Good. That has an excellent ultrasound department. What's happening at the moment?'

'Well, they were concerned about the blood flow, apparently, so yesterday she was taken over to Queen Charlotte's, where they have a foetal assessment unit, whatever that means.'

'It means they have the most up-to-date equipment to measure the baby's heart-rate, its growth, the blood flow in the cord and also to carry out the latest and most sophisticated test, measurement of the baby's cerebral blood flow.'

'Well, all those tests were apparently normal.'

'Excellent! That's great news.'

'So she was taken back to the West Middlesex and we're waiting to see what happens next. What is that most likely to be, do you think?'

'I'd imagine she'd have two steroid injections, twelve hours apart, to mature the baby's lungs, just in case it has to be induced early. It'll take forty-eight hours or so for the lungs to mature, then it'll have a reasonably good chance of survival.'

'What do you mean by "reasonably good"?'

But Thanet wasn't to find out. While they were talking the fireman who had gone down the well had been brought back up to the surface and now they began slowly to haul up the body. In a few minutes they would see her properly for the first time. Thanet braced himself as he moved forward with

Lineham and Mallard, conscious of the familiar symptoms: increased heart-rate, sweaty palms, sick feeling in the pit of his stomach. Nothing he could do, nothing he could tell himself, ever seemed to cushion the ripples of horror and dismay he invariably felt during these few moments. There was something so infinitely pathetic about the body of someone who had met a violent end. He had heard people who worked in hospices say that death could be a peaceful, even uplifting affair, but that could surely never be true for those who went unprepared to their graves. Thanet could do nothing to change that but he could and did vow afresh each time that he would do his level best to ensure that those deaths should not go unavenged.

And here she came, a limp, lifeless, sodden bundle. Gentle gloved hands reached out to protect her body from further damage as she was lifted over the wall and laid on the waiting stretcher. Thanet took several deep, unobtrusive breaths. Gradually the pounding in his ears subsided and he began to absorb what he was seeing. At first he was puzzled. Although he was certain they had never met, she looked vaguely familiar. Then he realised that it was her likeness to Rachel which was confusing him. Although disfigured by smears of dirt and an extensive graze on one side of her forehead, here were the same oval face, same bone structure, same slim, shapely body, its more mature curves mercilessly exposed to public gaze by the virtually transparent nature of the wet, clinging silk of the fuschia pink blouse and matching palazzo pants she was wearing. No underwear, Thanet noted.

'What a waste,' said one of the firemen. 'A real looker, wasn't she?'

'You'll go down again?' said Thanet to the man who had rescued her. 'I'd like a thorough search of the bottom of the well.'

The fireman nodded. 'Sure.'

Photographs taken, Thanet and Lineham waited while Doc Mallard finished his examination of the body. But the little doctor was unwilling to commit himself as to cause of death. 'You'll have to wait for the PM, I'm afraid.'

'But at a guess?'

The doctor struggled up. Thanet and Lineham knew better

than to offer a helping hand and a fireman who did not was simply ignored. 'Well, as you can see for yourself it looks as though she might have banged her head on the parapet as she went over and this could well have knocked her out. Then I'd say she probably drowned. If so, the diatom test will confirm it.'

Thanet escorted Mallard back to his car then returned to the courtyard.

'More or less what we expected,' said Lineham.

'Mmm. Better ask Mr Mintar if he wants to see his wife before they take her away, I suppose.'

They found him in the kitchen. Someone had cleared up in here since last night, Thanet noticed. Mintar had been watching proceedings from the window and not surprisingly declined Thanet's invitation. 'I don't want to see her like that.'

'There's the matter of formal identification, sir.'

'Later, if you don't mind. When . . . when you've . . . When she's been . . .'

'I understand. If we could just ask you a few questions, then, sir?'

'Better come into the study.'

23

THREE

Mintar's study was exactly as Thanet would have expected: spacious, book-lined, carpeted, well equipped with leather-topped desk, computer equipment and expensive dark green leather desk chair. His profession was immediately obvious from the serried ranks of bound law reports, copies of Archbold and *Current Law Statutes* and from the fat briefs tied up with distinctive red tape piled on the desk. Cardboard boxes stacked up along one wall presumably contained even fatter briefs. Thanet was well aware of the quantity of paperwork generated by a complicated case.

A large tabby cat lying on the desk sat up and turned to look at them as they came in.

Mintar walked around the desk and, scooping up the cat in what was clearly an habitual gesture, slumped into his chair and stared at a photograph in front of him. He seemed unaware of the two policemen.

The cat turned around three times and then settled down and started to purr.

Absent-mindedly Mintar began to stroke it.

Thanet cleared his throat, but Mintar did not respond. 'May we sit down, sir?'

With a visible effort the barrister dragged his eyes away from the photograph.

Thanet repeated his request and Mintar stared at him for a moment as if he were speaking in a foreign language. Then he blinked and waved a hand in invitation. 'Please do.'

Thanet drew a chair up in front of the desk and Lineham seated himself discreetly off to one side.

Mintar had returned to gazing at the photograph and suddenly he leaned forward, swung it around to face them and said savagely, 'That's why I didn't want to see her just now. That's what she was really like. And that's how I want to remember her.'

It was an enlargement of a family snap: Mintar, his wife and Rachel in tennis gear, arms linked and exuding enjoyment and well-being.

Virginia Mintar had indeed been a beautiful woman, Thanet thought. With their classical features, long blonde hair and slender figures, she and Rachel looked more like sisters than mother and daughter. 'Yes, I can understand that. Look, sir, I really am sorry to have to bother you at a time like this, but I'm sure you realise I have no choice.'

Mintar swung the photograph back around and returned to stroking the cat. 'Of course. By all means, proceed.'

'If we could begin by your telling me about yesterday?'

'Right. Yes.' A pause, while Mintar collected his thoughts.

As Mrs Mintar senior had told them, Jane Simons, Virginia Mintar's sister, and her boyfriend Arnold Prime were down for the weekend. They had arrived on Friday evening and as it was Prime's first visit to Kent, Jane and the Mintars had wanted to show him something of the county. Yesterday morning Ralph Mintar and his wife had taken them to visit the world-famous gardens created by Vita Sackville-West at Sissinghurst and in the afternoon Jane and Arnold had gone off by themselves to visit Leeds Castle, reputedly 'the most beautiful castle in the world'. The Mintars had stayed at home to play tennis with their next-door neighbours, the Squires, as they often did at weekends.

'My wife is . . . was, a very good player. She took it very seriously, always had coaching during the winter months, to keep her standard up.' Mintar gave a wistful smile. 'She was a great keep fit enthusiast. Belonged to a Health Club.'

They would return to Virginia Mintar later. At the moment Thanet wanted to get the facts clear in his head. 'So this tennis party would have finished at what time?'

'Around 4.30, I suppose.'

They had then had a cup of tea together before the Squires returned home. Normally that would have been the last the

25

Mintars saw of them that day, but as Jane and Arnold were staying, Virginia Mintar had thought it would be pleasant to have an informal supper party. The Squires had therefore been invited to return later.

'They are close friends?'

'Depends what you mean by "close". They are our nearest neighbours, we're on good terms with them and we do see quite a lot of them, yes, especially as we all enjoy a game of tennis. But that's as far as it goes.'

'So who would you say is your wife's closest friend?'

'Susan Amos,' said Mintar promptly.

Lineham took down her address.

'So what time did the Squires return last night?'

Mintar grimaced. 'They were uncomfortably prompt. Supper was to be around a quarter to eight and they were supposed to arrive in time for a drink beforehand. In fact they got here at about 7.15. Ginny was a bit put out, she hadn't finished the watering. It didn't matter too much, of course, as we know them well. It was just a bit inconvenient.'

'Where were you when they arrived?'

'Having a shower.'

'So you didn't see what your wife did in the courtyard after the Squires arrived? You don't know, for instance, whether or not she replaced the well cover before coming in?'

'No. You'd have to ask them. I only knew she hadn't finished the watering because she told me so, when she came up to let me know they were here. She asked me to remind her to do it later.'

'And did you?'

'No. I'm afraid I forgot.'

'And where were your sister-in-law and Mr Prime at the time?'

Mintar shrugged. 'In their room, I assume. They didn't get back from Leeds Castle until around 6.30, so I imagine they were changing. They came downstairs ten or fifteen minutes after me.'

'Miss Simons works in London?'

'Yes. In IT. She does something very sophisticated with computers, don't ask me what, it's far too technical for me to understand. Earns a fortune.'

'And Mr Prime?'

'He's a dentist.'

'Ah.' Why was it that dentists had such a bad press? Thanet wondered. Probably because everyone associated them with pain.

'Anyway, I hurried to finish dressing and joined Ginny and the Squires on the terrace for drinks.' He shrugged. 'Then the others came down and in a little while we had supper. We ate outside, it was such a beautiful evening.' His mouth twisted.

His wife's last, he must be thinking. 'When did Rachel and her fiancé arrive?'

Mintar gave a frown of displeasure. 'They weren't here for supper. They'd been out somewhere and they arrived just as we were finishing coffee.'

'What time would that have been?'

'Somewhere around half past nine, I should think. They'd come for a swim. They urged us all to join them. We'd only had a light meal, it was too hot to eat much, so most people said they would.'

'Not you, though.'

'No. I'd had one swim already, after playing tennis, and didn't particularly want to go in again. And in any case, as I told you last night, I had work to do, so I had a good excuse. Mother wasn't interested either.'

'So then what happened? If you could tell me in detail from here on, please.'

'We all got up from the table and everyone picked up something to carry into the kitchen – everyone who had eaten, that is. And we all trailed one behind the other along the corridor to the kitchen, dumped whatever we were carrying on the work surfaces and dispersed.'

'And what time was this?'

A moment's thought. 'Around ten to ten, I should think.'

'Where, exactly, did you disperse to?'

'I can't say for certain. Howard and Marilyn went home to change, I know that, but then I left to come in here. I assume Mother went back to the annexe and Jane and Arnold went upstairs, but I can't be certain.'

'And your wife?'

Mintar frowned. 'Again, I can't be sure. I imagine she would have stayed behind to load the dishwasher and clear things away in the kitchen – she liked to keep things neat and tidy.'

'So she wouldn't have been likely to leave the job half finished?'

'Definitely not, no. Why? Did she?'

'You didn't notice, then? She hadn't finished loading the dishwasher.'

'I'm afraid I was in no state to take in domestic details like that last night, Inspector. But under normal circumstances she certainly wouldn't have left the job half done.'

It was obvious that they were all thinking the same thing: *but these circumstances were far from normal.*

'Something must have interrupted her, then,' said Mintar, eyes narrowed. 'But what?'

If only we knew that, thought Thanet, we'd probably be more than halfway to a solution. 'What about Rachel and Mr Agon? What did they do when you all left the terrace?'

'Sorry, no idea. They were still there when we came in and they didn't follow us into the kitchen, that's all I know. I should think Rachel went up to her room to change and Agon went to the pool house.'

'How long have they been engaged?'

Mintar screwed up his mouth and sucked in his cheeks as though he had just bitten into a lemon and glanced at his watch. 'Approximately, let me see, twelve hours, or thereabouts.'

'They got engaged last night?'

'Yes. And no, Inspector, I can't pretend to be pleased. However, we had learned from bitter experience that it is expedient to be diplomatic in these matters, so I pretended to be delighted and said we'd crack a bottle of champagne.'

'And did you?'

'Yes.'

'You didn't mention this before.'

'No, well, I suppose I was trying to expunge it from my mind. It's all I need at the moment, to know that Rachel is serious about that . . . that shyster.'

'How did your wife feel about the engagement?'

'I never had a chance to discuss it with her, but I'm certain she

28

would have been as upset as I was. She certainly didn't approve of the relationship.'

'This "bitter experience" . . .'

'I shouldn't have mentioned it. It is irrelevant to the matter in hand.'

Thanet sighed. 'I'm sorry, Mr Mintar, but I can't agree. With all the work you have done at the criminal bar you must be aware that in circumstances like this anything and everything to do with your family is bound to come under the spotlight.'

'Oh, God.' Mintar leaned forward and put his head in his hands. 'This is unbearable.'

Thanet said nothing and after a few moments Mintar looked up. 'Yes, I do appreciate that that is so but I don't suppose for a moment you've ever been in this position yourself or indeed have ever been suspected of having committed a crime, so I don't think you can begin to understand just how intolerable it is. Not only to lose your wife but your privacy as well and, on top of all that, to know that inevitably you are bound to be a suspect.' He held up a hand. 'No, don't try to deny it. I'm absolutely certain that Ginny's death couldn't have been an accident, there's no point in pretending that it was, and we both know how often, in cases of domestic murder, it's the nearest and dearest who are guilty. There have been all too many well-publicised cases over the last year or two to ram this fact home to us.'

'I wasn't going to deny it, sir. You're right, of course. But you really are absolutely certain it couldn't have been an accident? Your wife never had any dizzy spells, for instance?'

'Not to my knowledge, no. And I'm sure I would have known, if she had. You can check with Howard Squires, of course. And in any case, the wall around the well is too high for someone of Ginny's height to topple over without extra momentum being applied, to shift the fulcrum.' He closed his eyes for a moment. The image his words conjured up must have been painful indeed. He cleared his throat before going on. 'So I really do think that you can rule out the possibility of it having been an accident. And I'm a hundred per cent certain it couldn't have been suicide. So, incredible as it may seem, that leaves us with only one alternative, doesn't it? And needless to say, I've spent the last few hours racking my brains as to who could possibly have wished to harm her.'

'And?'

'I've got absolutely nowhere. I really cannot imagine why anybody should want to . . .' Mintar's voice cracked and he stopped, took a deep breath. 'No, I'm afraid it's going to be up to you to find that out, Inspector. But believe me, I shall give you every ounce of assistance possible. That is why I have tried to be frank and honest with you – in my feelings towards Agon, for instance. I don't want you to think that I am trying to conceal anything. I have absolutely nothing to hide.'

'Thank you. It would make our job so much easier if everyone had the same attitude. But to return to what we were saying, I imagine you were referring to your other daughter's elopement.'

Mintar's eyes opened wide. 'My God, you don't waste much time, do you. How on earth did you find out about that?'

'It was Rachel, last night. She was so upset, and kept on saying her mother's disappearance was "Caro all over again." So I asked your mother what she meant.'

'I see.' Mintar sighed. 'Well, I don't think it's in the least relevant but if I must . . .' He stood up and, still carrying the cat, walked across to the window and looked out. 'There's not much to tell, really. Four years ago our elder daughter, Caroline, then just eighteen, fell in love with the gardener.' He gave a bitter little laugh. 'Very D.H. Lawrence, I'm afraid. It happens, I suppose. Her mother and I were none too pleased, as you can imagine, and tried to put a stop to it – a disastrous mistake, as it turned out. They eloped and we have never seen her since.'

'But you've been in touch?'

'No.' Mintar swung around to face them. 'And we have no idea where she is. So you can see why we were treading warily over this business with Rachel and Agon.'

'You did try to find out where she is?'

'Of course. And got absolutely nowhere. She left a note, you see, stating her intentions very clearly, so of course the police weren't very interested. Oh, they went through the motions, just to shut us up, but they got nowhere. Swain – that was his name – had never committed an offence of any kind so they couldn't trace him through the national database, and he apparently wasn't living on benefit, so far as they could find out, so that was that. And the Salvation Army didn't get anywhere either.'

'Really?' Thanet was surprised. The Salvation Army had an excellent record in tracing missing persons and would never give up until every possible line of inquiry had been exhausted.

'No. So there was absolutely nothing we could do about it, except hope that one day Caro would relent, and get in touch. Ginny never got over it.'

'Did the young man's family live locally?'

Another cynical little laugh. 'Oh yes. His mother lives in a cottage in the woods and has the reputation of being the local witch, so you can see why we didn't exactly consider him a desirable suitor for our daughter. She was as unhelpful as she could possibly be when we were trying to get in touch with Caro, still claims she doesn't have the faintest idea where they are and in fact seems to blame Caro for the whole thing. Says she turned her son's head.'

'He's her only child?'

Mintar nodded.

'So your present gardener . . . ?'

'Digby came as Swain's replacement.'

'I see. Well, thank you for explaining, sir. Just one or two further points . . . Your mother lives in the annexe, I gather. Has she been there long?'

'Yes, for many years – ever since I got married, in fact.' For the first time Mintar's expression lightened and he gave a slight smile. 'Oh, I know what you must have been thinking – that she's an unlikely candidate for a "granny annexe". And you'd be right, of course, she is. She's more than capable of running an independent establishment of her own and lives here purely for her own convenience. Perhaps I'd better explain that she's a botanist or, perhaps more accurately, an artist who is also a qualified botanist. She's always going off on far-flung expeditions and it suits her to be able to come and go as she pleases without having to worry about security and so on. We've lived in this house since I was in my early teens and when my father died we stayed on, although it was really too big for us. Mother found it rather a burden, I think, and she was relieved when I got married and Ginny and I took it over. We converted that little wing of outbuildings into a flat for her.' Again, the faint smile. 'I think Mother regards it more as a mini Dower House than a granny annexe. The arrangement has worked out well.'

'Did she and your wife get on?'

Mintar's eyebrows shot up. 'You're surely not suggesting my mother had anything to do with what happened to Ginny?'

'I was merely inquiring. It can be a difficult situation, I believe.'

'We don't exactly live in each other's pockets. And besides, as I said, Mother is away for long periods of time. They got on perfectly well, thank you.'

The door swung open.

'Daddy?'

Rachel stood in the doorway, swaying slightly. She had obviously just awoken from the sedative Dr Squires had given her last night: her eyelids drooped, her hair was tousled and she was wearing a very short white sleepshirt and an ankle-length deep blue silk kimono embroidered with huge white waterlilies. She steadied herself with one hand against the door jamb and said, 'Why is there a fire engine outside?' She noticed Thanet and Lineham and her expression changed, became more alert. 'Have you found her?'

She obviously hadn't looked out of any of the windows overlooking the courtyard, thought Thanet.

Mintar put the cat down, hurried across the room and put his arm around her shoulders. 'Rachel.' He cast an agonised glance at Thanet. *How am I going to tell her?*

Time for a tactful withdrawal. Thanet did not envy Mintar the next few minutes. He stood up. 'We'll leave you now, sir. If you could just direct us to your wife's room?'

Mintar's expression changed to – what? Thanet wondered. Something unexpected, certainly. Embarrassment, perhaps? Swiftly followed by resignation. 'Up the stairs, first on the right.' He turned to his daughter. 'Come along, darling. Let's get you back to your room.'

Still somewhat dazed, Rachel allowed herself to be shepherded up ahead of them. The two policemen tactfully waited for the door of Rachel's room to close before Lineham opened the door to her mother's bedroom. Then without warning he stopped dead on the threshold, so abruptly that Thanet bumped into him. 'Mike! Watch what you're doing. What are you playing at?'

But Lineham wasn't listening. He whistled softly. 'Just look at this, sir!' he said.

FOUR

'No-o-o-o!'

Thanet and Lineham froze as along the corridor floated a wail of despair. Mintar must have broken the news of her mother's death to Rachel.

'Poor kid,' muttered Thanet. Then, irritably, giving Lineham a little push, 'Move over then. I can't see a thing with you standing there like the rock of Gibraltar.'

Lineham moved aside and Thanet saw the reason for the sergeant's surprise – and also for Mintar's embarrassed reaction downstairs. The thought of having his wife's idiosyncracies exposed to the gaze of strangers would no doubt have made him squirm. For although the four-poster bed with its graceful hangings, the toning curtains and soft-pile carpet all proclaimed that this was the master bedroom, the room was dominated by a curious phenomenon. Piled up all around the walls right up to the ceiling, two and three deep in places, were cardboard boxes.

'Odd that none of the men commented on this last night,' said Lineham. 'What on earth do you suppose she keeps in them?' He crossed to the nearest pile, pulled out a box and peered at the lid. 'It says "T-SHIRTS, WHITE".' He opened it.

It was indeed filled with white T-shirts, mostly still in their polythene bags, all obviously unworn. Lineham picked some up, read the labels. 'Alexon, Jaeger, Ralph Lauren, Mondi . . . This lot must have cost a small fortune. Whatever did she want with them all?'

Thanet was opening another box labelled 'SWEATERS, PINK'.

34

This too was stuffed with top-quality garments in cashmere, lambswool, angora, all made by famous brand names.

They glanced at the labels on some of the other boxes: socks, pants, waist slips, full-length slips, nightdresses, pyjamas, cardigans, tennis shorts and tops, swimsuits, all in every colour of the spectrum. Then there were the accessories – belts, scarves, shoes, handbags, and gloves. The fitted wardrobe which took up one entire wall of the room was crammed so full of dresses, suits, skirts and trousers that it must have been difficult to put anything in or take anything out.

'No one woman could get through wearing this little lot in a lifetime,' said Lineham. 'There's only one explanation, isn't there? She was a shopaholic. I saw a documentary.'

'I agree, Mike.' Thanet put out a finger to touch the folds of a silk dress. 'And I wonder why. There must have been something seriously wrong.'

'I'll say. Doesn't look as though her husband slept in here, does it?'

And it was true that although there were two sets of pillows in the bed and two bedside tables, there was no sign of a masculine presence in the room.

'There's probably a dressing room through there.' Thanet nodded at a closed door. 'Quite common in certain sections of society, I believe.'

Lineham grunted. 'Not exactly the royal family, this.' Still, he went to check. 'But you're right. All very snug.'

Thanet had a look: another fitted wardrobe, single bed, trouser press, chest of drawers with silver-backed hairbrushes, bedside table with lamp and alarm clock. He turned back to the main bedroom. 'Anyway, it would take far too long for us to go through all these boxes. We'll put some of the team on to it and just take a quick glance around for now.'

But the search revealed nothing else of any interest apart from a small worn album of photographs in the drawer of one of the bedside tables. Thanet looked through it. The snapshots were all of a girl, from babyhood to teenage years, mostly alone but sometimes with another child who was recognisably Rachel. Caroline, presumably. Mintar had said that his wife had never got over losing her. Thanet had a sudden, vivid vision of

Ginny Mintar sitting up alone in the luxurious four-poster bed surrounded by all this evidence of an unquenchable thirst for fulfilment, obsessively turning over the pages of the album and mourning her lost daughter. Could there be a connection?

'I wonder why Mr Mintar never hired a private detective to find Caroline,' said Lineham, tuning in, as he so often did, to Thanet's thoughts.

'I wondered that, too. But there was something odd about his attitude to the whole business of Caroline's elopement, didn't you think?'

'In what way, sir?'

'I'm not sure. I could understand him not wanting to talk about it, but I just had the feeling he wasn't being frank with us, despite his protestations to the contrary.' Thanet replaced the album and shut the drawer.

'You're not suggesting anything sinister, are you, sir?'

'Oh no, I shouldn't think so for a minute. Though it might be worth just checking, to see what action the police did take.'

'To change the subject, it did occur to me . . .'

'What?'

'You know what you were saying about the work in the kitchen being left half done last night? And what Mr Mintar said about his wife asking him to remind her to finish the watering later? Well, I did notice that the sink is in front of the window, and that there's a clear view of the well from there. What if she was rinsing the dishes and happened to look out, remembered she hadn't done it? She'd have been busy all evening, serving supper. This might have been her first opportunity – her last, perhaps, if they were all going swimming.'

'Good point, Mike. So she thought she'd better see to it then and there, while she remembered. Then what?'

'Then she must have met someone.'

They stared at each other in silence, envisaging the scene. Thanet could see it all: Ginny Mintar hurrying across the court-yard to the well in the gathering dusk, the light from the kitchen spilling out behind her and a shadowy figure coming to meet her, or following her, perhaps . . . 'But who, I wonder?' He turned and made briskly for the door. 'Come on, Mike, we really haven't the faintest idea of what everyone was doing at the time. We've only got Mintar's assumptions to go on at the moment. We'll talk to Rachel later, when she's had a chance to calm down. Let's see if we can find Miss Simons and her boyfriend.'

They ran them to earth in the kitchen, seated at the big pine table. Jane was hunched over a mug of coffee, both hands clasped around it as though despite the heat of the day she was attempting to draw comfort from its warmth. There was a box of tissues on the table in front of her. Prime was sitting beside her, a protective arm around her shoulders. They both looked up as the two policemen entered. Jane had obviously been crying. Her eyes were bloodshot, the skin around them puffy and her mascara was badly smudged.

Not having seen Virginia Mintar until this morning, Thanet was surprised now to realise that there was a resemblance between the two sisters. It was as if Ginny's features had been blown up and distorted slightly so that whereas she had been beautiful, Jane had been aptly named. Not for the first time Thanet was struck by the infinite variations of the human face. Two eyes, a nose and a mouth, and apart from identical twins no two sets of features are exactly alike. A fractional adjustment here, a tiny shift of emphasis there and the result is completely different. No wonder portrait painters find it so difficult to achieve a satisfactory likeness, he thought.

Now, looking at Jane Simons, he wondered how it must have felt, having a younger sister so much more beautiful than she. Had it made her determined to shine in other ways, academically, perhaps? She had done very well for herself as far as her career was concerned, according to Mintar. Thanet suspected too that it had made her work hard to maximise her assets. Even this morning she had taken trouble with her make-up and although her cotton dress and matching jacket in a tawny mixture of black, browns and creams looked simple enough, Joan had long since taught him that such simplicity frequently carried a high price tag. Still, he felt sorry for these two. Apart from the considerable personal loss to Jane, it must be pretty dispiriting to set off for a light-hearted summer weekend in the country and find yourself caught up in what looked like a murder inquiry. 'May we sit down?'

She nodded.

Prime had sat back a little, but left his arm resting lightly on her shoulders.

'We're so sorry about your sister,' said Thanet as he and Lineham pulled out chairs and settled themselves. 'And I really do apologise for this, but I'm afraid that there are, inevitably, questions to be asked.'

She caught her lower lip beneath her teeth. 'I still can't believe it,' she whispered.

How often had he heard this from those caught up in the aftermath of a violent death? Thanet wondered. 'But sadly, it's true,' he said. 'So while last night is still fresh in your minds . . .'

'I do understand,' she said, and Thanet saw Prime's hand give her shoulder a little squeeze of approbation. 'What, exactly do you want to know?'

Thanet glanced at Lineham. *Take over.* He wanted to think, to observe these two. They intrigued him.

'If you would tell us about yesterday?' said the sergeant.

'What, all day?' said Prime, speaking for the first time, eyebrows climbing his bony forehead.

Thanet approved of Lineham's tactics. Talking about the earlier, innocent pleasures of the day would help Jane to relax. It did. By the time they had reached their return from Leeds Castle around 6.30 p.m. she had relinquished the coffee mug and was sitting back in her chair, one hand clasping Prime's on her shoulder.

'One small point before you go on,' said Lineham. 'Did you see Mrs Mintar when you got back?'

'No,' said Prime.

'I assume she was changing,' said Jane. 'She'd obviously done most of the preparations for supper. There were various dishes laid out on this table, with cutlery and dishes on trays, ready to be carried out.'

'Did you notice if she had been doing any watering in the courtyard?'

'Sorry, no.'

Prime also shook his head.

'Though I think I'd have noticed if the well had been uncovered,' said Jane. 'I don't *think* it was, but I can't be sure.' She looked to Prime for confirmation but he again shook his head.

'Sorry, I really don't think I would have noticed if it had been.'

Their account of the evening tallied with Mintar's and Lineham took them through it at a brisk pace until they reached the point at which they rose from the table. Then he followed the pattern which Thanet had set in his interview with Mintar and asked them to proceed in detail.

They glanced at each other.

'Well,' said Jane, 'we all picked up something to carry to the kitchen, to help clear the table. Ginny went first and we followed.'

'Along the corridor which leads from the terrace to the kitchen?'

'Yes. We deposited the various bits and pieces on worktops or the table then Ginny started to load the dishwasher. I offered to help, but she refused, said she could manage.' Jane pulled a face. 'She was fussy about things like that. You know, all the different dishes had to go in their allotted places, and the cutlery had to go in with knives on the right, forks on the left, spoons in between.'

'She was careful about detail, then.'

'Yes. And very tidy-minded. That was why . . .'

'What?'

'Well, that was why I was surprised, later, when we were all looking for her and I came in here, to find she'd left the job half done. That was when I first began to get worried, to think that there might be something wrong.'

'Was it you who finished clearing up later?' said Thanet.

'Yes. I couldn't sleep, so after you'd gone I thought I'd tidy up. Ginny hated coming down to a mess in the morning. I . . . I thought she'd be pleased to find I'd finished up for her.' Jane's voice shook. 'Stupid, really. It was as if, by assuming she'd turn up, I'd make it happen.' Her gaze drifted to the window. 'Well she did, didn't she?' Tears filled her eyes and spilled over. 'I really still can't believe it,' she said again, shaking her head.

Prime shook a tissue out of the box on the table and handed it to her. She wiped her eyes and blew her nose. 'Sorry.'

Lineham waited a few moments, then said, 'If we could go back to where you all put the dishes down . . . What did everybody do then?'

Jane was still dabbing at her eyes. 'Let me see.' She looked to Prime for help.

He narrowed his eyes, obviously thinking back. 'Ralph left straight away, went to his study, I presume. He'd excused himself from swimming, said he had work to do. Then all of us except Ginny went back and collected the rest of the stuff from the table, took it into the kitchen. Then Howard and Marilyn went off to change and so did we.'

'Where were Rachel and her fiancé?'

Jane didn't exactly wince at the mention of Agon, but her expression hardened. 'Still on the terrace.'

'When you went back, you mean?'

'Yes. To put it crudely, they were having a good snog.'

'You don't approve of Mr Agon, Miss Simons?' said Thanet.

She pulled a face. 'Slimy toad. I most certainly do not. The sooner Rachel dumps him the better.'

'You all toasted their future in champagne, I understand?'

'Yes. It was as brief and joyless a "celebration" as I have ever experienced. I couldn't help feeling sorry for Rachel, she must have realised how her parents felt – how we all felt, for that matter. But I imagine Ralph thought he really must at least go through the motions.'

'After what happened with Rachel's sister, you mean?' said Lineham.

'You know about that? Yes.'

'So, to get back to what we were saying, what time would you say it was when you went up to change?'

They agreed that it was probably between 9.50 and 10.

'And when you got back down?'

Prime hesitated. 'It must have been about a quarter past.'

Now that was interesting, thought Thanet. Up until now they had been consulting each other all the time, but suddenly it seemed to him that they were studiously avoiding looking at each other. He wasn't sure if Lineham had noticed this or not.

40

He had. 'A quarter of an hour's a long time, to change into swimsuits?'

Prime shrugged. 'There was no hurry. We chatted.'

What about? Thanet wondered. There was a stiffness in Prime's voice and although his arm still lay across the back of Jane Simons's chair she had released his hand. Had they quarrelled? And if so, had it been over something which had happened at supper?

'What about?' said Lineham.

Prime pursed his lips, wagged his head from side to side. 'This and that. The evening. The other guests. The engagement. Nothing very significant.'

'How can it possibly matter what we talked about up in our room?' said Jane. And there, too, was an edge which had been absent before.

'Perhaps it doesn't,' said Lineham. *And perhaps it does.* The words hung unspoken in the air. 'So when you got to the pool, who was already there?'

Thanet noted the glint of relief in Prime's eyes before he answered: 'They were all there except for Ginny – and Ralph and Frances, of course.'

'That would be Rachel and her fiancé and Mr and Mrs Squires.'

'That's right, yes.'

'Didn't it occur to you to wonder where your sister was, Miss Simons?'

'Yes, of course. That was why I asked if anyone else had seen her.'

But she wasn't being completely frank, thought Thanet. Her eyes had that evasiveness, that veiled look which frequently denotes an attempt to lie by a person who is by nature honest.

'So you were the first person to notice she was missing.'

'Yes. But we didn't realise she was, at that point. Missing. We just thought she'd been delayed for some reason.'

'Then we thought she might have changed her mind about coming for a swim, didn't we?' said Prime.

'That's right.'

It was interesting that once again they were united in their

41

responses, Thanet thought. They evidently thought that the tricky area had been successfully negotiated.

'But we did think it was odd she hadn't come out to say so,' said Jane.

'And then someone suggested she might have gone to bed,' said Prime.

'Not that anyone took that seriously. She never went to bed early and anyway she'd never have done so without excusing herself to her guests. So then Rachel went to look for her.'

'What time would this have been?'

Again they consulted each other with a glance.

'A quarter to eleven?' said Prime.

She nodded. 'Something like that.'

'Around half an hour after you got back downstairs, then.'

Again a flash of constraint before this time they nodded in unison. 'Yes.'

'But when Rachel came back, said Virginia wasn't in her room or indeed anywhere in the house, as far as she could tell, we began to feel concerned,' said Prime. 'We decided we'd have to look for her. So we all went and threw some clothes on and began to search. The rest, you know.'

But Jane Simons hadn't exactly thrown some clothes on, thought Thanet, remembering how well groomed she had appeared last night. Even in what was beginning to seem an emergency she had been determined to look her best. Perhaps that was an uncharitable view. Perhaps she didn't feel able to face the world without her full armour on.

The door opened and Rachel came in with her father. She was still wearing the blue silk kimono, now tightly belted around her narrow waist. Although she was very pale and, like Jane, her eyes were red and swollen, she looked fairly composed. 'Daddy says you'll need to speak to me,' she said.

Thanet and Lineham had risen. 'It can wait, Miss Mintar,' said Thanet. 'There's no rush.'

'I'd rather get it over with, if you don't mind.'

'I'll stay with you, darling,' said her father.

'No!' Then, more gently. 'Thank you, Daddy, but I'll be quite all right by myself.'

'But—'

42

'Daddy, please. I'm not a child any longer. Just go, will you?'

Jane Simons and Prime were already on their feet. Their relief was obvious. 'We'll go too,' she said. 'If there's anything else we can do to help . . .'

'Thank you.'

Thanet waited until they had all gone and Rachel was seated at the table. 'Would you like a cup of coffee?'

'No, thank you.'

He sat down opposite her and said, 'You're sure about this?'

She shook back her long blonde hair. 'Yes.'

'Right. We'll make it as brief as possible.'

'Take as long as you like.' The blue eyes filled with tears and she dashed them angrily away with the back of her hand. 'I want to do everything I can to help.'

FIVE

Rachel would find sympathy hard to cope with, thought Thanet. Best to be brisk and businesslike. 'Now, I understand that you and Mr Agon arrived here last night as the others were finishing their coffee. What time would that have been?'

'Around half past nine, I should think.' She was twisting a strand of hair round and round a forefinger.

Thanet took her quickly to the point where they all split up to change. 'I understand that you and your fiancé were the last to leave the terrace?'

There was a brief spark of joy in her eyes before she agreed that that was so.

It had probably been the first time that anyone had referred to Agon as her fiancé, Thanet realised, and like every newly engaged girl showing off her engagement ring, she was pleased that their new status had been acknowledged. As her aunt had said, despite the spurious celebration last night she was bound to be aware that her family was less than delighted about her choice of husband.

'So what did you do, after the table had been cleared?'

'I went up to my room to change.' She was still very tense, hanging on to the hair wound around her finger as if it were an anchor.

'And Mr Agon?'

'He changed in the pool house.'

'Which way did you go into the house? Through the corridor to the kitchen, or through the sitting room?'

'Through the drawing room. It's the quickest way into the hall.'

44

She wasn't correcting him, Thanet realised, just using the habitual way in which the family referred to that room. 'What about when you came back down?'

'The same.'

'And the others? Which way did they return?'

The brief, factual exchanges were beginning to have the calming effect Thanet had hoped for and now she released the lock of hair and sat back in her chair, frowning a little as she thought back. 'Well, Marilyn and Howard came through the courtyard, obviously, the same way they had gone. Jane and her man came through the—' She stopped. 'No, hang on. They came back separately. I remember wondering why they hadn't come together. I saw him come through the French windows in the drawing room but she wasn't with him. She turned up a few minutes later.'

Thanet and Lineham exchanged glances. Prime and Jane Simons had certainly given the impression that they had returned to the pool together.

'And did she come through the drawing room too?'

'I didn't notice, I'm afraid. I assume so. I just saw her getting into the pool, that's all. She asked me where Mum . . .' At this first mention of her mother, Rachel's fragile composure slipped. She swallowed, pressed her lips together and took a deep breath. 'She asked me where Mum was. Until then none of us had really noticed she wasn't there. And we still weren't worried. We knew how keen she was on leaving the kitchen spick and span. We just thought she was taking longer because she was clearing up.'

'Was it usual for her to clear everything away so thoroughly before guests had left?' Thanet tried to be tactful, not to sound critical. In his book it would have been downright rude.

'Not if it was a proper dinner party, no. But last night it was very informal, just Howard and Marilyn around for supper . . . Then when we suggested a swim, that made it even more so.'

'Yes, I see. So who was in the pool when you got back?'

'Just Matt.'

'And who arrived next?'

'Let me think.' Now that they were no longer talking about her mother she had settled down again. 'Howard, I think. Yes,

Howard. He came just after me. Then Marilyn, then Jane's boyfriend. Jane was last, as I said.'

'The Squires didn't arrive together either?' Thanet groaned inwardly.

'No.'

'Was there much of a time lapse between them?'

'I honestly didn't notice.' She gestured helplessly. 'We were fooling around in the pool. If I'd known it was going to be important . . . It was only a few minutes, I should think. But I don't really know.' Once again she was becoming agitated, twisting her hands together.

Thanet said, 'Never mind, it doesn't really matter,' intending to calm her down. Instead, his words had the opposite effect.

'But it does, doesn't it?' she burst out. 'Matter. It's only just dawned on me. Dad didn't say . . . I assumed it was an accident, but I wasn't really thinking straight. It couldn't have been, could it? There's no way Mum could have fallen over that parapet. Someone . . . Someone must have . . .' She stared at him wildly. 'And you think it was one of us, don't you? That's what all these questions are about. And . . . And . . .' She stopped.

Thanet opened his mouth to speak, trying to find words of reassurance – but what reassurance could he possibly give?

Before he could say anything Rachel said, 'But why? Who could possibly want to hurt her?' She put her elbows on the table and buried her face in her hands, shaking her head. 'No, I can't believe it, I just can't.'

'That's what we have to try to find out.'

There was a silence while she digested what had they had been saying. Then she looked up again. 'And all this stuff about who came back to the pool and when . . . It could have been any one of us, couldn't it? *We all came back separately.*'

'So it seems,' said Thanet with a sigh.

'So . . .' She twisted her head to gaze out of the window as if trying to see back into the past. Then, eyes full of misery, she looked back at Thanet and whispered, 'Not knowing who and why and how . . . It's going to be awful. I don't think I can bear it . . . All that uncertainty . . . And at the end of it, nothing will bring her back, will it? She's gone. Gone for ever, just like Caroline.'

'Your sister. Yes. Your father told me about that.'

'Oh, Dad. What does he care?' Her tone was bitter.

Thanet was surprised. Until now Mintar and Rachel had seemed to be on good terms. 'What do you mean?'

It seemed that the mention of Caroline had resurrected past feelings of resentment. 'He behaves as if she never existed.'

'That wasn't the impression he gave us.'

'No, well, he wouldn't, would he?'

'Why not?'

'He wouldn't want to be seen as an uncaring father. Bad for the image. When the police told us that as she was over age and had gone willingly – she left a note, you know – d'you know what he said? "Well, that's it. She's made her bed and she must lie on it. I wash my hands of her." How Victorian can you get? And he's never referred to her again to my knowledge, not once, in four years.'

Truly incredible behaviour in this day and age, Thanet had to agree. But he could now understand why Mintar had been uncomfortable, talking about Caroline. It wasn't just that the hurt had gone deep, perhaps he blamed himself for not having tried harder to find her before the trail went cold, especially if her loss had affected his wife as much as he had seemed to imply. 'That doesn't mean to say he didn't care.'

'Huh! Funny way of showing it!'

'He certainly seems to care for you.'

'I'm all he's got left now, aren't I? But I used to come pretty low in the pecking order, believe me. Mum came first, then Caro, then me. When Caro went I moved up a notch, that's all. And now . . .' She was silent a moment and then said, 'If he cared, why didn't he do something about it?'

'But he did. He contacted the Salvation Army. It wasn't his fault that they couldn't find her.'

'He did not! That was Mum! He was dead against it. They had terrible arguments about it and in the end she just went ahead and did it of her own accord. He wasn't too pleased, believe me! But by then the trail was cold, it was presumably too late and they never found her.'

Although Thanet knew that the Salvation Army frequently managed to trace people who had been missing for far longer

47

than Caroline, he did not contradict her. What was the point? It would only cause her further distress.

'Did your sister's elopement come as a complete surprise to you all?'

'Absolutely. Of course, looking back, you could see it must have been on the cards. I mean, there'd been awful rows about Caro going out with Dick and she told me she was absolutely fed up with it. But she didn't breathe a word about eloping to anyone.'

'And no one noticed she was unusually excited or tense?'

'No. That was probably because the night she went away, Gran came back unexpectedly from Turkestan or somewhere. She had been off on one of her trips for a couple of months. She's always going on these plant-hunting expeditions, she's a botanical artist. Anyway, we knew she was due back soon but there was some sort of mix-up or misunderstanding about dates and no one was expecting her when she arrived that evening. So of course there was general fuss all around and a celebratory dinner – she always produces a bottle of champagne the night of her return.' Rachel gave a brief smile for the first time and Thanet saw how beautiful she could be when warmth and animation informed her features. 'Gran always believes in doing things in style. I hope I'm like that when I'm seventy-seven! Anyway, we were all too busy listening to her traveller's tales to pay much attention to Caroline. As soon as we'd finished dinner, which took rather longer than usual, Caro excused herself, said she had a headache.'

'You didn't look in on her later, to see how she was?'

'She'd hung her "DO NOT DISTURB" notice on the door. I didn't think anything of it, just assumed she'd gone to sleep. So it wasn't until next day that anyone realised she'd gone. By then, of course, they must have been well away.'

'Your father said your mother never got over it.' Thanet still couldn't understand why, if Mintar was so fond of his wife, he had been so set against trying to find Caroline, when it obviously meant so much to Virginia. Was it simply stiff-necked pride that had prevented him from backing down?

'No, she never did. She seemed to carry on as normal, but . . . Well, you've seen her room, haven't you?'

'All the clothes, you mean?'

'Yes. She was never like that before. Oh, she used to enjoy shopping, who doesn't, but not like that, not to that extent. I tried to get her to see she needed help, but she wouldn't acknowledge there was a problem, wouldn't even talk about it.'

'Did she ever think of hiring a private detective to find Caroline?'

'She actually did hire one, sometime last year. But he didn't get anywhere either. It didn't help that Dick's mother was so uncooperative.'

'Do you think she knows where they are?'

'Not by the way she behaves – she blames Caroline, you know, for causing her to lose her son. As if he hadn't had anything to do with the elopement!'

'What was he like, Dick?'

Another smile. 'Drop dead gorgeous!' she said, sounding like a normal teenager for the first time. 'In fact, I have never been able to work out how such a hideous old woman could produce anything so scrumptious. I had a terrific crush on him myself and I wasn't a bit surprised when Caro went overboard for him. I was green with envy when they started going out together.' She grimaced. 'He was a great deal more pleasant to have about the place than Digby, I can tell you.'

There was a knock at the door. Lineham answered it. The firemen had finished, apparently.

'Tell them we'll just be a few minutes,' said Thanet. He turned back to Rachel. 'Digby. Why don't you like him?'

She pulled a face again. 'Him and his camera. He gives me the creeps.'

'Camera?'

'It's his hobby. Photography. Wildlife, supposed to be. And to be fair, he is a very good photographer. He's got an exhibition on at the moment, in the branch library in the village. Not exactly the Tate, but still . . .'

'What did you mean by "supposed to be"?'

She looked uncomfortable. 'Perhaps I shouldn't have said that.'

'No, please, I'm interested.'

'Well, I'm never quite sure that he doesn't sometimes photograph people.'

'You, you mean?'

She nodded. 'I'd never sunbathe in the nude when he's around, for example. And I'm careful to choose my spot if I'm wearing a bikini.'

'Have you told your father this?'

She shook her head. 'I'm not certain about it, you see. I've never actually caught him at it. It's just a feeling I have. And the way he looks at me. Slyly. As if he knows all my secrets.' She gave a shiver of distaste.

'I'm sure your father would want to know, if you feel like that. I know I would, if it were my daughter.' At the thought of Bridget Thanet experienced another shaft of anxiety. What was happening to her now? He was suddenly overwhelmed by the need to ring Joan and find out. He rose. 'Well, thank you very much for your help, Miss Mintar—'

'Rachel. Call me Rachel.'

'Very well. Thank you, Rachel. I know it can't have been easy for you. You've been very brave.'

To his dismay he saw that the compliment had brought her to the verge of tears again and he kicked himself for not keeping the tone impersonal. Still, nothing and no one was going to keep her on an even keel for long today, he guessed.

Outside the firemen were all packed up and ready to go. Laid out neatly on a sheet of polythene was an array of objects which had been brought up from the bottom of the well. 'Anything interesting?' he said.

The fire chief shook his head. 'I shouldn't think so. Anyway, there it is. We'll leave you to it. Good luck.'

Thanet thanked them, then went and sat in the car for a few moments to ring Joan in privacy. But there was no news as yet and he returned to the well, where Lineham was studying the finds: assorted bottles and jars, some broken and some intact; various bits of shaped wood, probably pieces of ancient toys; a trowel with a broken handle; a number of pieces of clay pipes; an old biscuit tin; a little stack of broken china and some unidentifiable pieces of rusty metal.

'Nothing much there,' said the sergeant.

'Doesn't look like it.'

'So what now?'

'Mrs Mintar senior, I think. But first I'd like to take a closer look at the swimming pool, get a better idea of the lie of the land.'

They left the SOCO bagging the objects retrieved from the well, then, taking the route the Squires must have followed when returning to the pool last night, walked past the end of the annexe. This had a small, private garden of its own at the rear, Thanet saw, surrounded by a tall yew hedge which also flanked the raised terrace on to which the French windows of the drawing room opened. Below that, down a short flight of steps, lay the swimming pool. Beyond it was a tennis court and over to the left a small single-storey building.

'The pool house?' said Lineham.

They went to have a look inside. There were two changing cubicles, a shower, and a lavatory.

'Simple, but adequate,' said Thanet.

'Not so simple and more than adequate,' said Lineham, opening another door. 'Look, there's a sauna. Very nice, too.'

'Don't see the attraction, myself,' said Thanet.

'Have you ever had a sauna?'

'Can't say I have.'

'There you are, then! How can you pass judgement till you've tried it? It's great! Very relaxing.'

'Not my cup of tea.'

'You ought to give it a whirl some time, sir. You might be surprised.'

'You're not advertising a health club, Mike.'

They went outside again to take a closer look at the pool area. It was paved with non-slip tiles and, except for the side nearest to the house, was surrounded by a neatly clipped waist-high box hedge affording shelter and some degree of privacy for sunbathers. On the poolside, across one of the shorter ends, was a long roller with a heavy blue plastic pool cover rolled up on it. There were comfortable sun loungers with yellow and white striped cushions and a slatted cedarwood table with matching chairs, shaded by a large cream canvas Italian umbrella. Conscious of the sun beating down on his head, Thanet walked

51

around to the side furthest from the house, then, turning to look back at the house, squatted down. Yes, from this side of the pool and probably to about halfway across anyone in the water would have a clear view of the drawing-room windows and the door to the corridor leading to the kitchen. Only the roof of the annexe was visible; it too must have a small terrace but the yew hedge which surrounded it shielded it from view. Mrs Mintar senior would have been able to hear the swimmers last night, but she wouldn't have been able to see them. On the other hand, some of her windows overlooked the courtyard . . .

The water lay as flat and calm as a steel mirror and its blue depths looked infinitely inviting. Thanet leaned forward to test the temperature. It felt pleasantly warm.

'Thinking of having a dip, sir?' said Lineham, eyes wide with mock innocence.

Thanet scowled and stood up. 'Old Mrs Mintar,' he said. 'Now she's had time to think, perhaps she saw or heard something last night.'

SIX

Lineham rang Mrs Mintar's doorbell.

No reply.

He rang again.

Still no response.

'Try the door,' said Thanet.

It opened. Thanet put his head in and called.

'Who is it?' A voice from the left, sounding annoyed.

'Inspector Thanet and Sergeant Lineham.'

'Go into the sitting room. I'll be out in a minute.'

The door to the sitting room stood ajar and they stepped inside. It was furnished in bright, clear colours: blues, greens and turquoise, with a touch of purple here and there. Not the room of an average seventy-seven-year-old. But then her son and granddaughter had made it clear that she was anything but that. Glazed doors stood open on to a little terrace and Thanet glimpsed a huge Chinese ceramic pot overflowing with summer bedding plants and a narrow border crammed with roses and summer-flowering perennials.

On the walls hung groups of striking botanical paintings and as Thanet stepped across to take a closer look he kicked something lying on the floor. He bent to pick it up. It was a small brown pill bottle. Automatically he read the label: *Glyceryl Trinitrate 300 mg. Take one as directed.*

'Looks as though she has angina,' he said to Lineham. He put the bottle on the mantelpiece.

'Wonder how that affects her expeditions.'

'Quite.' Thanet returned to the group of paintings: *Pulsatilla ambigua,* he read, *Pulsatilla occidentalis, Pulsatilla campanella.*

53

'Beautiful, aren't they?' Mrs Mintar had come into the room. 'Commonly called pasque flowers, from the French. '*Pâques*,' she explained to his uncomprehending look.

'Of course,' he said, digging into his memory. 'Easter.'

'Quite. Hence *passefleurs* – "Easter flowers".'

'Did you do these after one of your expeditions?'

She looked amused. 'You know about those. You really have learned a lot about us in a very short time, haven't you? Yes. But not one expedition. Several.'

The pill bottle was no longer on the mantelpiece, he noted. She must have removed it while he was taking another look at the paintings and was no doubt hoping they hadn't noticed it. So she didn't want them to know of her condition. Interesting. 'Do you go away often?'

'A couple of times a year. More often if I can.' Talking about her work she became more animated. 'I've been very lucky, really. Expeditions are very expensive to mount and there are always loads of botanists anxious to get out into the field. But fortunately I've got this other string to my bow, being able to draw and paint. The sponsors often want more than just a photographic record, and I've gradually carved out a niche for myself. This year, for instance, I was in South America from just after Christmas to the beginning of March and I hope to go to south-west China in November.'

'Have you always done this work?'

'Oh yes. Barristers' wives have to develop their own interests, their husband's work is so time-consuming that they'd go mad if they didn't. I would have, anyway.'

'So your husband was also in the legal profession.'

'He became a High Court judge, as a matter of fact.'

'You don't use your title?'

She made a dismissive gesture. 'I don't go in much for that sort of thing. I'd rather paddle my own canoe.'

The metaphor was apt. He could just imagine her white-water rafting down the Amazon. Though the angina must somewhat cramp her style these days – if, that is, she made any concessions to it. Which, he guessed, she probably didn't. She was the type who'd rather die on a mountain than of old age in a hospital bed. He turned back to the paintings. 'These are really lovely.'

'Thank you. I just thought they'd make an interesting group.'

'Pastel, aren't they?'

Her eyebrows rose slightly. 'Yes, they are.'

'It's unusual to see botanical paintings in pastel. I thought they were invariably in watercolour.'

'They are. The ones I do for the RHS magazine, for example, are always in watercolour. These I do for my own pleasure and they aren't strictly botanical, more interpretations of the botanical, shall we say.'

'And much more exciting, if you ask me. More . . . dramatic.'

'It's very kind of you to say so. But I don't imagine you've come here to discuss my work, Inspector. I know we could stand here having an interesting conversation for the rest of the morning, but I'm sure you're anxious to get on.' *And if you're not, I am.*

She was wearing wide-legged cotton trousers and a loose cotton smock smudged with pastel dust. She must have been working when they arrived, which was, no doubt, why she had sounded so annoyed at being interrupted. But painting? Only a few hours after her daughter-in-law's body had been found?

'I can see you're thinking I must be pretty heartless,' she said, 'to be working under these circumstances. But there's no point in pretending that there was any love lost between Virginia and myself. I am sorry for my son's sake, of course, but as far as I'm concerned it's good riddance.'

'You don't mince your words, do you?' said Thanet.

'What's the point? Waste of time, in my opinion.'

'Well, it certainly makes my job much easier.'

She shifted from one foot to the other, obviously impatient to get back to her work. She hadn't invited them to sit down and had remained standing herself.

Well, he wasn't going to be rushed, thought Thanet. It was time he made it clear who was in charge here. 'May we sit down?'

She hesitated. She was so forthright that he almost expected her to refuse, but good breeding took over and she made a grudging gesture. *If you must.* She herself perched on the very edge of an upright chair as if to emphasise the fact that she hoped the interview would be brief.

'Naturally,' said Thanet when they were all settled, 'in view of what has happened, we're trying to piece together everyone's movements yesterday.'

'Quite.' She folded her arms as if to contain her impatience. *Well, get on with it, then,* her body language shouted.

'If you would take us quickly through the day?'

'The *whole* day?'

'Please.'

She gave an exasperated sigh before beginning her account. She had stayed at home all day, apparently. She had worked in the morning and had a leisurely afternoon, going for her daily swim before settling down to read the paper. After tea she had showered and changed before joining the others for pre-supper drinks.

'What time was this?'

'About 7.30.'

'And you had drinks on the terrace?'

'That's right.'

'Which way did you go to get to the terrace? Did you go outside and around the side of the annexe, via the courtyard, or is there a connecting door to the house?' Thanet was annoyed with himself that he hadn't checked this point. He did seem to remember seeing a door in the corridor leading to the kitchen which might give access to the annexe, but he hadn't investigated.

'Yes, there is a connecting door, and that was the way I went.'

'Along the corridor from the kitchen to the terrace?'

'Yes.'

Pity. 'Would you have happened to notice if the well cover was on or off at that point? You might have glanced out when you locked the front door, for example?'

'I didn't. So no, I didn't notice.'

They skipped quickly to the point where the dinner party broke up and once again Thanet heard the by now familiar account of what had happened. As the others had already told him, after carrying some dishes through to the kitchen Mrs Mintar had retired to her own quarters. 'I'd had enough of being sociable by then.'

'So then what did you do?'

'Read a book until Ralph came to ask me if I'd seen Virginia. Then, of course, I got caught up in all the commotion.'

Thanet glanced at the back wall of the sitting room, where a small window overlooked the courtyard. 'Did you hear any noises from the courtyard, between the time you got back and your son's arrival?'

She hesitated.

So there was something. 'Well?'

But still she hesitated. Then she said, 'I'm just not sure.'

'What do you mean?'

'Well, you know what it's like, when you're reading, when you're really engrossed in a book. You're often not even aware of it when someone has spoken to you directly.'

'So?'

'So I *think* I might have heard something. Voices. But as I say, I can't be certain.'

Thanet's scalp prickled. 'In the courtyard?'

She nodded.

The chances were slim but he had to ask. 'Did you recognise them, by any chance?' He was aware of Lineham's pencil poised motionless over his notebook as they awaited her answer.

'No. Definitely not.'

'Please, Mrs Mintar, do try to remember. This could be very important.'

'I'm not an idiot, Inspector, I'm aware of that! But I can't be any more specific. Believe me, I only wish I could, if only because it would help to clear up this whole mess much more quickly, and get the police out of our hair. I'm sorry, I don't mean to be rude, but I really do resent having my life disrupted like this.'

'Do you have any idea what time it was?'

'No. There really is no point in pursuing this. It's just a vague impression, that's all, which is why I hesitated to mention it in the first place.'

She was right. It seemed pointless to persist and they left. Outside Thanet glanced at his watch: 1.30. 'Come on, Mike, let's go to the pub, have a bite to eat. We'll walk. It'll clear our heads.'

57

'Not exactly bowed down with grief, was she?' said Lineham as they set off down the drive.

'No.'

They walked in silence for a while, thinking back over the interview, turning left after passing through the wrought-iron gates.

A little further on they came to the driveway leading up to the windmill. Thanet had noticed earlier that it had obviously been converted into a house: there were curtains at the windows and cars parked in front. 'That must be where the Squires live,' he said. 'We'll interview them next, after lunch. It'll be interesting to see what it's like inside. I've never been in a converted windmill before.'

He expected Lineham to comment, but the sergeant hadn't been listening. He was still brooding on Mrs Mintar. 'She's downright self-centred, if you ask me,' he said. 'Very wrapped up in her work. I don't suppose her son had much of a life. I bet he was dumped on a nanny most of the time and then packed off to boarding school at the earliest possible moment, while she swanned off to foreign parts.'

'Yes. And if so, that could well be why he reacted as he did when Caroline left. As a child he would probably have found it less painful to try to put his mother completely out of his mind, than make himself miserable thinking about her all the time. So when Caroline went—'

'Sir. Sorry to interrupt, but isn't that Mr Prime ahead?'

Arnold Prime's tall, loose-limbed figure was immediately recognisable. He was strolling along at a leisurely pace, hands in pockets, taking in his surroundings. 'Looks like it. Probably wanted to get away from the house for a while.'

'Don't blame him. Not exactly a fun weekend, is it?'

'That's what I was thinking earlier. Still, it could be useful to have a word with him by himself. He might be more willing to give us a frank account of his impressions of the supper party last night. He was the only outsider, after all, apart from Agon who didn't arrive until later.'

They speeded up and soon caught up with their unsuspecting quarry. 'Sorry about this, Mr Prime,' said Thanet as they came alongside. 'I expect you thought you were going to have a

58

bit of peace and quiet. But we would like another word with you.'

Not surprisingly, Prime didn't look too pleased. But he gave a resigned shrug. 'Go ahead.'

The two policemen fell into step with him.

'All this must have ruined your weekend, sir,' said Lineham.

'I'm very sorry that Jane is so upset, obviously. But I hardly knew her sister, so I can't pretend to be grief-stricken.'

'And that is precisely why we wanted to talk to you,' said Thanet. 'You're the only person there last night who – apart from your relationship with Miss Simons – wasn't actually involved with any of those present. Up until now, everyone has been saying that the supper party was absolutely without incident, but it's very difficult to believe that nothing unusual happened.'

'Why? What bearing has that got on what happened later?'

'Oh come, Mr Prime. Aren't you being rather naïve?'

Prime compressed his lips, but said nothing.

'I suppose the theory in the family is that some intruder came along and pushed Mrs Mintar down the well?' said Lineham.

'It's a possible answer,' said Prime defensively.

'Possible, but unlikely,' said Thanet.

'Statistically, the chances are that it was someone in the family,' said Lineham.

'Or at least, someone close to them,' said Thanet. 'And if so, we have to ask ourselves not only who and why but why then? Why did whoever was responsible choose that particular moment rather than any other? Did something happen during the evening to precipitate matters? Which is why we're asking you, as an unbiased observer, if you would think back very carefully and try to recall if there was anything, anything at all which could be relevant. I know it's a lot to ask, but we really would appreciate it.'

Prime had heard them out but now he shook his head. 'I'm sorry, I really don't feel I can do that.'

'I appreciate your reluctance. Mr Mintar is your host and you are close to Miss Simons. But everyone seems to agree that Mrs Mintar's death couldn't have been an accident, so we are talking about murder. And I'm afraid that in a case of murder normal social conventions just have to be put aside. I don't want to sound pompous and talk about duty and an obligation to help the police, but the fact remains that a woman has been killed. And that you might be able to help us find out who's responsible.'

There was nothing more to say. They couldn't force Prime to talk if he didn't want to and silence fell while they let him think over what had been said.

Thanet had already taken off his jacket and slung it over his shoulder but he was still conscious of his shirt sticking to his back, of the ferocity of the sun's rays beating down upon his head. It was now the hottest part of the day and ahead of them the tarmac shimmered. Already the verges at the side of the road and the grass in the fields were turning brown and crisping in the unremitting drought. If this went on, Thanet thought, England's green and pleasant land would become green no longer and in the long term the changing climate would have a disastrous effect on the native deciduous trees. Starved of water they would surely eventually die. Perhaps in a hundred years time this landscape, which probably looked very similar now to the way it had a century ago, would have changed beyond recognition. He took out a handkerchief and mopped his forehead. Thoughts of a cold shower or, failing that, a long, cool drink danced in his head. What would the Super say, he wondered, if he turned up for work tomorrow wearing shorts, sandals and sunhat?

This entertaining fantasy was interrupted by Prime. 'Very well,' he said. 'I take your point. I'll try to help, if I can. What, exactly, do you want to know?'

Thanet looked about. They had just reached the junction of Miller's Lane with the village street. To their right, at tables set out beneath the trees on the wide pavement in front of the Dog and Thistle, a number of families were lingering over a late lunch. Otherwise, apart from a young couple with a toddler in a pushchair, Paxton dozed in an early Sunday afternoon torpor. Across the road, against the churchyard wall, was a conveniently empty bench in the shade of a huge horsechestnut tree. That long cool drink would just have to wait. 'Let's go and sit over there.'

They crossed the road and sat down. 'Well, to begin with,' said Thanet, 'can you recall any particular incident which indicated, for instance, that there was any bad feeling, any animosity or resentment between any of the other guests and Mrs Mintar? Perhaps we'd better call her by her Christian name, to avoid confusion with her mother-in-law.'

Prime frowned, pondering. Eventually he shook his head. 'Not a specific incident, no, but . . .'

'What?'

'It's difficult to put my finger on it, really. I suppose the best way I can describe it is to say that I was conscious that there were a lot of undercurrents. And they seemed mostly to centre on Virginia.'

'Could you elaborate?'

He shrugged. 'As I say, it's difficult. It's just that I was aware that there were things going on below the surface, things I didn't understand.'

'How did these undercurrents manifest themselves?'

'Innuendoes. Glances.'

'Directed at Mrs . . . at Virginia?'

'Mostly, yes.'

'Directed by whom?'

'That was the thing. By practically everybody. By her husband, certainly, by her mother-in-law – there's no love lost there, I can assure you – and even by the Squires.'

'Both of them?'

Prime shrugged again. 'I'm only telling you of my impressions.'

'Was it Virginia's behaviour at supper last night which provoked these reactions, do you think, or were they a hangover, so to speak, of past events?'

Again a hesitation. 'It was difficult to tell. I was sitting next to her, you see, so without making a point of it I couldn't actually see her face a lot of the time.'

He was holding back on something here, Thanet was sure of it. But why? 'Did she say anything, then, to upset anyone?'

Prime sighed. 'Not that I can remember.'

But again there was a reservation in his voice. Perhaps, Thanet

61

thought, this was because it somehow concerned Jane Simons and he didn't want to get her involved. Was this the moment to tackle him about the way the couple had misled them earlier, about their return to the pool? No. Prime was fairly relaxed at present. He didn't want to put him on the defensive until he was certain there was nothing else to be learned. 'You said just now, when you were talking about undercurrents, that they were *mostly* directed at Virginia. What others were there?'

'Well, take Mrs Mintar senior, for instance. She was sitting next to Howard Squires but I can guarantee they didn't exchange a word, all evening. And Marilyn Squires hardly took her eyes off her husband, except to look at Virginia.'

'Are you saying you think there might have been something going on between Howard Squires and Virginia? And that his wife was aware of it – or, at least, suspected it?'

'I don't know. Howard certainly spent a lot of time looking at Virginia, but then she was sitting directly opposite him. And you have to understand that Virginia was the sort of woman who automatically attracted a lot of attention from men.'

'Did she set out to do so?'

'I'd say so, yes.'

Again Prime was uncomfortable and suddenly Thanet twigged. Ten to one, Virginia Mintar had been flirting with Prime, the new man at her table. Her sister would naturally have resented this and when she and Prime went up to change for the swim, they might well have had a row about it. And that could have been why they went down again separately. More sure of his ground now he decided to go on the offensive. 'Mr Prime, why did you and Miss Simons deliberately mislead us this morning?'

'What do you mean?' He was pretending to be surprised but it was obvious that he knew what Thanet meant.

'You gave us the impression you returned to the swimming pool together.'

He had to drag the information out of Prime but he managed it eventually. His guess was right. Virginia had set her cap at her sister's boyfriend and Jane had been so upset by her behaviour that it had taken considerable effort to convince her that Prime had not been taken in by Virginia's charms.

'It must be very difficult to have a younger sister as beautiful as that,' said Thanet.

'Exactly,' said Prime eagerly. 'And Jane's past experience hasn't exactly led her to trust Virginia, as far as men are concerned. More than once, when they were younger, Virginia just waltzed in and purloined Jane's boyfriends. In fact, Jane was very reluctant to bring me down here to meet her sister and brother-in-law at all. We've been going out together for almost a year now and she's been putting it off and putting it off, making one excuse after another. In the end I managed to get her to tell me the real reason for her reluctance and persuade her that she had nothing to worry about.'

'She was afraid that Virginia would lead you astray.'

'Yes. Jane said, well, I hesitate to speak ill of the dead, but Jane said that Virginia "found it difficult to keep her hands off anything in trousers". That was the way she put it.'

'And could she? Did she? You said you were sitting next to her.'

'I must admit she did come on a bit strong. I have a fairly realistic appreciation of my charms, I think, Inspector, and I know I'm no oil painting. Beautiful women don't exactly throw themselves into my arms. But there's no doubt that Virginia was flirting with me. I'm not surprised Jane was upset.'

'What about Mr Mintar? How did he react to this?'

'He didn't seem particularly worried. As I said, he did watch his wife a lot, but I suppose if she always behaved like that he must have got used to it, over the years.'

'And the others?'

'Her mother-in-law wasn't amused, I assure you. As for the Squires, well, I just don't know what was going on there. Anyway, I was quite relieved when the young people turned up with their big news.'

'Because it provided another focus of attention?'

'Exactly. Though, as Jane told you earlier, there weren't exactly any cries of delight. Oh, Ralph put on a good enough show, I suppose, producing champagne and so on, but you'd have to have been an idiot not to see that he was really pretty miffed about it. And the same goes for Virginia and her mother-in-law too. I knew about Rachel's sister, though, so I could understand their dilemma.'

Thanet glanced at Lineham, raising his eyebrows. *Anything else you want to ask?*

Lineham shook his head.

'Thank you, sir,' said Thanet. 'You've been very helpful.'

'That's it?' Prime's relief was clear.

'For the moment. When did you intend returning to London?'

'This evening.'

'I'm afraid that won't be possible. This will apply to Miss Simons too.'

'But I have a whole list of appointments tomorrow, Inspector. I can't just cancel the lot, let my patients down without warning like that.'

'I'm sorry, sir, but I have to insist. We'll let you go back at the earliest possible moment, I assure you.'

Looking thoroughly disgruntled Prime stalked off up the village street.

'Not too happy about that, sir, was he?'

'Can't be helped.' Thanet glanced across the road. Most of the tables were now empty. 'Come on, Mike. If I have to wait any longer for a drink I shall expire.'

They both ordered bacon and mushroom baguettes and carried their drinks outside. Thanet only ever allowed himself one drink at lunchtime while he was working so in addition to a bottle of lager he ordered a glass of sparkling water with a dash of lime. The second they sat down he drank this straight off, feeling himself revive as it flooded his system. 'Ah, that's better,' he said.

Lineham was watching him with a grin. 'You were thirsty, weren't you?' He took a leisurely swallow from his glass.

'I can't imagine why you weren't.' Thanet poured out half of his lager and sat back. 'You must have the metabolism of a camel. Anyway, what do you think was going on over that meal last night?'

'Sounds to me as though our Ginny liked to have all the men at her feet. I bet you're right, and she was having an affair with Howard, who didn't like it when she switched her attentions to

Jane's boyfriend. And it sounds as though Mrs Squires had a good idea of what was going on. As for poor old Mintar, doesn't sound as though he had much choice but to sit back and watch, does it?'

'And presumably her mother-in-law disapproved, which is why she is so anti-Virginia.'

'And anti-Squires, perhaps?'

'Possibly. Ah, thank you.'

Their food had arrived. It smelled delicious and Thanet's mouth watered in anticipation. He took a large mouthful, his tastebuds singing alleluia as they came into contact with the fresh, crusty bread, the warm, juicy mushrooms and crispy bacon.

'Mmm, this is a bit of all right,' mumbled Lineham.

They concentrated on eating for a while, then the sergeant said, 'Well, as I said last night, the old lady has certainly got it in for Howard. That could be why.'

'And has it occurred to you, Mike, that if there was something going on between Squires and Virginia, he could have had a major problem on his hands?'

'With his wife, you mean?'

'No. With his professional position. "Our family doctor" was what Mintar called him last night.'

'Yeees,' breathed Lineham. 'I see what you mean. Affairs with patients are strictly *verboten*.'

'Precisely. It'll be interesting to see what he has to say for himself.'

SEVEN

'Must be nice to be able to afford a place like this,' said Lineham as they toiled up the drive to the windmill. Although they had walked at a gentle pace they were still sweating by the time they had covered the short distance from the village.

'Mmm.' Thanet was wishing they had taken one of their cars instead of choosing to walk. He mopped at his forehead and paused to glance up at the distinctive structure ahead of them. Although there are a number of windmills open to the public dotted around Kent, some of them restored to working order by groups of enthusiasts or, latterly, by the KCC, he had never been this close to one before. Very few have been converted into private houses and now, of course, conservation being the order of the day, it would be virtually impossible to get planning permission.

To his untutored eye this looked a magnificent specimen. Octagonal in shape, with a base of tarred brick and the upper portion of white weatherboarding, it stood on a slight rise, dominating the surrounding countryside by virtue of its height and the distinctive silhouette of its sails. It had been maintained in excellent condition and its elegant simplicity had not been marred by inappropriate domestic embellishments such as wrought-iron coach lamps or hanging baskets.

'Better get on, Mike.'

They trudged the last few yards up to the front door but there was no reply to their knock.

'They can't be out,' said Lineham. The windows were all open and there were three cars in the drive, a BMW, a Golf and an ancient Ford Escort.

66

'Probably in the garden on a day like this.'

They walked around to the back of the house. Thanet was right. It was an idyllic summer Sunday afternoon scene: comfortable wicker chairs and table in the shade of an old apple tree, jug of lemonade and tall glasses. Squires and a woman, presumably the elusive Marilyn, were reading the Sunday papers and a teenage girl in a bikini was sunbathing on a rug spread out on the grass nearby.

'Sorry to disturb you,' said Thanet. 'We knocked, but there was no reply.'

Squires, who was wearing crumpled khaki shorts, polo shirt and espadrilles, jumped up with the ease and elasticity of a man who took the trouble to keep himself fit. He was in his forties, with thick brown hair which flopped over his forehead in a boyish manner. 'Ah, Inspector . . . ? I'm sorry, I can't remember your name.' He held out his hand, somehow managing to exude warmth and sincerity and at the same time maintain a gravity appropriate to the occasion.

Thanet shook it. 'Thanet. And this is Sergeant Lineham.'

'I don't believe you've met my wife. She had to go home last night, she wasn't feeling well.'

Mrs Squires smiled. 'I invariably get a headache if I go swimming after a meal. I should have known better and not given in to temptation.'

Or perhaps she hadn't wanted to leave her husband free to cavort in the pool with the delectable Virginia in a bathing suit, thought Thanet. Marilyn Squires was several years younger than her husband, he guessed, and tiny, with sharp, pointed chin, cropped black hair and a flat-chested, almost adolescent figure. She was wearing lime green shorts and halter top and huge sunglasses with tortoiseshell frames.

'And this is Sarah,' said Squires, indicating the girl, who had sat up.

She was around fifteen and looked more like her father than her mother. 'Hi,' she said.

'You'd better scoot,' Squires said to her. 'I'm sure the Inspector wants to talk business.'

She scowled. 'Must I?'

'Actually,' said Thanet, 'I'd prefer to go inside, if you don't

67

mind. It would be cooler.' Also less informal. And he wanted to get rid of those sunglasses. He liked to see the eyes of witnesses when he was interviewing them.

'By all means.'

'A fascinating house you live in,' he said as Sarah lay down again and the rest of them trooped across the lawn and around to the front door. There appeared to be no other means of egress from the house into the garden and Thanet wondered what would happen in the event of a fire.

It was as if he had pressed a button.

'It's a Smock Mill,' said Squires enthusiastically, 'built in 1820. It was a working mill right up until just after the end of the First World War. Then it became virtually derelict until the early sixties, when it was sold and converted into a house. We bought it a couple of years ago.'

'I imagine there must be problems, converting a building like this.'

'Obviously.'

They had reached the front door and now stepped into a pleasantly cool dining hall with ancient oak refectory table and ladder-backed rush-seated chairs. The octagonal space was bisected by a partition wall with two doors in it. Kitchen and cloakroom perhaps? There was a distant but distracting beat of pop music. Thanet was pleased to see that the sudden transition from bright sunshine to the interior of the house had made Mrs Squires remove her sunglasses. Without them she looked considerably older.

Squires went straight to the foot of an open-tread staircase against the left-hand wall. 'Edward?' he shouted. 'Turn it down a bit, will you?'

There was no response and with an apologetic grimace he ran halfway up the stairs and called again. This time the music faded.

'Sorry,' he said as he returned. 'Where were we? Ah, yes, you were asking about the problems of converting a windmill. The trickiest, of course, is how to get from one floor to the next in a building this shape.' He gestured at the staircase and Thanet could see what he meant: there was an awkwardly shaped gap between it and the wall. 'That's the obvious way of course and it does look more authentic, but as you can see it wastes a lot of space and means that on each floor the size of the living accommodation is restricted by the amount of room needed for the flight of stairs. The best solution would be to have custom-made staircases built in against the walls but that's a very expensive option and so far we've held off from launching into it – it would also involve putting in new partition walls on each floor, to enlarge the rooms, otherwise there'd be no point.'

'How many floors are there?' said Lineham.

'Two in the base – this one and the sitting room above – and three in the windmill proper. That's the section above the staging. I'll show you, if you like.'

It was clear from Lineham's face that he was longing to accept the offer, and Thanet too was sorely tempted, but that was not the reason why they were here. Squires would obviously prefer to postpone the interview as long as possible and was prepared to go on discussing windmill conversions indefinitely. 'Thank you, sir, but I think we'd better get on. Shall we conduct the interview here?'

'Oh. Yes, of course. Or we could go up to my study?'

Where you would no doubt seat yourself authoritatively behind your desk, thought Thanet. 'No, this will do very well. Shall we sit down?'

'This is a dreadful business,' said Squires, when they were all settled around the dining table.

'We still can't believe it,' said his wife. She put her hand on his lap. 'Can we, Howard?'

Had Thanet imagined the beginnings of an instinctive flinch away from her?

'No,' said Squires. 'We can't take it in.'

'And to think that Sarah was here alone last night!' she went on. 'It doesn't bear thinking about . . . You never imagine this sort of thing can happen to anyone you know, do you? It doesn't seem real, somehow.' Her eyes were beautiful, very dark, almost black, and she opened them wide as she stared at Thanet, as if begging him to tell her that actually it had all been a mistake and Virginia was alive and well.

She appeared calm but Thanet was close enough to see that the pulse in her temple was beating rapidly – too rapidly, surely.

'All too real, I'm afraid,' said Thanet. 'Which is why we must ask you some questions about last night.'

They both nodded and looked cooperative.

'Anything we can do to help,' said Squires.

As arranged, Lineham took them quickly through their movements the previous day until they reached the point at which they returned to the Mintars' house in the evening. Then he glanced at Thanet and they continued the questioning in tandem.

'You walked, I presume, being so close,' said Thanet. 'Which way did you go?'

'There's a gate in the fence which divides the two gardens,' said Squires. 'We had it put in for ease of access. Ralph is very generous and lets us use the tennis court whenever we want to, if it's free.'

'So you walked through this gate and along past the front of the Mintars' house . . .'

'And around the side into the courtyard. Yes.'

'Why didn't you knock on the front door?'

'Because Ginny had said, "Supper at about a quarter to eight and drinks on the terrace before", so we went straight around to the back of the house. It was a very informal occasion, we didn't have to announce ourselves, it wouldn't have mattered if Ralph and Ginny weren't there. We knew they'd join us when they were ready.'

'And were they? There?'

'She was doing the watering in the courtyard.'

'Where was she drawing the water from?' said Lineham. 'The tap or the well?'

They looked at each other.

'Did you notice?' Squires asked his wife.

She shook her head. 'No. I was too busy thinking she obviously hadn't expected us to be quite so early and wishing we'd delayed for ten minutes.'

'Try to think,' said Lineham. 'Where, exactly, was she when you first saw her, as you came into the courtyard?'

'Watering one of the tubs by the annexe door,' said Marilyn Squires.

So as they suspected, she had been interrupted while watering

70

the camellias, thought Thanet. In which case the well cover would almost certainly have been off.

'That's right,' said her husband.

'So what did she do?'

'Looked up, said, "Hullo", and walked across to meet us.'

'What did she do with the watering can?'

They stared at him, trying to recall.

'I remember,' said Marilyn. 'She put it down next to the well wall, when she was halfway across.'

'And then?'

Marilyn shrugged. 'She continued on her way. She just sort of dipped to one side to put it down then went on walking.'

'So can you remember now whether the well cover was on or off?'

'I really couldn't say,' said Squires, but his wife screwed up her eyes, then closed them to concentrate.

They all waited.

'I'm trying to visualise it,' she murmured.

A further silence.

Then, 'Got it!' she said, and her eyes flew open. 'It was off!' she said triumphantly.

'You're sure?' said Thanet.

'Certain.'

Thanet saw no reason to doubt her. 'Thank you, that's a great help. Now, please consider very carefully. Assuming you're right, Mrs Squires, and the cover was off at that point, could you tell me if she replaced it while you were in the courtyard?'

They both shook their heads.

'Definitely not,' she said.

'She walked straight around to the terrace with us,' said her husband.

'What about later? Both of you must have walked through the courtyard at least – what, three times? Once on your way back here to change for the swim, once on your return to the pool, and once to come home again later on. And you, Mr Squires, must have gone to and fro yet again, to put some clothes on before helping to look for Mrs Mintar. Now, on any of those occasions did you notice whether the well cover was off or on?'

71

'Oh, my goodness,' said Marilyn Squires, pulling a face. 'We'll have to think.'

Silence. They were both frowning, trying to remember.

Once again she closed her eyes and Thanet watched her hopefully. Eventually she shook her head. 'It's no good. I'm sorry, I just didn't notice.'

'Nor did I,' said Squires. 'We're so used to seeing that well we never notice it any more, it's practically become invisible.'

'Please, do give this some more thought,' said Thanet. 'It really could be important. Cast your minds back.'

A further silence. More head shakes. Then, 'Hang on,' said Howard suddenly.

'What?' said Thanet and Lineham simultaneously.

'Later on. I remember now. When we were looking for her. There was a stone in my shoe so I had to stop to remove it. I was crossing the courtyard at the time and I put my foot up on that low wall around the well to tie the lace. And I'm sure the cover was on, or I'd have noticed the black hole in front of me, because it would have been different from normal. Yes. Now I think about it, I'm sure that's right.'

'And what time was this, sir?' said Thanet.

A shrug. 'I'm not sure. It was soon after we started looking, so just after eleven, I should say.'

'You simply assumed Mrs Mintar had put the cover back on?'

'I didn't assume anything, because I hadn't noticed, earlier, that it was off! If, indeed, it was.'

Squires was becoming exasperated and it was obvious that nothing was to be gained by pursuing the matter so on Thanet's nod Lineham took them back to the beginning of the evening. With wide-eyed innocence they assured him that it had been the most congenial of occasions, that nothing untoward had happened, that all had been harmony and conviviality. But Thanet, watching closely, observed the signs: from time to time Marilyn would moisten her lips with the tip of her tongue and her husband would rub his nose or tug at his ear, all good indications that they were either lying or trying to conceal something. If Howard had indeed been involved with Virginia no doubt they were desperate to keep it quiet. As Thanet had said to

Lineham, the consequences could be disastrous for Howard's career as a GP.

'Right,' Lineham was saying. 'Could we now move on a little. We understand that you did not return to the pool together. Is that right?'

Thanet groaned inwardly. Oh, Mike. Too soon, too sudden. The sergeant should have continued patiently moving on through the evening step by step. Then, possibly, they might have made a mistake, thought it was safe to say they had returned to the pool together. And then there would have been something to pick them up on, rattle them. Thanet was becoming more and more convinced that beneath her apparent calm Marilyn Squires was very much afraid. But of what, precisely? he wondered.

But it was too late now. The question had been asked and they were both looking disconcerted. Perhaps they had been intending to lie about it, or perhaps it was simply that they were put out to discover that Thanet and Lineham had already been checking up on their movements.

Squires was the first to recover. 'That's right,' he said, smooth as silk. 'Not that I can see it has any relevance whatsoever.'

Lineham, quite rightly, ignored the implicit request for an explanation. 'Why was that, sir?' he said, politely.

Marilyn Squires lifted thin shoulders. 'There's no mystery about it. I had a phone call. You can check, I'll give you the number, if you like.'

'Thank you. Yes, we would.'

She looked taken aback. She obviously hadn't expected him to take her up on the offer. She glanced nervously at her husband before reeling it off. 'Sturrenden 842963. It's a Mrs Bettina Leyton, a friend of mine.'

Lineham wrote it down. 'Thank you.'

'Might as well get that cleared out of the way,' said Thanet. 'Is Mrs Leyton likely to be at home now, do you think? Good. Then may we use your phone?' He nodded at the telephone on the desk.

They did not miss the implications of his request: he wasn't going to give them a chance to get in first and prime Mrs Leyton to give the right answers.

But the information had been genuine, he discovered. Just unfortunate timing for them. As it was, Howard confirmed what Rachel had told them: he got back to the pool between 10 and 10.15 and was the first to arrive after Matt and Rachel. Marilyn arrived shortly afterwards, followed by Arnold Prime and Jane.

'They arrived back together?'

'I didn't notice,' said Squires.

'Separately,' said his wife. 'Arnold first, then Jane, a few minutes later.'

'A few?'

'Sorry, I can't be more precise.'

'Did you happen to notice which door they came through?' said Thanet, mentally crossing his fingers. Mrs Squires was obviously much more observant than her husband.

'Arnold came through the drawing-room door and Jane through the door to the corridor leading to the kitchen.'

'You're sure?'

'I was sitting on the edge of the pool facing the house at the time,' she said. 'I was still dithering about going in. As I said, I often get a headache if I swim after a meal – which is, in fact, what happened. I really should have known better.'

'Thank you,' said Thanet, rising. 'You've been most helpful.'

'All right, all right, don't say it!' said Lineham, the second they were out of earshot, holding up a hand like a traffic policeman. 'I jumped the gun there, didn't I?'

'In the event, I don't think it mattered too much,' said Thanet. 'Come on, we'll go back through the gate in the fence.'

But Lineham was annoyed with himself and kept muttering about it.

'Mike!' said Thanet sharply. 'I said, forget it. It really didn't matter. The main thing is that you realised what you'd done. Apart from which we gleaned some very useful information – about the well cover and the fact that Jane Simons returned to the pool via the kitchen, for example.'

'But—'

'I said, that's enough. If you could just try to focus on the job in hand, and tell me what you thought of those two . . .'

'Shifty!' said Lineham promptly. 'And very, very nervous. I wonder why.'

'I agree. And yet, I don't know what you thought, but I didn't think they were actually lying about anything you asked them.'

'Which means, of course,' said Lineham gloomily, 'that I couldn't have asked them the right questions, could I?'

'You asked them everything I would have asked at the moment. I suppose the answer is we just haven't found out enough, yet, to know what those right questions are. I certainly don't feel that it would have been advisable at this point to come straight out and ask him if he was having an affair with Virginia Mintar.'

'No. Perhaps that was what they were afraid of, though.'

'Or perhaps not. At this stage we've got to keep an open mind.'

'Anyway, they're hiding something, that's for sure.'

'Yes. But leaving aside the possibility of his involvement with Virginia, the point is that we have no idea whether that something is relevant to our inquiries or not. You know what people are like. They're always giving the wrong impression by trying to cover up things in which we wouldn't be even remotely interested. No doubt all will be revealed, in time.'

'So what next, sir? Do we tackle Jane Simons again?'

'Not yet.' Thanet had been thinking. 'Digby said that he always watered the camellias during the week and Virginia Mintar did them at weekends. Which would imply that he was normally off duty on Saturdays and Sundays.'

'I see what you mean,' said Lineham. 'So what was he doing here this morning?'

'It didn't occur to me to ask. Stupid.'

'Me too.'

They were back in the courtyard by now. 'Well, it should be easy enough to find out,' said Thanet. 'We'll go and ask the old lady. She should know.'

Mrs Mintar senior was clearly annoyed to be interrupted again and her answer was brief and unequivocal. Digby never worked on Sundays, and she couldn't think what he had been doing here this morning. She slammed the door behind them the moment they turned away.

75

'So do we want to talk to him again at the moment?' said Lineham.

'I'm not sure. There was something about his attitude . . .' said Thanet.

'That smirk, you mean?'

'It's just that I had the feeling he thought he had the laugh on us. That he knew more than he was saying.'

'He's well placed to observe what goes on in the family.'

'Exactly.' Thanet made up his mind. 'Yes, I think we will have another word.'

But Digby was nowhere to be found. Apparently he had disappeared soon after the body had been retrieved from the well.

'Probably went home once the excitement was over,' said Thanet. 'Have you got his address?'

'Yup. Made a note this morning. He lives in the village.' Lineham leafed through his notebook. 'Here it is.'

'What would I do without you, Mike?'

It sounded as though Thanet was joking but Lineham looked gratified. They both knew Thanet meant it. They had worked together for so long that without the sergeant Thanet felt that he was working with one arm tied behind his back. It wasn't just that Lineham was efficient over minor details like this, but that over the years he and Thanet had built up so close a rapport that there was often no need to communicate in words. A gesture, a lift of the eyebrow, or the flicker of a glance were usually enough.

It was too hot to walk into the village again so they drove. After asking directions they found Digby's cottage some two hundred yards off the main street, at the end of an unmade-up track. An ugly little building of yellow brick, it crouched alone behind an unusually tall and overgrown privet hedge.

Thanet believed that the houses in which people lived invariably had something to say about their owners and his first reaction to this one was: *What has he got to hide?* 'Is he married?' he said as they pushed open the sagging picket gate and approached the front door. Nobody had expended much love on the place. The paint on windows and door was peeling, the gutters sagged and although the little squares of lawn on either side of the path had been cut, a minimum of effort had been expended on the garden.

76

'No idea. What makes you ask?'

'No one seems to care much what this place looks like.'

'Maybe it's rented, and he's got a bad landlord.'

'Possibly.'

Digby didn't look too pleased to see them and stood aside only grudgingly to let them in.

By contrast with the external appearance of the place, the room into which the front door opened was, if not particularly attractive, clean and well ordered. Its most striking feature was a group of three framed black and white photographs on the wall above the fireplace. Thanet also noted well-stocked bookshelves as well as a mini CD system. Interestingly, there was only one armchair, conveniently placed for viewing the television set which was tuned in to a golf programme. Did the man never have visitors? Thanet's interest sharpened. Digby's profile was becoming more interesting by the minute: male, almost certainly unmarried, a loner . . .

Digby switched off the set. 'What do you want?' he said to Thanet. 'I've gone over it all twice already and I can't see what else I can tell you.'

'It's surprising what people can remember, when they've had time to think, sir,' said Lineham.

'Maybe I've got better things to think about,' said Digby.

They were all still standing.

'May we sit down?' said Thanet, looking around in vain for a chair.

With an exaggerated sigh Digby went into a room at the rear and came back carrying a kitchen chair and a camping stool.

The man apparently had only one chair in his kitchen, too!

Lineham set the stool against a wall and opened his notebook. 'Just one or two more questions, then, sir,' he said as he sat down, somewhat gingerly.

The stool held, however.

Thanet suppressed a grin. 'You don't usually work on Sundays, we gather, Mr Digby. Would you mind telling us why you went in this morning?'

'I'd left something in the pocket of my overalls.'

'What?'

'A couple of films.'

Thanet's eyebrows went up. It was an unexpected reply, though perhaps it shouldn't have been, in view of the photographs on the walls and what Rachel had told them.

Digby took this as disbelief and launched into an explanation. 'I bought them in the town, yesterday morning, when I had to go in to pick something up for Mr Mintar. I put them in my pocket and forgot to bring them home last night. I wanted to use them this morning.'

'Ah yes,' said Thanet. 'Miss Mintar told us that you are an accomplished photographer.' He stood up and went to take a look at the mounted prints. 'These are yours, I presume?'

'Yes.'

The photographs were very unusual. They reminded him of the puzzle photographs which one occasionally sees in newspapers and magazines, when readers are asked to identify weird-looking objects which invariably turn out to be something mundane. It was a moment or two before he realised that all three were close-ups of garden plants. One was of the unfurling leaf of a fern. In another the prominent stamens of a lily thrust themselves skywards, the petals curling elegantly back behind them like unfolding wings. The third, a study in tone of strange, twisting shapes, he failed to recognise. 'What is this one?' he asked, pointing.

'A close-up of the bark of *Acer griseum*, the Paperbark Maple.'

'Do you do all your own developing and printing?' Thanet said, still looking.

Digby's lip curled. 'Of course.' *Stupid question.*

'These really are very good. Interesting. Original.' Thanet meant it. He was aware of Lineham shifting restlessly on his stool. *Shouldn't we be getting on with it?* He returned to his chair. 'You have an exhibition on at the moment, I believe.'

'Only in the local village library. It's not exactly the National Gallery.' But Digby was obviously pleased by Thanet's compliment.

'We must drop in and take a look,' said Lineham.

'Are you interested in wildlife?'

'Some forms,' said the sergeant.

The double meaning was not lost on Digby and his expression

78

darkened again. 'Look, could we get on?' His eyes strayed to the television set.

'Of course. You want to get back to the golf,' said Thanet. 'Well, we won't keep you long. So, you went to the Mintars' house this morning to fetch your films. I imagine you intended just to pick them up then come straight back.'

'That's right.'

'You said it was the watering can which alerted you to the fact that something might be wrong?'

'I told you. Mrs Mintar was a very tidy-minded lady. Everything had to be just so. It was unusual, that's all. So I went to tidy it away.' He shrugged. 'It was automatic.'

'That was very conscientious of you. It was your day off, after all. A lot of people wouldn't have bothered.'

Another shrug.

'Do you see much of your employers?'

'A fair bit, I suppose.'

'A good family to work for?'

'Pretty good, yes.'

'Would you say they got on well together, Mr and Mrs Mintar?'

Digby was no fool. He saw at once where this line of questioning was leading. 'If you're thinking of trying to pin this on Mr Mintar you're way off beam,' he said at once. 'I know what you lot always say about domestic murder, but he wouldn't have harmed a hair on his wife's head. Potty about her, he was. He's a good bloke.'

'And Mrs Mintar? What was she like?'

'Very nice. Polite, appreciative, not like some.'

But Thanet had the impression that Digby was deliberately keeping his expression bland. He was, as Lineham had said, well placed to observe the comings and goings in the Mintar household. If Mintar was away a lot, as he must be, and if Virginia Mintar was as man-mad as her sister seemed to imply, perhaps she might have felt that it was safe to bring her boyfriends (lovers?) home. And if she was involved with Howard Squires, Digby would no doubt know more about it than anyone else.

'And a very attractive woman,' said Lineham.

There was a wary look in Digby's eyes as he said, 'So?'

'She must have had admirers.'

79

'If she did it was none of my business.'

'It must have been lonely for her, with Mr Mintar away so much.'

Digby shrugged.

'Was there anyone special?' said Thanet softly.

Digby compressed his lips and said nothing.

'Oh come, Mr Digby. Being there most of the time you must have been aware of any regular visitors.'

Digby rubbed the side of his nose. 'I said, none of my business, was it?'

'Not then, maybe. But it is now. Don't you want to help us find out who killed her?'

'I suppose.'

'Then please, cast your mind back and tell us if there was anyone you saw her with on a regular basis, either some time ago or more recently.'

'There's that friend of hers. Mrs Amos.' The sardonic twinkle was back in Digby's eye.

Thanet felt like shaking him. The man knew something, he was certain of it. 'What about male friends, Mr Digby?'

Digby pulled down the corners of his mouth and shook his head. 'Not to my knowledge.'

Whatever he knew, he wasn't going to tell, that was clear. Thanet tried another tack. 'Could you tell us something about her activities?'

'What activities?'

Thanet saw Lineham stir. The sergeant was finding this interview equally frustrating. 'You must have some idea where she went, whom she saw?'

'Not really.'

'You have no idea at all? She never said, "Oh, Digby, I'm just going to such and such a place. If anyone calls, tell them I hope to be back by lunchtime", for example?'

'I don't recall her ever saying exactly that, no.'

Thanet was keeping his temper with difficulty. 'Mr Digby. I don't know if you are being deliberately obstructive, but I would like to remind you that your employer, a woman whom you say you liked, has been murdered. She is dead, Mr Digby, and someone is responsible.'

'So what do you want me to say?' Digby flared up. 'I was her gardener, not her minder. She didn't give me a list of her activities, did she? I know she spent a lot of time at that Health Club. And she did an awful lot of shopping, she was always coming back with those glossy carrier bags. But apart from that . . . I imagine she went to coffee mornings, had lunch with her friends, all that sort of stuff.'

As Thanet had hoped, anger had loosened the man's tongue. Careful now, not to phrase the next question in a negative manner. 'And were there any special male friends?'

'I told you! Not to my knowledge!'

Thanet and Lineham exchanged brief glances. *He's lying.*

But perhaps now was the moment to get at the truth about another of Virginia Mintar's relationships. 'How did Mrs Mintar get on with her mother-in-law?'

Digby pounced upon the change of topic with relief. 'Ah well, now that's a very different kettle of fish.'

'Oh?'

'Always rowing, they were.'

'About what?'

'This and that.'

'Can't you be a little more precise?'

'She's an interfering old bag. Always thinking she knows best and trying to tell me what to do. She was the same with Mrs Mintar.'

'She criticised her, you mean.'

'Too right, she did!'

'About?'

'Mrs Mintar couldn't do a thing right in her eyes.'

Digby was being evasive again. But now a gleam of malice appeared in his eyes. 'As a matter of fact, they had a hell of a ding-dong yesterday.'

'Oh? When was this?'

'Dinner time. I was just knocking off and I was walking past the side of the annexe when I heard them arguing.'

'Where were they?'

'In her studio. There's a window on the side. It was wide open.'

'Could you hear what they were saying?' Thanet guessed

that the temptation to eavesdrop would have been irresistible.

'I'd guess the old bag had been going on at her again about something because young Mrs Mintar was saying that if she didn't shut up and stop her nagging she'd tell Mr Mintar about her heart condition, and that would put a stop to her gallivanting off to foreign parts for good and all.'

EIGHT

Outside the heat of the day was trapped between the high hedges of the narrow lane and the interior of Lineham's car was like an oven. They opened all the doors to cool it down and waited for a few minutes before getting in.

'Ouch,' said Lineham as he touched the steering wheel. 'This is almost too hot to handle.' He switched on the blower and a stream of torrid air gushed out at them. 'If the climate goes on changing like this they'll have to start putting in air conditioning as standard.'

'Mmm.' Thanet was thinking about Digby. 'Doesn't sound as if there was much love lost between Virginia Mintar and her mother-in-law, does there?'

'Nor between Digby and the old lady, either.'

'Are you suggesting he might have been exaggerating, in order to get her into trouble?'

'It's a thought, isn't it?'

'And the row, yesterday lunchtime?'

Lineham did not answer immediately. He was pulling out into the main street. His caution, however, proved unnecessary. Not a single person was in sight. Presumably they were all, like the Squireses, prostrate in their back gardens or shut up indoors like Digby, watching television. Thanet didn't blame them. He was sweating so much that his back was sticking to the car seat and he leaned forward a little to separate them and allow air to pass between.

'Oh, I should think that bit was true enough,' said Lineham. 'I don't see how he could have known about old Mrs Mintar's heart condition otherwise.'

'No. The interesting thing is that her son obviously doesn't know and her daughter-in-law did. Now how did that come about, I wonder? It certainly doesn't seem that they were on sufficiently good terms for her to have confided in Virginia. In fact, I should have thought she'd have been anxious to keep it a total secret, for the very reason Digby mentioned.'

'No more expeditions, you mean?'

'Yes. Did you notice her whip that pill bottle out of sight when we were looking at the paintings?'

'No, I didn't.' Lineham looked chagrined. He hated to feel he had missed something.

'You weren't supposed to. It was real sleight-of-hand stuff.'

'You noticed, though, didn't you?'

Thanet ignored this. Lineham was always putting himself down. 'The point is, I should guess her work is more important to her than anything else, and those expeditions are what she enjoys most of all. The only time she seemed to come to life was when she was talking about them.'

'I agree that I can't see her telling Virginia about her condition voluntarily. Unless, of course, Virginia found out by accident – she could have had an attack while Virginia was present, for instance.'

'Possible, I suppose. But she's a tough old bird. In those circumstances, unless it was a very bad attack, I could just imagine her gritting her teeth and making an excuse to get away without letting on, so that she could take her medication in private. No, Mike, if we're right and Virginia was involved with Dr Squires I think it much more likely that that's how she found out.'

'Pillow talk, you mean?'

'Yes.'

Lineham tutted. 'Getting in deeper and deeper, isn't he? An affair with a patient and then breaking another patient's confidentiality . . . If he did tell her, that would explain why he's so unpopular with the old lady. She would be bound to realise how Virginia found out.'

'Quite. But this is all speculation at the moment, remember, Mike. Still, I think another word with him is next on the agenda. But leaving aside the question of how Virginia found out, we can't ignore the point Digby was making.'

'That Virginia and the old lady had a row yesterday afternoon, you mean.'

'And that Virginia was threatening to spill the beans to her husband.'

'You think that might have been a strong enough motive to shove her down the well?'

'Think about it, Mike. Mrs Mintar senior's front door is only a matter of yards away from the well and by her own admission she was in the annexe at the time. It was a hot night and she might well have left her front door open when she went in, to cool the place down. And the circumstances were ideal – it was dark, everyone was out of the way, Virginia would have been alone, the well cover was off . . . So say Virginia remembers she hadn't finished watering the camellias. She goes out to the well, bends over to pick up the watering can, or leans across to reach the bucket or whatever . . . Mrs Mintar sees her chance and grabs it. It wouldn't have taken much strength. Virginia was only slight. If she was caught off balance . . .'

'What about the voices Mrs Mintar claims to have heard in the courtyard?'

'There's no corroboration, as yet anyway. She could well have made them up, to throw us off the track.'

Lineham slammed on the brakes. They were in the lane approaching the Squires' house now and a tabby cat had just shot across the road in front of them. 'Sorry, sir! Stupid animal,' he muttered.

'That was Mintar's cat, I think,' said Thanet. 'You wouldn't have been too popular if you'd run him over.'

'If it carries on like that it won't be long before someone does,' said Lineham. 'Shall we park in the Squires' drive, or next door?'

'Next door, I think, and we'll walk through.'

Squires was not pleased to see them again so soon but with a bad grace took them back into the hall. 'What is it this time, Inspector?' He perched on a corner of the table as if to emphasise the fact that he expected the interview to be brief and gestured to Thanet to sit down.

Thanet shook his head, remained standing. He had no intention of giving Squires the psychological advantage of looking down on him. Lineham propped himself against the wall and took out his notebook.

'We've just been to interview Digby.'

Squires looked surprised. Whatever he had expected or feared, it wasn't this. But he was intelligent enough to realise that Thanet wouldn't have used this oblique approach without good reason. 'The Mintars' gardener? So?' *What has it got to do with me?*

'Mrs Mintar senior is a patient of yours, I believe?'

Squires' expression remained impassive but his left eyelid twitched. 'Please get to the point, Inspector.'

But Thanet persisted. 'She *is* a patient of yours, isn't she?'

A terse nod. 'But I still don't see—'

'Digby apparently heard Mrs Mintar and Virginia Mintar – we'll use her Christian name to avoid confusion – arguing yesterday. He said that Virginia was threatening to tell her husband about Mrs Mintar's heart condition.'

Squires said nothing.

'Perhaps you could confirm that, Doctor?'

'Confirm what? That they were arguing? How can I? I wasn't there.'

This was wilful misunderstanding and it was an effort for Thanet to conceal his rising irritation. 'That Mrs Mintar has a heart condition,' he said.

'I *could* confirm – or deny – that, yes. But I won't. You're asking me to break patient confidentiality.'

'I don't think so. We already knew of Mrs Mintar's condition. She had dropped her bottle of pills and I picked them up. It was obvious what they were for.'

'Why bother to ask me, then? Anyway, drawing your own conclusions is one matter. My breaking patient confidentiality is another. In any case, I don't see what conceivable relevance this has to your investigation.'

'Don't you? Shall I just say that we'd have to be very stupid not to have realised that there was little love lost between Mrs Mintar and her daughter-in-law.'

Squires stared at him. 'My God,' he said. 'You're surely not suggesting that Mrs Mintar . . . That *is* what you're suggesting, isn't it?' Thanet could almost hear what the man

86

was thinking: *If they suspect the old lady, that'll take the heat off me.*

'I think you'd agree that Mrs Mintar's work means a great deal to her?'

'Certainly.'

'And that she would be deeply disappointed if she were unable to go on any more of her plant-finding expeditions?'

'I imagine so, yes.'

'And that if she does suffer from a heart condition and the organisers knew of it, they wouldn't be too happy about allowing a seventy-seven-year-old with angina to accompany them? It would be too much of a responsibility, I imagine.'

'Such expeditions are very strenuous, I believe,' said Squires carefully.

'And that if Mr Mintar knew of his mother's condition, he would almost certainly take steps to stop her from going?'

'Steps? Mrs Mintar is a very determined woman.'

Thanet waved a hand. 'Inform the organisers. Whatever.'

'I suppose Ralph would take fairly drastic action, yes.'

'Don't you think it's time we stopped this charade, sir? Why don't you come straight out and admit that yes, Mrs Mintar does have a heart condition.'

Squires's mouth set in stubborn lines. 'I can't do that.'

'Very well. But perhaps you can tell us something else. What interests us, you see, is how Virginia Mintar learned of her mother-in-law's state of health.'

Squires was no fool. He saw at once where this was leading and his face went blank as the shutters came down.

'They weren't exactly on the best of terms, were they?' said Thanet. 'I can't see Mrs Mintar deciding to confide in Virginia, can you? And it seems to us there's only one other way Virginia could have found out.'

Squires folded his arms across his chest as if to contain – what? Anger? Fear? Dismay? 'I hope you're not suggesting what I think you're suggesting?'

'And what would that be, sir?'

'That it was I who told her.'

'Did I suggest that? I was merely asking you for possible explanations as to how Virginia could have found out.'

'Don't give me that! And I deeply resent the implication. Surely, the very fact that I have steadfastly refused, under considerable pressure, I might say, to enlighten you on the matter, underlines the fact that I take patient confidentiality very seriously indeed.'

'You might well have acted out of concern for your patient, in the hope that somehow Mrs Mintar could be stopped from doing something you are bound to have regarded as foolhardy?'

Squires was tempted by this suggestion. Thanet saw the man consider and reject it before he said, 'Certainly not!'

'Then how could she have found out?'

'For God's sake, man, it's obvious, isn't it? The same way that you did! By accident!' Squires stopped, obviously aware that implicit in this statement was the very admission he had been trying to avoid. With an exclamation of disgust he slid off the table and went to stand with his back to them, looking out of the window.

Thanet said nothing and eventually Squires swung around. His tone was weary as he said, 'Congratulations, Inspector. Very neat.'

'So how did she find out, sir?'

Squires dragged out one of the dining chairs and slumped down on it, underlining his sense of defeat. 'She went across to see her mother-in-law one day and Mrs Mintar had an attack while she was there. She said Mrs Mintar wouldn't actually admit what was happening, but that it was obvious to anyone with a grain of intelligence. She consulted me because she wanted to know the best course of action to take should it happen again.'

He was lying, Thanet was certain of it. The doctor's prevarications had at least given him time to concoct a story – though if it weren't true, he was taking a risk: Thanet might well decide to check on it with the old lady herself. 'When was this?'

'A month or so ago.'

'Did she ask you about the wisdom of Mrs Mintar going on these trips?'

'Yes, she did. And I told Virginia that it would be most unwise for her mother-in-law to go on any more, that I had told her so, but that she wouldn't listen to me.'

'Did you know that Virginia had not informed her husband of his mother's condition?'

'No I didn't. I assumed she had.'

'Why didn't she, do you think?'

'I have absolutely no idea.'

But it was obvious, really. Knowledge of this nature was power, and power over her mother-in-law was something that Virginia Mintar would not readily have relinquished. Had she paid for it with her life? 'Well, I think that's all for the moment. Thank you, sir.'

Squires's relief that the interview was at an end was obvious, and did not escape Lineham either.

'More porkies, don't you agree, sir?' said the sergeant when they were outside again.

'Yes, I do. And plenty more where those came from, I should say.' It was marginally cooler now but the sun was still beating down from a Mediterranean sky. 'I'm absolutely parched! I only wish I'd thought to bring a bottle of water with me. I certainly shall tomorrow.'

Lineham grinned. 'I've got a Thermos in the car.'

'Anyone could tell you were a boy Scout, Mike! Lead me to it!'

While they drank the tea they discussed their next move. They both agreed: in view of what Digby had told them they would have to talk to Mrs Mintar again.

'Wonder what sort of welcome we'll get this time,' said Lineham as they approached the open door of the annexe.

'Perhaps she'll have finished painting by now and be a bit more cooperative.'

And this, to their surprise, proved to be the case. She was positively affable, taking them into the sitting room and even offering them tea. Her work must have gone well, Thanet thought, and she was on a temporary high. She had changed out of her painting gear into a flowing jade green caftan with a panel of embroidery down the front. He would have loved another cup of tea but he refused it. This could be a difficult interview and he wouldn't have felt comfortable accepting hospitality from her. 'I apologise for bothering you again,' he said.

She waved a dismissive hand. 'I'm the one who should be

apologising. I'm afraid I was really rather rude this morning. You were only doing your job, after all. Shall we sit down?' She waited until they were settled and then said, 'I'm afraid I'm notoriously bad-tempered when my work is interrupted.'

'I can understand that.'

'Perhaps. I think that only another creative person really can – a composer, perhaps, or a writer. When you are engaged in a creative activity of that nature you become completely absorbed in it. But it's a very special kind of absorption, very difficult to describe. It's as if you are existing on a different level, as if . . . well, as if you take a deep breath and then sink beneath the waves, don't come up for air until you have finished.' She gave an embarrassed laugh. 'I'm not explaining myself very clearly, am I?'

'Oh, but you are. It's fascinating.'

'The point I'm trying to make is that if that concentration is disrupted it's often very difficult to get back to the point where you were. The thread is broken. And I'm afraid I react very badly when that happens. So . . .' She sat back and folded her hands, the picture of attentive cooperation, '. . . tell me how I can help you this time.'

Best to delay tackling her about the row with Virginia, Thanet decided, and take advantage of her helpful mood by finding out a little more about Caroline. 'We've heard quite a bit more about Caroline's elopement this morning, both from your son and from Rachel. I believe you were here at the time?'

Her eyebrows had gone up. 'I really don't see—'

Thanet sighed. He didn't see why he should have to explain himself, but he didn't want to annoy her by being too peremptory. 'It's just that in a case like this . . .'

'A case like what, Inspector?'

'Mrs Mintar. I know that everyone here would like to believe that your daughter-in-law's death was an accident. But equally, the consensus of opinion is that it couldn't have been.'

'She could have had a heart attack and fallen in. Or a stroke. People do, even at her age.'

'It's possible. Unlikely, in view of the height of the wall, but possible. And if she did, the post-mortem should confirm it. But we can't afford to sit around and twiddle our thumbs while we're waiting for that. So, as I was about to say, there are two other alternatives . . .'

'Suicide and murder.'

Irascible she might be, but it was refreshing to interview a witness who didn't beat about the bush. 'Quite.'

'And as we can rule out the former . . .'

'Precisely. Furthermore, although the family would no doubt love to subscribe to the theory of a psychopath who just happened to stray into the courtyard last night and push your daughter-in-law down the well—'

'All right, all right. No need to spell it out. I'm as aware of the statistics as most, I dare say.'

'The point being that in order to work out what happened last night we have to try to understand the people involved.'

'And that includes dragging up something that happened four years ago?'

'Such events have repercussions which can last for many years, for a lifetime even. We understand that your daughter-in-law was deeply distressed by Caroline's elopement and her unhappiness is bound to have had a profound effect on her behaviour. This, in turn, would have affected those around her and their attitudes to her. Surely you can see therefore that we are bound to be interested in what happened?'

She stared at him without expression, clearly considering what he had said. 'Oh very well,' she said at last. 'If you really think it will help.'

Thanet glanced at Lineham, who pretended to consult his notebook.

'To go back to the night Caroline left, then,' the sergeant said, 'we understand you arrived back from one of your trips that very evening.'

'That's right. I got back shortly before dinner. I wasn't expected until the following day but there'd been a real muddle over our flight booking and three of us had to come back a day early. Anyway, with the benefit of hindsight, I should have known something was up as far as Caroline was concerned.'

'What do you mean?' said Thanet.

'I suppose, having been away for some time, I was looking at everyone with a fresh eye. And Caroline was like a cat on hot bricks.'

'In what way, precisely?' said Lineham.

'She kept on glancing at her watch when she thought no one was looking, for instance. And she scarcely touched her food.'

'What did you think was the matter with her?'

'I wasn't too concerned. You know what young girls are like. If it isn't PMT it's boys. I suppose I simply assumed she was anxious to get off and meet that lout she was so keen on.'

'You didn't like him?' said Thanet.

Mrs Mintar lifted her chin. 'He simply wasn't suitable for Caroline. Their backgrounds were too different.'

Thanet could hear Lineham thinking, *What a snob!* and as he expected the sergeant couldn't resist a comment.

'They seem to have made a go of it, anyway,' said Lineham.

'Who can possibly tell? She hasn't come running back, certainly. But she took after me in many ways and she had a certain stubborn pride.'

'You're saying that even if the marriage had been a disaster she wouldn't have come home again?' said Thanet.

'Possibly.'

Thanet wondered what that said about the Mintar family. He hoped that if either of his children were ever in trouble they would know where to turn first for help and support. His stomach clenched as he thought of Bridget's current problem. One of the worst aspects of the situation was that he was absolutely powerless to do anything about it. *Oh, Bridget.*

'If they ever got married at all,' Mrs Mintar was saying, with a disapproving sniff. 'Living together seems to be much more fashionable these days.'

'I understood that both her mother and her father were very fond of Caroline.'

'Oh they were. Too much so.'

'What do you mean?'

'I think she felt stifled, found the situation at home claustrophobic. I think that was one of the reasons she kicked over the traces so thoroughly, first in making a completely unacceptable choice and then by running off with him.'

'They disapproved of him as strongly as you did?'

'Of course they did! Oh, he was a handsome creature, I grant you that, in an animal sort of way, but without a grain of refinement or intelligence. Anyone could see with half an eye that what she felt for him was purely physical and would wear off in no time at all. That was why I was all for letting the thing run its course. I could see that by making such a fuss about it Ralph would only make her more determined. Which is, of course, what happened.'

'There were rows about her seeing this man?' Lineham consulted his notebook. 'This Dick Swain?'

'Endless rows, I gather. I was away when they were at their peak, of course, but I believe my son did stop short of actually forbidding her to see him, just. Not that it made any difference in the end, she went anyway.'

'I understand he's not too happy about this engagement of Rachel's, either,' said Thanet.

'An understatement, if ever I heard one.'

'There doesn't seem to be much he can do about it.'

'Oh, I wouldn't say that. Matthew Agon is a very different kettle of fish. We can always resort to the traditional solution. In fact, I've been trying to persuade Ralph to do so. But apparently Virginia was against the idea for some reason.'

'The traditional solution?' said Lineham.

'We're talking about a financial inducement, I imagine?' said Thanet.

'That's right. Bribery. I believe in calling a spade a spade.'

Not much doubt about that! thought Thanet. 'You think it might work?'

'If it were substantial enough, yes. And it would be worth every penny, to get rid of that toad.'

'But your daughter-in-law was against it, you say? Why was that?'

'I think she was afraid it could go disastrously wrong and turn Rachel against them if Agon refused the offer and told Rachel about it. But I think Ralph had hopes of bringing her around.'

'He wouldn't have gone ahead without her agreement?'

She hesitated. 'I'm not sure, if it came to the crunch.'

She had been so cooperative that Thanet was now reluctant to broach the subject which had precipitated this second interview. It had to be done, however. How to achieve a smooth transition, though? 'Your daughter-in-law was not an amenable sort of person?'

A cynical little laugh. 'Shall we just say that she liked her own way.'

'And usually got it?'

'Usually, yes.'

'As far as her husband was concerned, you mean?'

'I didn't say that. I have no intention of discussing their relationship with you, Inspector, if that's what you're hoping.'

'What about your own relationship with her?'

'What about it?'

'You said yourself, this morning, that there was no love lost between you, that as far as you were concerned it was good riddance.'

'So? I hope you're not suggesting what I think you're suggesting, Inspector?'

Thanet said nothing, waited.

She gave a little laugh. 'You don't seriously think that *I* was responsible for her death? An old woman like me?' She shook her head in mocking disbelief. 'I'd have thought there were far more likely candidates, wouldn't you?'

'Such as?'

'I'm afraid you'll just have to work that out for yourself.'

Was she serious, or just trying to deflect him? 'I'm merely trying to find out how deep this mutual antipathy was. Because as you've already admitted, it was mutual, wasn't it?'

'I've never pretended otherwise.'

'I have to tell you, Mrs Mintar, that you were overheard having a serious quarrel with your daughter-in-law yesterday lunchtime.'

This shook her. She stared at him and her self-control slipped long enough for him to catch a gleam of panic in her eyes before the guard went up again. Her reaction could imply guilt, of course, but he guessed that she was remembering what the row had been about and wondering if the eavesdropper had been close enough to hear what was being said. He guessed, too, that she was torn between denying the whole thing and wanting to find out exactly what Thanet knew. The need to know won. Her chin went up as she said defiantly, 'What of it?'

'Oh come, Mrs Mintar, don't pretend to be naïve. Your daughter-in-law is murdered and we find out that only hours before that you had what was described to us as "a hell of a ding-dong" with her. What are we supposed to think?'

' "A hell of a ding-dong". That could only be Digby, the creep! Typical of him, to listen in on people's private conversations! I'm right, aren't I? What lies has he been telling about me?'

'What makes you think they were lies?'

'I wouldn't trust him further than I could spit! What did he say?'

She was desperate to know if her secret was safe and Thanet couldn't help feeling sorry for her. This woman's work was her life and she was terrified of having her richest source of enjoyment and inspiration snatched away from her.

'That your daughter-in-law was threatening to tell your son that you suffer from angina.'

Her hand went defensively up to her chest as if he had dealt her a mortal blow and the colour drained from her face, leaving her skin the colour of tallow. Suddenly she looked her age.

Thanet was alarmed. In view of her condition, perhaps he should have broken the news more gently. 'Are you all right?' he said.

She compressed her lips and shook her head dismissively. 'I'm fine.' Slowly, experimentally, she lowered her hand. 'Have you told my son about this?'

'No.'

'Then I must ask you not to do so.' Her mouth twisted. 'That wretched man!'

'We already knew of your condition.' Thanet explained how.

She leaned forward, tension in every line of her body. 'You must promise not to tell Ralph!'

'If the matter has no relevance to our investigation I see no reason why we should.'

At last she relaxed, leaning her head against the back of the chair as if exhausted. 'Thank you.' After a few moments she straightened up again and gave a wry grin. 'So I really am a suspect!'

'It's obvious how important to you it is, that he shouldn't find out. If your daughter-in-law was threatening to tell him . . .'

She waved a hand. 'You didn't know Virginia, Inspector. It was an idle threat.'

'Why should you believe that?'

'Firstly because it was the only stick she had to beat me with and she wasn't going to throw it away in a hurry. And secondly because if she did, she might have been stuck with having me living here all the time instead of just part of the time. And believe me, that wouldn't have suited her one little bit.'

Thanet had to admit that from what he had heard of Virginia so far, this made sense. 'What was the row about?'

'The usual thing. Virginia's behaviour.'

'In what way, specifically?'

'Specifically, the way she couldn't resist throwing herself at any new man who came along, in front of my son. I couldn't bear seeing him humiliated like that.'

'In this case you are referring to . . . ?'

'Her sister's boyfriend.' She hesitated, gave Thanet an assessing look. Then she got up, strolled across to a side table, opened a heavily carved wooden box and took out a long, slim, brown, elegant cigarette. With a lift of her eyebrows and a wave of her hand she offered them one and when they shook their heads she took her time over lighting up.

Thanet guessed that in view of her angina this was a rare indulgence, the need probably triggered by the stress of the interview.

She blew out a thin stream of smoke before speaking again. 'Especially . . .' she said, deliberately.

Thanet caught the malicious gleam in her eye and could guess what was coming. She had decided to relinquish any idea of preserving family privacy in order to turn the spotlight away from herself. If she had to sacrifice her son's dignity and reveal him as a cuckold – good old-fashioned word, Thanet had always thought – then so be it.

'Yes?' he said, as she had known he would.

'I'm sure you've already worked out for yourself that it was unlikely in the extreme that I should voluntarily have told

Virginia about my little problem. So of course you must have asked yourself precisely how she did find out?'

She was going to tell him about Virginia's affair with Squires! He experienced the spurt of excitement and satisfaction which invariably accompanied this turning point in an interview, when he knew that he had succeeded in manipulating a witness into revealing what s/he had every intention of concealing.

'Naturally.'

'And I suspect you have already guessed the answer.'

'Perhaps.'

'Then let's see if you've guessed correctly.'

NINE

Mrs Mintar blew out another plume of smoke and gave him a mocking, challenging grin.

But Thanet was too old a hand to be caught out like that. What if he were wrong? He smiled back, benignly. 'I'd much prefer to hear it from you,' he said.

Abruptly her expression changed and she turned to stub out her half-smoked cigarette with angry, stabbing movements. Then she returned to her chair. 'Have you got any children, Inspector?'

'Two.' His stomach clenched. What was happening to Bridget right now?

'Married?'

'One is.'

'Then I hope he or she has a faithful partner. You can't imagine what it's like to have to stand by and see your son betrayed, not once or twice but over and over again, to have to watch him watching his wife flirting shamelessly with other men. Virginia simply could not resist the temptation to exercise her charms on every new male that came her way. You should have seen her last night, with Jane's boyfriend! Smiles, fluttering eyelids, oh-so-friendly hand laid upon his thigh . . . I tell you, it was a disgusting performance. And apart from the fact that Ralph was present, it was downright embarrassing for the rest of us, and especially for Jane.' She paused, and again the malicious gleam appeared in her eye. 'The big plus, of course, was that it made that parody of a doctor squirm.'

Now they were getting to the point. 'Dr Squires, you mean.'

'Who else? I must say I did enjoy seeing him suffer, after what he did to me. Oh yes, Inspector, I can see you already know. But I will spell it out for you. Virginia knew of my condition because her lover told her. Pillow talk, no doubt. Our charming Dr Squires is not only an adulterer but he has betrayed his profession, firstly by having an affair with a patient and secondly by breaking patient confidentiality. And the infuriating thing is, I haven't been able to do a thing about it. If I complained to the General Medical Council Ralph would find out about my heart condition and I couldn't afford to risk that.'

'You could change your doctor.'

'True. And I shall. But that wouldn't have helped the current situation.'

Unless you got rid of Virginia, thought Thanet. 'How long had this affair been going on?'

A shrug. 'No idea. All I know is that when I got back at the beginning of March it didn't take me long to realise what was happening. So I must say that last night I did relish the spectacle of watching him see her flirt so outrageously with another man. Believe me, he didn't enjoy that one little bit, though he tried to hide it, of course.'

'What about his wife? Did she know about this, do you think?'

'If she didn't she must be blind or deaf. He was absolutely besotted with Virginia, couldn't keep his eyes off her.'

'But you don't actually know whether or not Mrs Squires knew?'

'Not to be positive, no. But I suspect she did. I think that, like me, she was rather enjoying seeing her husband's nose put out of joint last night.'

'How did Mr Prime react to these attentions?'

'I gave him ten out of ten for being Virginia-resistant.'

'He didn't respond, then.'

'Only by looking uncomfortable. But of course, this just made Virginia redouble her efforts.'

'What about her sister?'

'Jane? Oh, she was furious with Virginia, as you can imagine. She didn't actually say anything, I don't think she would have wanted to embarrass Ralph, she's very fond of him, but you could tell that underneath she was seething.' Mrs Mintar leaned back in her chair with an air of finality and waved a graceful hand, the green silk of her flowing caftan sleeve falling back to reveal a tanned, muscular arm. 'So there you have it, Inspector, the full picture. Believe me, it wasn't a very pleasant social occasion and not one that I would wish to repeat in a hurry. Not that there's any possibility of that now, of course, thank God. And then, of course, to cap it all, Rachel came waltzing in with the news of her engagement. Ralph put a brave face on it, naturally, what else could he do? We all did. But after the charade with the champagne was over I can assure you I had no wish to prolong the evening by participating in the jolly swimming party they proposed. I couldn't wait to get back and immerse myself in a book. So consoling, the printed word, don't you think? And much less wearing than people.'

Thanet rose and Lineham followed suit. 'Well, thank you for being so frank with us, Mrs Mintar. You've been most helpful.'

'Not at all.' The sardonic gleam was back in her eye. *Given you plenty of food for thought, haven't I?*

Outside Thanet hesitated. They needed to interview Howard Squires again in the light of what Mrs Mintar had told them, but first he'd like to chew matters over with Lineham. 'Come on, Mike, let's go for a stroll, clear our minds.'

They walked down the drive and turned right, away from the village. Although it was now late afternoon the sun continued to beat mercilessly down and the air was suffocatingly hot and still. Perhaps this hadn't been a good idea after all, thought Thanet. Though he felt he really had needed to get away from the Mintars' house, to distance himself a little from the intensity of the emotional situations in which all of those involved in this crime seemed to have been locked. 'Let's see if we can find some shade.'

A couple of hundred yards further on they came to a five-barred gate conveniently shaded by a big oak tree and they stopped with sighs of relief, taking out handkerchiefs to mop at sweating foreheads.

'That's better,' said Lineham. 'Been a real scorcher today, hasn't it?'

Thanet automatically felt in his pocket for the familiar bulge of his pipe, and experienced the usual little thud of disappointment that it wasn't there. At times like this, when he wanted to relax, he still felt bereft without it. For years he had remained determined to hold out against the anti-smoking brigade but in the end, as the places where it was possible to smoke and still feel comfortable about it grew fewer and fewer, he became fed up with being made to feel a pariah. Even then he would have continued out of sheer perversity but for Bridget's pregnancy. No one these days could be unaware of the dangers of smoking near babies and the prospect of being unable to light up either in Bridget and Alexander's house – or indeed in his own home when they came to visit – was the deciding factor in making him stop. It had been a great relief to Lineham, he knew, though neither of them had ever referred to it, and the sergeant had put up with his tetchiness in the early days of deprivation without a word, look or gesture of resentment.

Now, Thanet merely sighed and joined Lineham in resting his forearms along the top bar of the gate and gazing at the vista before them. The lane ran along the spine of a slight ridge and from here the land fell away in the irregular patchwork of fields bordered by hedges and punctuated by specimen trees which is the essence of the English countryside, sadly destroyed only too often in recent years by greedy farmers but, mercifully, here in this area of Kent so far preserved for posterity. Though born and brought up in Sturrenden, the small country town where he lived and worked, Thanet had always loved the countryside in general and the Kent landscape in particular. In his opinion it was some of the most beautiful in England. Earlier on in his career he had had to live elsewhere for brief periods but he had been delighted to return to Kent and now had no intention of leaving if he could help it. He had often been berated for his lack of ambition but had steadfastly refused to climb further up the promotions ladder, knowing that the higher you scrambled the more likely it was that you would have to be prepared to move around. Anyway, in his view, the further you climbed the more desk-bound you became and the more distant from the work which had attracted you in the first place. No, he had found his niche and was content to stay in it. If it weren't for this constant, nagging anxiety over Bridget . . . Perhaps he ought to ring Joan? No, what was the point? If there were any news she'd have been in touch right away. But it made him sick to the stomach to think of what Bridget must be going through now. And to know that there was very real danger for her as well as the baby . . .

'You all right, sir?'

Thanet nodded, lips compressed.

'Worried about your daughter?' Lineham was aware of the situation.

'I can't help it, Mike. Well, you know what it's like. You've been through it yourself, when Louise had Richard.'

Lineham nodded. 'The worst of it is, you feel so helpless.'

'I just can't stop thinking about it.'

'I know. It's just there, all the time. I found the best thing was to concentrate on work.'

'You're right. I must make more of an effort. But first – I've been meaning to ask but kept on forgetting – tell me how your mother is settling in at Abbeyfield.'

Widowed young, old Mrs Lineham had had a struggle to bring up her only child and, naturally perhaps, had become fiercely possessive. Lineham had had to fight to achieve independence, firstly in his choice of career – Mrs Lineham considering police work much too dangerous – and secondly in his choice of wife, his mother recognising that in Louise she would have far too strong-minded a rival. It had always amused Thanet that his sergeant had managed to break away from one dominating woman only to choose to marry another.

The result was that Lineham spent most of his life in a balancing act, trying to reconcile the needs of each with the demands of the other, and the latest crisis had arisen last year, when the old lady had decided she no longer wished to live alone and had started angling for an invitation to move in with her son and his family – a recipe for disaster if ever there was one. For some time Lineham had prevaricated, knowing himself to be in a cleft stick, but had finally been rescued by a suggestion of Thanet's, who had via his own mother heard of an excellent organisation called Abbeyfield. This was a charity which provided at very reasonable cost accommodation for small groups of elderly people who found living alone hard to bear. Residents had their own rooms with their own furniture and as much or as little freedom and company as they wished, and there was always a resident housekeeper to keep an eye on them and to provide the main meals of the day. Although initially resistant to the idea, after visiting the Abbeyfield House in Maidstone and talking to the residents there old Mrs Lineham had soon changed her mind and had put her name down on the waiting list for the new Abbeyfield House due to open in Sturrenden this year. She had moved in a month ago.

'Fine. It's early days yet, of course, but touch wood, so far she seems to be settling in well. I can't tell you how grateful we are that you came up with the idea.'

'Don't thank me, thank my mother. Pure luck, really, that she had happened to mention it to me. Anyway, I'm glad it seems to be working out. I assume she hasn't sold her house yet?'

'No, she's hedging her bets at the moment, until she's sure she wants to stay.'

'Good.' Reluctant still to return to the topic of the murder, Thanet resumed his contemplation of the landscape. 'Did you know you can tell the age of a hedge by counting the number of native species in it, Mike? One per century.'

'No, I didn't. Not that I'd recognise them anyway.'

'Ben did a nature project. I thought it was fascinating. We used to go out counting species at weekends. Let's see if I can remember . . .' He turned to look at the hedge behind them, across the road. 'Hawthorn – the most common one; dogwood – that's the one with the reddish stems; elder; hornbeam – that goes a wonderful golden apricot colour in the autumn, hazel . . . How many's that?'

Lineham grinned. 'Five. You're showing off, sir.'

Thanet laughed. 'You're dead right, I am. But just think. Five hundred years old.'

'It's a load of rubbish if you ask me. Anyone planting a country hedge would mix up the species, and in ten years' time no one would know the difference.'

'You know the trouble with you, Mike? There is no romance in your soul!'

'And no bad thing, if you ask me. Look at that lot back

there.' Lineham jerked his head in the direction of the Mintars' house.

The sergeant obviously considered it time they got down to work again. He was right, of course.

'I don't know whether I'd quite call that romance, Mike. The emotions flying around last night were a good deal more earthy than that, don't you think?'

'There were plenty of them, anyway. Not my idea of a good night out!'

Thanet grinned. 'Nor mine. Still, we're beginning to get a pretty good picture of what went on, don't you think?'

'She's a really hard nut, that's for sure.'

'Old Mrs Mintar, you mean.'

'Yes. Coming on strong about how she couldn't discuss her son's relationships and then, the second her own neck is threatened, opening up the whole can of worms no matter what sort of light it put him in.'

'She really got up your nose, didn't she, Mike?'

'Like I said earlier, I just think she's a selfish old harridan, that's all. Whatever she says about how upset she used to get on Mr Mintar's behalf, I think that all she really cares about is herself and her work. I don't think she'd let anything stand in her way. And as you said yourself, she was perfectly placed to nip out and shove Virginia down that well. I'm sure she's strong enough. I know she's got this heart problem, but apart from that she must do an awful lot of walking and climbing with all those plant-hunting trips she goes on. Did you notice the muscles in her arm just now?'

'Yes, I did. And you may well be right. Though whether we'll ever manage to prove it, if so, I don't know.'

'There could be fingerprints on the well cover.'

'Possibly. With any luck. Though I'm not sure that would really help, in this case. Defence would argue she's had a thousand and one opportunities to put them there. But in any case it'll take days to get the results of all the comparisons through and we can't afford to hang around doing nothing. And anyway, there are a number of other likely possibilities . . .'

'True,' said Lineham reluctantly. It was obvious that old Mrs Mintar was his preferred candidate for the role of murderer.

'. . . which we have to consider,' said Thanet firmly. 'The interesting thing about last night's dinner party was the degree to which Virginia was the focal point for all that negative emotion. Just think about it, Mike. Practically everyone there – except Mr Prime, perhaps – could be said to have a motive. Next to the old lady, who I grant you comes pretty near the top of the list, there's Dr Squires. If you ask me, his motive is just as strong as hers. Imagine the power Virginia had over him – and I'm not talking only about how she was making him suffer last night, but the power over his career. If she'd chosen to blow the whistle on him, he'd have been finished. And he had the opportunity too. He and his wife returned to the pool separately, remember. What if Virginia was at the well when he came back and he grabbed his opportunity to have it out with her over her flirting with Prime?'

'There wouldn't have been time, surely, for a quarrel to escalate to that degree? According to Rachel Mrs Squires was only a few minutes behind her husband.'

'Oh, I don't know. It all depends on how angry he was when he tackled her, if that was what happened. An awful lot can happen in a few minutes. I certainly don't think we can rule it out.'

'I suppose not.'

'Then there's Mrs Squires herself . . .'

'We don't actually know, yet, whether she knew her husband was having an affair.'

'True. Though if she didn't, that meant Virginia had even more power over him, if she was threatening to spill the beans. But from what old Mrs Mintar said it just wasn't possible for Mrs Squires not to have noticed. It certainly doesn't sound as though Squires took much trouble to hide his feelings. So maybe his wife felt she couldn't stand it any longer. And she had just as much opportunity as her husband. So did Jane, who according to Prime has had to put up with this sort of behaviour from Virginia in the past. Who knows, perhaps this was the last straw?'

'I wonder if that's why Jane didn't go back down to the pool with Mr Prime? What if she told him to go on ahead because she wanted to have it out with her sister? Yes! That could be why she came out of the passageway door, not through the sitting room, which is the quickest way back to the pool! She went to the kitchen first! And if her sister had just gone out to finish the watering, she could have followed her. So they argue, Virginia Mintar laughs at her perhaps, for making a fuss, and on impulse . . . ? Jane's no lightweight, is she, sir, she'd have had no problem tipping her sister over that wall.'

'True. I must admit she doesn't strike me as the most likely possibility but all the same, you're probably right about that being why she returned to the pool through the corridor. We'll bear that in mind when we next see her. But finally we mustn't forget that last, but not least—'

'There's the husband. Yes. Nobody saw him after they'd cleared the table, until Rachel went to tell him Virginia was missing. He says he stayed in his study, but he could easily have come out again while everyone was changing. I should think he'd had it up to here with her behaviour. Why did he put up with it, that's what I want to know? I couldn't, that's for sure! Imagine what it must be like, to have to sit there and watch your wife carrying on like that!'

'Obviously he must have felt quite differently about it. Some men do. I suppose it's partly a question of temperament but I imagine it also depends on the price they're prepared to pay to keep their wives. Remember that surgeon, what was his name? The one whose wife was pushed off a balcony?'

'Mr Tarrant. Yes, I remember. You're right. His attitude was he didn't care what she did as long as she stayed with him.' Lineham shook his head. 'Beats me. I couldn't stand it.'

'No, neither could I.' Though there was no danger of his having to, with Joan, thank God. Memories flitted through Thanet's mind of the torture he had undergone at one time when Joan was away finishing her probation training and briefly he had wondered if she had indeed fallen for someone else. He had been wrong, of course, and had felt thoroughly ashamed of himself afterwards, but he found it virtually impossible to imagine how it must be to have a wife who behaved so blatantly at her and her husband's own dinner table. Surely, whatever façade Mintar presented to the world, underneath he must have suffered, found the humiliation hard to bear?

'Ah well, we mustn't stand around here all day, pleasant though it may be. Come on, Mike. Let's see if Dr S. can wriggle out of this one.'

TEN

It was marginally cooler now and Squires was mowing the lawn. He had removed his shirt, revealing a tanned, well-muscled torso without an ounce of superfluous fat. No doubt about it, he really was a good advertisement for healthy living.

'Stripes!' murmured Lineham, admiring the doctor's handiwork. 'I can never get my lawn to look like that.'

'Perhaps you ought to ask him to give you a lesson, Mike.' One of the cars was missing, Thanet noticed, the Golf.

Engrossed in his task, it was some minutes before Squires saw them. He waited until he had reached the end of a strip and then switched the mower off and came across, pulling a spotted handkerchief out of his pocket to mop at face and neck. 'Look, I don't want to be unreasonable, Inspector, but three times in one day is a bit much.'

'Sorry, I'm afraid it can't be helped,' said Thanet. 'We really do need to have another word.'

Squires compressed his lips but said nothing and once again they all trooped into the house.

'You'll have to excuse me,' said the doctor and without waiting for a response took off up the stairs.

Lineham raised his eyebrows at Thanet who said, 'Gone to wash, I imagine. Or put on a shirt. Must make you feel more vulnerable, being half naked.'

A few minutes later Squires called from the top of the stairs, 'Come up, Inspector.'

So the doctor wanted to conduct the interview on his own terms. Thanet could have refused but it wasn't worth making an issue of it.

Squires was waiting for them at the top, fully clothed and looking refreshed. There were two doors on the little landing and he led them through the left-hand one into his study, which had obviously been sliced off the sitting room. It was a narrow slot of a room with three slightly angled walls and one straight one covered with floor to ceiling bookshelves. 'Thought we might have a change of venue,' he said.

'Why not?' said Thanet amiably.

Squires sat down behind his desk, which had been positioned across the far end of the room, and gestured them to a couple of upright chairs. 'Right, then, Inspector, what can I do for you this time? Do sit down.'

'Your wife is out?'

'At the moment, yes. She's taking Sarah to a friend's house. Why, did you want to see her? She won't be long.'

'No. I was only wondering because I want to discuss a rather delicate matter and I should think you would prefer her not to be present.'

This shook him. His expression of polite inquiry changed, grew wary. 'I can't think what you mean.'

'Oh come, sir, you must realise what I'm talking about. I'm referring, of course, to your affair with Mrs Mintar.'

Silence. Thanet could see that the man was thinking furiously. *How much do they know?* Obviously, if he were to deny the affair he must do so quickly, to make his reaction believable. On the other hand, if he denied it and they somehow had incontrovertible proof of it, his credibility would be destroyed.

Squires gave a forced laugh. 'What absolute rubbish! Someone's been telling you stories, Inspector.'

So he had decided to gamble on it. A risk worth taking, probably. And it could well pay off. They had no proof, after all, only hearsay, and so far as they knew the only person who could confirm or deny the accusation was dead.

Thanet tensed. Was that the distant sound of a car door being shut? He couldn't be sure. This room was at the back of the house, on the side away from the drive. In any case, Squires obviously hadn't heard it, he was concentrating too hard on the conversation.

'Who was it?' said Squires, leaning forward, eyes narrowed.

109

'Virginia Mintar was a patient of mine, and such a rumour is highly defamatory. It could land me in serious trouble.'

'I can imagine,' said Thanet drily. 'But I'm afraid I can't tell you. If untrue, I can assure you that it will go no further, as far as we are concerned.'

'*If* untrue?' said Squires angrily, abandoning all pretence of affability. 'Are you questioning my word?'

'I'm simply saying that if the story is untrue you have nothing to fear on our part. But if—'

'If what? No, that simply isn't good enough, Inspector. I need to know who this person is, so that I can put a stop to this nonsense!'

'Howard?' Light footsteps could be heard running up the stairs.

Squires leaned forward and said urgently, 'Inspector—'

Concentrating on getting his timing right, Thanet continued smoothly, raising his voice, '—but if not, I really do advise you to tell your wife.'

The words hung in the air as the door swung open. Marilyn Squires stood on the threshold. She ignored the two policemen and her eyes locked with those of her husband.

Excellent, thought Thanet, she must have heard, surely. 'Ah, Mrs Squires,' he said, rising. 'We were just leaving. We'll see ourselves out.'

Lineham barely managed to hide his surprise at this abrupt end to the interview and as soon as they were outside in the hall he whispered, 'Why the sudden departure, sir? Just when we had him by the . . .'

'Shh.'

When leaving the room Thanet had shut the door loudly and then, banking on the fact that the Squires would be so caught up in the highly charged atmosphere that they wouldn't notice, had quickly released the catch again so that it rebounded a little, leaving a crack to which he now put his ear. Normally he disapproved of eavesdropping but conversations between possible suspects in a murder case were a different matter and this wouldn't be the first time he had had to resort to such tactics, sometimes with invaluable results. Having been given this heaven-sent opportunity he had no intention of missing it.

Lineham cottoned on immediately, and bent to follow suit.

Thanet was right, the Squires weren't aware of his ruse. Almost at once Marilyn's voice rang out. 'Tell me what?' Her tone was ominous, accusatory.

She already knows, thought Thanet.

Squires had obviously been thrown off balance by his wife's untimely arrival, and failed to come up with a convincing reply. 'Oh, nothing important.'

'I see. Nothing important, you say. Well, I think I can guess what the Inspector was referring to.'

Silence. Squires wasn't going to risk an answer.

Marilyn's tone changed. 'You shouldn't be so careless, my love, leaving things like this in places where other people might come across them.'

Thanet and Lineham raised eyebrows at each other. *What?*

'Where did you get that? You've been going through my pockets!'

'And I'm supposed to feel guilty about that? *I'm* supposed to feel guilty, after what you've been up to? Big joke. All's fair in love and war, you surely know that, my darling. Did you really think I didn't notice your reaction yesterday morning when this arrived? The guilty, hunted look, the swift transfer to your pocket?'

A letter, then, thought Thanet.

'I suppose you couldn't risk burning it, just in case the worst came to the worst and you should ever need it as proof of blackmail, but you really should have been more careful about where you put it.' Marilyn's tone changed, became once again charged with anger. 'How could you have been so stupid, so bloody, bloody stupid? You must have known you were putting everything – your reputation, your career, our marriage, the children's well-being – everything at risk, having an affair with a patient! And for Virginia, of all people, that worthless—'

'Shut up, do you hear me? Stop it! I won't listen to you running her down. She's dead, isn't that enough for you?'

'And being dead sanctifies her, is that it? Well, I'm sorry but I'm afraid I can't see it like that.'

'I'd just like to get my hands on the person who sent that—'

'Typical! Things are never your fault, are they? You always

111

try to wriggle out of them by trying to cast blame elsewhere. But I'm afraid that in this case that just won't wash. And you needn't blame whoever sent this for my finding out. I'd have had to be one hundred per cent stupid, and blind into the bargain, not to have noticed what was going on. It just confirmed what I suspected, that's all. Idiotic of me, wasn't it, to hope that if I just ignored it the whole thing would eventually blow over, just fizzle out. Well it didn't, did it? And now look where you've landed us. It's obvious the police have got wind of it.'

'I'm not going to listen to any more of this!'

'That's right. That's your next tactic, isn't it? If you can't shove the blame on to someone else, just avoid the issue altogether and walk out.'

Thanet and Lineham straightened up as the door swung open. Squires came to an abrupt halt, his face a study in dismay. *How much have they heard?* Almost at once, however, he recovered. 'My God,' he said in disgust. 'A pair of eavesdroppers. I didn't think you'd stoop quite so low, Inspector.'

Thanet had no intention of being put on the defensive. 'Not as low as a witness who lies in a murder case,' he said. 'I think you owe us an explanation, don't you, sir? Please.'

And he put out an arm to usher Squires back into the room.

The doctor complied reluctantly.

'And I think we'll take that, Mrs Squires.' Thanet held out his hand. He had not missed Marilyn Squires' attempt to hide the letter behind her back.

Slowly, reluctantly, she complied but Squires was almost too quick for them. He lunged forward in an attempt to snatch it from her. 'That's my property!'

But Lineham was too quick for him. His arm shot out and he grabbed Squires' wrist just as his fingers touched the paper.

Thanet glanced at the sergeant. *Well done, Mike.* 'Thank you,' he said, taking it.

And it wasn't a letter, he now saw, but a photograph: Squires and Virginia Mintar, both in tennis gear and clearly identifiable, locked in a passionate embrace on a wooden bench beside a tennis court – the Mintars', probably. Squires' hand was invisible between her legs beneath the brief pleated skirt and there could be no doubt whatsoever about their relationship. He turned the photograph over. Printed on the back in block capitals was the message: 'WANT TO SEE THE REST? I'LL BE IN TOUCH.'

Thanet handed it to Lineham to look at.

'And this arrived yesterday morning?'

A sullen nod from Squires.

'Have you any idea who sent it?'

Squires hesitated. 'No.'

He's lying, thought Thanet. He suspects, but he's not sure. The best policy now would be to let the man stew. 'Very well, Mr Squires, we'll leave it at that for the moment. But I'm sure you realise that this puts you in a very difficult position with regard to Mrs Mintar's death and I strongly advise you to be frank with us in future. Once we know that someone has lied to us we naturally regard anything else he tells us with some suspicion. I hope that neither of you has plans to go away at present? No? Good.'

And on this ominous note Thanet left.

'That'll have put the wind up him!' said Lineham. 'His face, when he opened that door and saw us there!'

'Mmm. Who do you think sent the photograph, Mike?'

Lineham didn't hesitate. 'Digby. Rachel said she was sure he was always creeping about, spying on her. And whoever sent that photograph had to have printed it himself. It's hardly the sort of thing you'd take to Boots.'

Thanet nodded. 'My guess too.' He made up his mind. 'We'll get a search warrant in the morning, see if we can find the rest of them. Interesting that Digby didn't breathe a word about Virginia and Squires when we were interviewing him. I suppose he wasn't going to risk losing a potentially lucrative source of income.'

'No. He was far more interested in pointing the finger at the old lady.'

'Yes, he was, wasn't he? But it does occur to me, Mike . . .'

'What, sir?'

'If he really was in the habit of spying and, as we now suspect, of taking photographs, who knows what else we might turn up?'

'Ye-e-e-s!' breathed Lineham. 'You're right.'

They had reached their cars and Thanet paused to glance at his watch. Six-thirty.

'What next, sir?'

'We'll call it a day here, I think. Better get back to the office, do some reports. The Super'll expect every last detail in the morning. Actually, come to think of it, I'd better give him a ring tonight, in case he's back.'

It was a quarter to ten by the time they had finished and, anxious to put work behind him when he left the office, Thanet tried Superintendent Draco's number. The answerphone was still on and he didn't bother to leave a message. It would have to wait until tomorrow.

On the way home his anxieties about Bridget came rushing back and when he got there he was dismayed to find the house in darkness and Joan's car missing. Something must have gone wrong. Why hadn't she got in touch with him? He must ring the hospital at once.

Heart-rate accelerating he hurried into the house, switching on lights everywhere. There was a note propped against the telephone on the table in the hall. He snatched it up.

2.30. Can't stand hanging around waiting for news. Am driving up to visit Bridget in hospital. Back for supper. Love, J.

Back for supper? They usually ate around seven. Where was she? Perhaps there had been a crisis at the hospital and she was staying on? If so, she would surely have let him know? He saw that there was one message on the answerphone. Perhaps it was from her? But it wasn't, it was from Ben.

Ben, their son, who was still determined on eventually making a career in the police force, had graduated in computer studies from Reading University and was now on a VSO scheme in Africa. Thanet was annoyed and disappointed to have missed him as living out in the wilds Ben rarely had the opportunity to get to a telephone.

'Hi, Mum, Dad. Just to let you know everything's OK. And I was wondering about Bridget, of course. Not long now, is it? I'll ring again as soon as I can. 'Bye.'

Perhaps it was just as well that they had both been out when

114

he rang, after all. Bridget and Ben had always been close and it would be especially worrying for him if he knew what was happening, when it was so difficult for him to keep in touch. With any luck, by the next time he managed to get through it would all be over, for better or for worse.

Joan had left the hospital number beside the phone and he rang it, listening impatiently to the recorded messages and pressing the appropriate keypad numbers when necessary. At last he was through to the maternity ward. No, there was no change in Mrs Highman's condition, which was being closely monitored. Visiting hours finished at eight and the nurse had no idea whether or not Mrs Highman's mother had been in earlier. Thanet asked her to give Bridget his love and rang off.

So where was Joan? Even if she'd stayed until the end of visiting time, she should be home by now. It took only an hour and three-quarters to drive back to Sturrenden – but via the M25, the most crowded stretch of motorway in Europe. There must have been an accident. One was always hearing tales of horrendous delays because of overturned lorries, collisions on contraflows and multiple pile-ups. Please God, if there had been, Joan had not been involved.

He crossed to the window and peered out. The last remnants of light were fading from the sky. If she were simply held up, why hadn't she rung him on her mobile? He could try ringing her.

But there was no reply. Another phone call, to the police operations room, ascertained that no, there had been no major incident on the M25 and traffic was flowing normally.

Keep calm, he told himself. There's probably some perfectly simple explanation. Perhaps she's got a puncture, or the car has broken down. Suppressing memories of the many occasions when, as a young policeman, he had had to break the news of a fatal road traffic accident to a stunned family, Thanet went into the kitchen and began to hunt around for something to prepare for supper. She would be hungry when she got home.

He was defrosting an M&S ready meal in the microwave when the phone rang. He rushed to answer it, flooded with relief when he heard her voice. 'Joan! Where are you?'

And the explanation was, after all, just as mundane as he had tried to convince himself that it might be. A puncture on the slip road leading from the M25 to the M26 had complicated a relatively simple repair job. In that situation it had been too dangerous for her to attempt to change the wheel herself and she had had to walk to the nearest telephone and call the RAC.

'Why didn't you ring them on your mobile?'

'I daren't tell you.'

'You left it behind!' exploded Thanet.

'Just as bad, I'm afraid. Flat battery! I'm using the repair man's.'

'Oh, Joan, for God's sake . . .' Thanet caught himself up. What was the point of recriminations? She was safe, that was the main thing. 'How long do you think it'll be before you get home?'

It was, in fact, almost midnight.

'Don't ever do that to me again!' he said as she walked in. He held out his arms and she came to him, laid her head against his shoulder.

'I'm sorry, Luke.'

'Never mind. You're here now, that's all that matters.' He pulled away, studied her face. 'You look exhausted. Are you hungry? I'm keeping something hot in the oven.'

She shook her head. 'It's too late and anyway I'm too wound up for a proper meal. It was such a ghastly place to break down, Luke, the cars come whizzing around the bends on those slip roads.'

'I know. It must have been awful for you. What would you like to do now? Go straight to bed? I could bring you up some tea and toast, if you like.'

'Would you? That would be lovely.'

'Why don't you have a quick bath first, to relax you.'

'Perhaps I will.'

Joan dropped her handbag on the table and trailed wearily up the stairs. Thanet waited until he heard the bath water running out and then made the tea and toast, taking up a cup for himself.

'It's such a relief to be home, I can't tell you,' said Joan as he sat down on the edge of the bed. 'I just hate driving on the M25. And believe me, I've learned my lesson about making sure my mobile is charged up.'

116

'I should think so! Honestly, love—'

'I know, I know!' Joan took a bite of toast then sipped at her tea. 'Oh, this is lovely.'

'So,' said Thanet. 'Tell me how Bridget is.'

Joan pulled a face. 'She's putting a brave face on it. What else can she do? But they're obviously both worried to death, you can tell.'

'Alexander was there?'

'Oh yes, I think he's staying with her all the time he's allowed to. He's being wonderful.'

'And what, exactly, is happening at the moment? Doc Mallard was saying something about some injections she might have. To mature the baby's lungs?'

'That's right. She has to have two, twelve hours apart. She had one at ten this morning and she'll have had the second by now. After that they have to wait forty-eight hours before they induce. Then the baby should apparently have a good chance of survival.'

'It's definite that they will induce?'

'Oh I should think so, yes. There doesn't seem to be any question of that. They just can't get her blood pressure down.' Joan shook her head and squeezed her eyes tight shut, trying hard not to cry, but despite her efforts tears began to roll down her cheeks. 'Oh Luke, I'm so frightened for her.'

Thanet moved the tray on to the floor and put his arms around her. 'I know.'

Joan pulled away, reached for a tissue and wiped her eyes, then blew her nose. 'I'm sorry, darling. There's no point in carrying on like this, is there? Tell me what you've been doing today.'

'Chasing my tail, as usual on the first day of a case. Do you ever recall Bridget mentioning a girl called Caroline Mintar? She also went to Sturrenden High, but she'd be – let me see – about three years younger than Sprig.'

Joan repeated the name. 'It does have a familiar ring. Yes. Wasn't there some sort of scandal? But it was several years after Bridget left school.'

'That's right. Four years ago. She eloped with the gardener, when she was eighteen.'

'Of course, I remember now! It was in the local paper, caused quite a stir at the time.'

'Yes, well it's her mother who was found dead this morning. Apparently she never got over it.'

'She committed suicide, you mean?'

'I don't think so, no. Everyone seems to rule that out.'

'How is her family taking it?'

'Badly. Especially as they never saw or heard from Caroline again.'

'Oh Luke, how awful.'

'Yes. And to make matters worse, Rachel, her other daughter, who is now the same age as Caroline was when she eloped, has just become engaged to someone equally unsuitable. I've met him and believe me, I'm only too thankful that Bridget never got tangled up with anyone like that. Ralph Mintar, the husband, is bound to be a suspect, of course, but I can't help feeling sorry for the poor bloke.'

'We've been very lucky so far, haven't we, Luke?'

'Yes, we have.'

Then they were both silent, thinking of Bridget.

So far.

ELEVEN

Lineham was hard at work when Thanet arrived at the office next morning. It wasn't that Thanet was late, just that the sergeant was always early.

'Morning, sir. Going to be another scorcher, by the look of it.'

'Yes. I remembered to pick up a couple of bottles of water on the way. And to bring a cool bag to put them in.'

'So did I,' said Lineham with a grin.

'Well, at least we won't get dehydrated!' Thanet sat down at his desk. 'So, anything interesting come in?'

'Doc Mallard looked in. The PM's starting around now.'

'Good. Anything else?'

'Not unless you count Tanya's interview with the local witch.'

WDC Tanya Phillips was proving to be a useful member of the team. She had been with them over a year now.

'Local witch?' Thanet remembered what Mintar had said. 'Ah, yes, the mother of the lad Caroline eloped with.'

'There's nothing relevant to our case in Tanya's report, but it's just up your street. Look.'

Thanet took the proffered paper. 'What is my street, Mike?'

'Anything a bit off-beat.'

'Mmm,' said Thanet, reading. 'I see what you mean. Real Hansel and Gretel stuff, isn't it.'

The interview with Marah Swain had been part of routine house-to-house inquiries. In the literal sense she was, like the Squires, Mintar's next-door neighbour, although her house was half a mile further on down the lane and invisible from the road, being in the middle of a clearing in a wood.

She claimed not to have seen or heard anything unusual the night of Virginia Mintar's death and appeared to be unmoved by it. At the end of the report Tanya had written: *Thoroughly uncooperative. Locally has the reputation of being a witch.*

Intrigued, Thanet called Tanya in. 'This Mrs Swain,' he said, tapping the report. 'Bit of an oddball, by the sound of it.'

'Miss, actually, sir. Apparently she's never made any secret of the fact that her son was illegitimate. But yes, you can say that again!' Tanya laughed, eyes sparkling at the memory. She was in her mid twenties, a stocky girl with a mop of unruly dark curls. 'It wasn't exactly the easiest of interviews. I don't know if she's a bit deaf but her radio was playing full blast the whole time I was there, and requests to turn it down were simply ignored. And you ought to see the inside of that cottage! It's like something out of the Middle Ages!'

'In what way?'

'Well, it's dark and gloomy, doesn't look as though it's been cleaned for about a hundred years, with bunches of dried herbs and stuff hanging from nails all along the beams in the ceiling and every windowsill crammed with jamjars full of things I wouldn't like to examine too closely.'

Lineham grinned. 'What, frogs legs and eyeballs and such-like?'

Tanya shuddered. 'Something like that, I imagine. As I said, I didn't really want to know. And the cellar is apparently stuffed with more of the same, according to a girl I interviewed in the village. She – the girl – is married to a man who went to school with Dick Swain. The two boys used to play together after school and Dick took him down to the cellar one day. Dick's mother caught them there and was furious, apparently, forbade the boy ever to come to the house again.'

'All right, so she's a bit weird. But this comment at the end of your report . . .'

'About her being a witch, you mean?'

'Yes. Somewhat far-fetched, isn't it?'

Tanya shrugged. 'Before interviewing her I would have agreed. But now, well, I wouldn't be too sure.'

'Why?'

'She looks the part, for a start. She's got long, grey hair

which straggles down over her shoulders and chest, and the way she dresses is like something out of the nineteenth century – shapeless ankle-length black skirt, woollen shawl, thick stockings and old leather boots which look as though they once belonged to a tramp. Put a witch's hat on her and sit her on a broomstick and she could model for the illustrations in a book of fairy tales any day.'

Thanet was amused at the graphic description.

'Then there's the way she looks at you, sir. Suspicious and sort of well . . .' Tanya groped for the right word. 'Malevolent, yes, that's it. Malevolent.'

'Charming!' said Lineham.

'She certainly sounds something of a throw-back,' said Thanet. 'Is she supposed to practise? If that's the right word for it?'

Another shrug. 'Rumour is that she does. Though I gather it's all very clandestine, no one would actually admit to consulting her. And frankly, I can't see anyone going there unless they were desperate. The place absolutely stinks – and I really do mean stinks! Handkerchief over the nose stuff!'

'Glad it was you not me, then,' said Lineham.

But Thanet rather wished he had interviewed Dick Swain's mother himself. Not that there had been any reason to do so, but Lineham was right, the off-beat always intrigued him. 'Thanks, Tanya. How's the house-to-house going?'

'Slowly, as usual. We're just on our way back out there now.'

'Good.'

When she had gone Lineham said, 'Not surprising the Mintars were dead against Caroline going out with Dick Swain, is it? Can't say I blame them. His mother doesn't sound exactly the sort of mother-in-law I'd choose for my children. And on top of that Swain was illegitimate too. I wonder who his father was? Probably the tramp she got the boots from!'

Thanet glanced at his watch. 'I'd better go.' If he wasn't careful he'd be late for the morning meeting and Draco did not take kindly to unpunctuality. Added to which, Thanet thought it quite likely he would be hauled over the coals for not having contacted Draco over the weekend. Leaving Lineham to arrange the morning's appointments, he hurried downstairs.

He made it with one minute to spare. They were all waiting for him in characteristic manner, Draco drumming his fingers impatiently on his desk, Chief Inspector Tody with his self-deprecatory half-smile, Inspector Boon with his ironic twinkle.

'Ah, Thanet,' said Draco. 'Perhaps we may now begin.' *At last,* his tone implied. He sat back in his chair, fingers steepled beneath his chin, snapping dark eyes focused on Thanet like laser beams. Even his shock of black curly hair seemed to crackle with energy. 'With a report on the Mintar case, I think.'

His tone was ominous and Thanet's heart sank. He was definitely in for it later. Why did Draco always succeed in making him feel he was back in the headmaster's study? Still, at least the Super showed consideration in such circumstances. He was not in the habit of reprimanding his men in front of colleagues.

Succinctly, he made his report.

'So,' said Draco when he had finished, 'you seem pretty certain it wasn't suicide, or an accident.'

'I don't think it could have been, sir. Not one of the people who knew her thought it could have been suicide and the wall around the well really is too high – about the height of her hips – for it to have been an accident.'

'Even if she had a heart attack and collapsed on to it?' said Tody.

'I think in that case she'd have been found slumped across it. It's a pretty thick wall. She'd have needed extra momentum to tip right over.'

'In that case you're looking for someone pretty strong, aren't you?' said Boon.

'Not necessarily,' said Thanet. 'I don't think it would have been too difficult. She was fairly slight. One good shove would have done the trick, I should think.'

'Pointless discussion!' said Draco, who had been impatiently tapping a pencil on his desk throughout this exchange. 'Let's find out the cause of death before we start speculating. Do we know when the PM is?'

'It's taking place now, sir, I believe.'

'Good. Now, the search warrant for this photographer's place . . . I agree, it sounds a sensible idea. But to justify it before the magistrates I think we really must be certain that this is a murder case and Mrs Mintar did not die of natural causes. So again, we wait for PM results, right?'

'Yes, sir.'

After this the meeting was quickly wound up. Thanet had reached the door and was thinking that he had got away lightly after all when Draco called him back.

'Why was I not informed of Mrs Mintar's death until I arrived at work this morning?'

'You were away, sir—'

'I know I was away! But as you are well aware, I always leave a contact number.'

'To begin with we didn't realise it was so serious, sir. As I said, we thought Mrs Mintar might well turn up overnight. And then, well, we got caught up in things.'

'That is no excuse whatsoever!'

'I know. I'm sorry, sir. I did try to ring you last night—'

'There was no message on my answerphone.'

'It was late, sir. I thought it could wait until this morning.'

'*You* thought! Thanet, it is I who am in charge here. It is I who am ultimately responsible for what goes on here and it is I who make such decisions. I have made it abundantly clear in the past that if anyone so much as sneezes on my patch, I want to know, and my attitude has not changed. Is that clear?'

'Yes, sir. Perfectly.'

'What is your next move?'

'I want to see Matthew Agon, Mr Mintar's daughter's fiancé. He's the only person present when Mrs Mintar went missing that we have not yet interviewed.'

'Mr Mintar does not approve of this relationship, you said.'

'None of the family does.'

'Hmm. And after you've seen Agon?'

'I'm hoping to go and see a friend of Mrs Mintar's, sir. A Mrs Amos. I thought she might be able to help us with some background.'

'Hot on background, aren't you, Thanet?'

'I do find it helps, sir.'

'And after that?'

123

'I'm not sure yet, sir.' Thanet hated being pinned down like this.

But Draco wouldn't let it go. 'But probably?'

The Superintendent was punishing him for his slip-up, Thanet realised. 'Probably back to Mr Mintar's house.'

'And I imagine you'll then be there for some time. Most of the afternoon, perhaps?'

'I expect so, sir. Unless we're able to apply for the search warrant this morning, and it's granted. In which case—'

'It's just that I'd like to take a look at the crime scene for myself. But it needn't be a problem. We'll make it early afternoon – say around 1.30? Then you'd have plenty of time to do the search later.'

Draco breathing down his neck, the ultimate punishment. Thanet's heart sank. 'Right, sir.'

Back in the office Lineham took one look at his face and said, 'What's up, sir?'

'We are to have the honour of an on-site visit from the Super this afternoon, Mike. Entirely my fault, for not making sure he was informed about the Mintar case.'

'Ah.' Knowing that Thanet would not allow criticism of a superior officer Lineham made no further comment, but his tone spoke volumes.

'Also, we're to defer the application for a search warrant until we've heard the PM results. We'd better ask Doc Mallard to ring them through. Did you manage to fix both appointments?'

Lineham had, and they were soon on their way.

The Leisure Club where Matthew Agon worked was attached to a country house hotel. Melton Park, for centuries the home of the Purefoy family, had, like many English country houses, become in the end an impossible financial burden and when the last owner had died a few years ago death duties had been the last straw. His heir had sold up and moved to a different part of the country, declaring that he could not bear to watch the indignities his family home would undoubtedly suffer in the hands of the new owners, a consortium which specialised in running upmarket hotels.

Application had at once been made, and permission granted, for extensive improvements. Outbuildings had been converted into a glamorous indoor swimming pool and leisure complex, parkland 'landscaped' into an eighteen-hole golf course, and a range of other outdoor activities catered for.

'Ve-ry nice,' said Lineham, looking about as they walked into the reception area of the Club. No expense had been spared. In the centre was a dolphin fountain, the soothing sound of trickling water a welcome change in Thanet's opinion from the ubiquitous pop music which assaults the ear in so many public buildings these days. The terracotta floor tiles had been buffed to a soft sheen and the reception desk looked as though it had been hewn out of one huge slab of marble.

'Prepare to pay through the nose, all ye who enter here,' murmured Lineham as they approached it.

'How may I help you?'

The girl behind the desk was predictably young and pretty, presenting a suitably healthy image to clientele: shining shoulder-length blonde hair and a smile which would have enhanced any toothpaste advertisement. She was wearing a crisp white T-shirt with the club logo and the briefest of brief white shorts. Her smile dimmed a little when she heard why they were there. 'Matthew? He's coaching at the moment, but he'll be free in about twenty minutes. Perhaps you wouldn't mind waiting . . . ?' She gestured in the direction of a group of armchairs. 'I could order some coffee for you.'

The message was clear. *We don't want to upset our clients.*

But Thanet was interested to see Agon in action. He smiled benignly. 'That's very kind, but thank you, no. We'll just stroll around to the courts and wait until he's finished. Where are they exactly?'

Reluctantly she gave directions and Thanet turned away.

But Lineham lingered. 'Have you a membership leaflet?'

The gleaming white teeth reappeared. 'Of course, sir.' She rummaged beneath the desk and produced one. 'If you have any queries, please don't hesitate to ask. After the initial joining fee we do prefer clients to pay by monthly direct debit. It's more convenient all round.'

'Thank you.'

Thanet waited until they were outside then said, 'Thinking of taking out a second mortgage, Mike?'

'I'd need one! Just listen to this! The joining fee is £2,000 – *two thousand quid!* And that's just for a single membership. A family membership is £3,000! And then on top of that the annual fees range from £1,000 a year to £2,000 a year, depends on which option you go for. Ah well, it's all right for some.' Lineham screwed up the leaflet and threw it into a conveniently placed waste bin.

'No point in wanting things you can never hope to get.'

'Perhaps when I win the lottery . . .'

'If, you mean. Complete waste of money, in my opinion.' Apart from which, Thanet disapproved of the whole business. In his view the winning of huge sums of money never did anyone any good and in many ways was a positive force for harm. The introduction of the National Lottery, coupled with a dramatic rise in the number of slot machines and the easing of controls in the gaming industry, had resulted in a vast increase in the number of people with gambling problems, to the degree that a charity called Gamcare had been launched to help them. He himself had never bought a lottery ticket and had no intention of doing so.

Lineham grinned but said nothing. They had already discussed the matter *ad nauseam* and he knew that nothing would change Thanet's mind. 'Looks as though there are plenty who can afford the membership fees, anyway.'

The tennis courts were tucked away at the back of the building and as they walked around the side they had a clear view of the golf course. There were small groups of golfers at every hole.

'What I can never understand,' said Lineham, 'is how they can afford to belong to a club like this if they're out there playing golf instead of working their backs off to earn enough money to join.'

Thanet laughed. 'But you know perfectly well that they are working, Mike, at least in the sense that a lot of them are making or cementing important contacts from which they hope to earn money in the future. Not that that applies to everyone who plays, of course, far from it, I'm sure. But golf in particular is notorious for that.'

'So they say. I think we're in the wrong profession.'

'Oh come on, Mike. Can you honestly say you'd rather be out

there knocking a ball about and buttering people up instead of being about to interview a witness in a murder case?' It was getting hotter by the minute; Thanet took off his jacket and slung it over his shoulder.

Lineham pulled a face and followed suit. 'You're dead right. I wouldn't.'

They had turned the corner and come in view of the tennis courts.

'There he is, sir.'

Thanet put a hand on Lineham's arm to restrain him. 'Wait a minute, Mike'. He wanted to seize the opportunity to watch Agon unobserved.

On the court nearest to them Agon was coaching a slim, attractive woman in her thirties. They were both standing at the base line with their backs to the two detectives and were obviously working on the woman's service. Agon stood back and watched as she served several balls.

'You're not bringing your racquet far enough down behind, so you don't get up enough momentum,' he said. 'Look.' He demonstrated, sending a couple of balls skimming over the net at speed.

She tried again. He was right, Thanet could see.

Agon put down his racquet and went to stand behind her. 'See if you can feel what I mean.' He moved in closer and curling his left arm around her waist put his right hand over hers on the handle.

'"Feel" being the operative word,' whispered Lineham in Thanet's ear.

With a sinuous little wriggle she pressed her body back against his and turned her face sideways and upwards. It was a clear invitation. And, thought Thanet, not the first time it had been tendered – or accepted.

'Very cosy!' said Lineham.

But on this occasion Agon simply murmured something which made her laugh and they both addressed the task in hand. After demonstrating the serving movement once or twice he released her. As he did so he ran his left hand lightly up her bare thigh.

'See that, sir?'

Thanet nodded.

The woman cast a coquettish glance at Agon over her shoulder. In doing so she spotted the two men watching and her expression changed. She nodded in their direction and said something to Agon, who turned.

'Don't let us disturb you, Mr Agon,' said Thanet, raising his voice. 'We're happy to wait until you've finished.'

Agon glanced at his watch. 'I just about have.' He turned to his pupil and they had a brief conversation. The woman nodded, picked up a sweater from the bench at the side of the court, then sauntered off, hips swaying provocatively. She gave the two policemen a resentful glance as she passed.

'See you tomorrow, same time,' Agon called after her.

The most casual of nods showed that she had heard him.

'Now, Inspector,' said Agon with a cooperative smile, 'how may I help?'

Despite the heat and the exercise he looked cool and unruffled in his tennis whites. Thanet envied him his shorts and polo shirt.

'Is there somewhere cooler we could sit?'

Agon nodded. 'This way.'

He led them along the side of the row of tennis courts and around a bank of shrubs to a shady area where tables and chairs had been set out in front of a small rustic bar serving snacks for the convenience of club members. There were a few people sitting about.

'Fancy a coffee? Or a cold drink?' said Agon.

Much as he would have liked to accept, Thanet refused. Agon would presumably have had to pay for them, and he didn't want to be beholden to the man. He led the way to a table where they would not be overheard.

'It's about the night before last, of course,' he said, and glanced at Lineham. *Take over, Mike.*

Lineham took out his notebook.

'Ah yes,' said Agon. 'Saturday night.' And briefly, malice sparked in his eyes. 'A very interesting occasion.'

'In what way, sir?'

TWELVE

Agon ran his tongue over his lips. 'Sure you don't want a drink? No? Mind if I get myself one?'

They watched him walk across the grass to the little bar, exchanging an occasional greeting with some of the other people scattered around. One young woman put out a hand to detain him and they spoke together briefly.

'Fancies him, doesn't she?' said Lineham. 'Very popular with the ladies, our Mr Agon.'

'Looks like it. Not surprising, I suppose. He's a very good-looking young man.'

'I wonder what Rachel thinks of it. It must be very uncomfortable, being engaged to someone who's such a magnet to the opposite sex, don't you think?'

'I imagine she's so head over heels she doesn't care, just feels delighted that she's the one he's chosen. Anyway, I expect he watches his step when she's around.'

'It'll be different after they're married, I bet. He won't need to be so careful then.'

'You're a cynic, Mike. Perhaps she's the love of his life.'

Lineham gave a derisive snort. 'Think he really needs a drink, sir, or d'you think he's just playing for time while he makes up his mind what he's going to tell us?'

'A bit of both, I imagine.'

When Agon returned Thanet tried to avoid looking at the glass of lemonade he was carrying. Tall, beaded with moisture and chinking with ice it looked far too inviting for Thanet's comfort.

Agon took a long swallow and then sat back with a sigh of satisfaction. 'Ah, that's better. It's hot work out there. Now, where were we?' He crossed his legs, resting right ankle on left knee, and looked expectantly at Lineham.

Thanet had been trying to work out what it was about the man which had provoked that immediate reaction of dislike, the night before last. It wasn't that he automatically mistrusted good-looking men. Alexander, for instance, was very good-looking. *When would there be more news of Bridget?* True, Agon's eyes were set rather close together. Was there any justification for the old adage that this denoted shiftiness? Perhaps he, Thanet, was being unfair. He must be on his guard. Prejudice clouds the judgement.

'You were going to tell us about that night, sir,' said Lineham. 'You said it was interesting.'

'Ah, yes.' Agon took another swig from his glass. 'Well, if you've been talking to the family, as I'm sure you have, you'll have gathered I'm not exactly *numero uno* around there and on Saturday night they were all shook up, as Elvis would have put it, by our little bombshell.'

'That you and Miss Mintar had just got engaged, you mean.'

'That's right. You a married man, Sergeant?' Agon eyed Lineham speculatively. 'Yes, you are. I can always tell. They have that – what? That *settled* look.'

Lineham ignored this. 'You had a little celebration, I believe? Mr Mintar opened a bottle of champagne.'

'Huh! Celebration? Wake, more like it. Oh, they put as good a face on it as they could bring themselves to, for Rachel's sake, but you didn't have to be a mind-reader to know what they were all thinking. I'm only surprised it wasn't me who ended up at the bottom of the well.'

'Oh come on, sir. Aren't you exaggerating a bit?'

'You weren't there, Sergeant. I was.'

'Yes, well, as I said, perhaps you could give us your account of the evening.'

Agon obliged, with the occasional snide comment. He was obviously enjoying the opportunity of openly displaying his resentment of the Mintars' attitude towards him. With Rachel, of course, he probably wouldn't dare, for fear of putting her off.

His story tallied with the others. After everyone had left the terrace he and Rachel had remained behind for a few minutes 'for obvious reasons' – he gave a salacious wink here – and had then separated. Rachel had gone into the house via the lounge, as he called it, whereas he had returned to his car to fetch his swimming trunks before changing in the pool house. He had been first into the pool, closely followed by Rachel and then the others in the order already described.

'Where had you parked your car, sir?'

'In the courtyard, as usual. Everyone parks there.'

'So to fetch your swimming things you had to walk along the side of the annexe where old Mrs Mintar lives, and across the far side of the courtyard?'

Lineham's tone was factual, low-key, and betrayed no hint of the excitement which, like Thanet, he must be feeling. Were they about to be given one last glimpse of Virginia Mintar, before she died?

Agon was looking impatient. 'Well, yes, obviously.'

'Matt!' A short, powerfully built man in tennis whites was hurrying across the grass towards them. He was swinging a racquet. 'Sorry I'm late!'

Of all the moments to be interrupted! thought Thanet. Lineham was looking equally frustrated.

Agon glanced at the two policemen. 'My next lesson.' He started to rise. 'I'm afraid you'll have to excuse me.'

Thanet couldn't believe it. Agon actually seemed to think they were going to let him walk out on them, in the middle of an interview! 'I'm afraid your client will just have to wait until we've finished, sir.'

The short man raised his eyebrows at Agon, who gave a rueful shrug. 'Sorry, Mr Martin, you heard the man. If you'd like to go on court and practise some serves I'll be with you as soon as I can.'

Martin was not amused. He glanced at his watch. 'This is very annoying. I'm pressed for time as it is. No, I can't hang around at your convenience, Agon. I'll just have to cancel.' And swinging around he headed back towards the clubhouse.

'I'm not going to be very popular with my employers,' said Agon, giving Thanet a baleful glance. 'I'm sure he'll be making a complaint.'

'I'm sorry to have inconvenienced you,' said Thanet. 'But I don't think you quite appreciate the seriousness of the matter. A woman has died, Mr Agon, and we have to try to find out how and why.'

'No need to get up on your high horse,' said Agon. 'Just let's get it over with as quickly as possible, shall we, before my next session is due to start. I don't want any more trouble.' He drank off the rest of his lemonade and put the glass down with an angry thump.

'We were talking about when you went to fetch your swimming trunks from the car,' said Lineham.

'So?'

'So we want you to think very carefully indeed,' said Thanet.

'About what?'

'Precisely what you saw and heard when you were crossing the courtyard.'

Agon shrugged. 'Nothing special.'

Thanet inwardly cursed Martin's arrival. Before, Agon had been reasonably cooperative. Now, smarting from his client's reaction, resentment was making him impatient and antagonistic. And Thanet himself hadn't helped, by being sarcastic just now. A climb-down was necessary.

'Please, sir, we really would be grateful if you'd cast your mind back and try to remember. Even the smallest thing would help.'

Agon stared at him, clearly torn between maintaining his hostile stance and getting rid of them quickly by cooperating. Prudence won. His tone changed. 'Sorry, Inspector, but I really don't think I can help you. I just went straight to the car, got my swimming stuff out, and went back to the pool house.'

'Perhaps it would help if you shut your eyes and tried to visualise the scene,' suggested Lineham.

Agon sighed and rolled his eyes, but complied. After a minute or two he said slowly, 'I think . . .'

'What?' Lineham was trying not to sound too eager.

'I'm not sure, but I think the lights were on in the kitchen.'

'And?'

'I just have the impression of someone moving about in there.'

'Would you try hard to recall who it was?'

Agon was silent for a moment longer, then shook his head and opened his eyes. 'No, sorry. It was just a vague impression and I should think I took it for granted it would be Virginia. But I certainly couldn't say for sure. I wasn't paying much attention. If I'd known it was going to be important . . .'

Familiar words indeed. Now it was Thanet's turn to sigh. Time to change tack and if he wanted to steer the interview in the way he wished it to go, it would have to be an oblique approach. He glanced at Lineham. *I'll take over now, Mike.* He knew Lineham wouldn't mind, would appreciate that he simply wanted to follow a particular line of questioning.

'How long have you been working here, sir?'

'Since last October. There's one indoor court, which we use during the winter months. A lot of people like to brush up on their strokes during the winter.'

'Virginia Mintar for one, I believe.'

Not surprisingly, perhaps, Agon's eyes grew wary. 'I did coach her for a short time earlier in the year, yes.'

'So you'd have some idea what she was like, as a person.'

'I suppose.'

'It's just that it would be useful to have an impartial view of her, from someone outside the family circle.'

Agon seemed to relax. 'You see all sorts here, and she was one of the obsessive types.'

'How do you mean?'

'Obsessive about exercise. She practically lived here – came every single day, weekends included. And not just for a quick swim. No, it would be forty-five minutes in the gym or on the tennis court and then another forty-five doing lengths in the pool.'

'We understand, from talking to other people, that Mrs Mintar was – it's difficult to put this tactfully – very interested in the opposite sex.'

'You can't expect me to gossip about members' private lives.'

Oh no? thought Thanet. Well, there were other ways of getting Agon to do just that. Time for the gloves to come off. 'And you yourself are, as I'm sure you're aware, a good-looking young man.' Deliberately, Thanet glanced across at the girl who had

133

spoken to Agon earlier. The implication was clear, but just to be sure Agon got the message he added, 'It was quite interesting watching your coaching methods just now.'

'Now hang on a minute, what are you implying?'

'Just that two and two often make four. Mrs Mintar liked men, you're an attractive man, therefore—'

'Stop right there, Inspector. I do have some discrimination, you know. Virginia was *middle-aged*, for God's sake.'

'But still very attractive. And a lot of men like older women.'

'Well, I'm not one of them! Why eat mutton when you can have lamb? That's what I always say. And believe me, there's plenty of lamb available around here.'

Poor Rachel. What have you got yourself into? 'I'd hardly expect you to admit it, would I? After all, sir, just think about it. You were actually there in the courtyard, alone, at the time she disappeared—'

'I wasn't the only one to have the opportunity!' exploded Agon.

His raised voice made heads turn and noticing this he leaned forward and hissed, 'There were plenty of others who did. I've been thinking about it and as I told you, every single one of them came back to the pool alone. And if you really want me to point a finger in the right direction, look no further than next door to the Mintars.'

Thank you, thought Thanet. It had been only too easy. 'You're surely not implying that there was something going on between Dr Squires and Mrs Mintar? She was his patient, I believe.'

'Precisely! But patient or not, it was common knowledge amongst the staff here. Not that he and Virginia weren't discreet, they were, but you could tell, all right. Dr Squires comes here every day too, to work out. I suppose it was inevitable they'd get together sooner or later. As you say, Virginia was man-mad and her old man seems to spend more time away than at home. I hate to say this about someone who was going to be my mother-in-law, but the story is, she'd worked her way through most of the available men in the Club.'

'Anyone in particular?'

'Not since I was here. It's been the doctor for months. He'd really have been for it, if anyone had blown the whistle on them.

134

I thought he was crazy, putting himself at risk like that. But he couldn't seem to help himself. I've seen it all before. If a woman like that gets under your skin . . . I steer clear of them, I can tell you. You should have seen the way she was carrying on that night, making eyes at her own sister's boyfriend!'

'How did Dr Squires react to that?'

'Jealous as hell. He couldn't hide it, even though his wife was there, sitting at the same table! And Virginia's sister wasn't too impressed either, I gather.'

'What do you mean?'

'Rachel overheard her aunt and Arnold arguing about it, when she went up to change. She said Jane was really upset, sounded as though she was in tears. I'm telling you, it's not surprising Virginia ended up the way she did.'

'He's right, isn't he?' said Lineham as they walked back to the car. 'It isn't really surprising, is it?' Then, with a sideways glance at Thanet, 'D'you really think Agon might have had something to do with it?'

'I doubt it. I was just trying to needle him into telling us about Squires and Virginia.'

'And you succeeded, too. He was desperate to point the finger anywhere but at himself.'

'Yes. All the same, I don't think we ought to rule him out.'

'Cold-hearted bastard, isn't he, sir? "I prefer lamb to mutton", indeed. And "there's plenty of lamb available around here, believe me"! I suppose that's what Rachel is. A lamb to the slaughter, more like, poor kid. Are you still calling me a cynic, as far as he's concerned?'

'I have to concede there, Mike.'

'I tell you what did occur to me, sir, while you were questioning him.'

They had reached the car and they got in.

'What?'

'That we might just be wrong about Digby being the blackmailer. Seems to me Agon's such a nasty bit of work he'd fit the bill nicely.'

'The thought did cross my mind, I must admit. If we're wrong about Digby, that's where we'll focus next. But I still think Digby's the best bet, because of the photographs. I'm sure you're right about them having been developed and printed at home.' Thanet glanced at his watch. Eleven o'clock. Time was getting on, if they wanted that search warrant. 'Surely we ought to have heard from Doc Mallard by now?'

'He did say he'd ring, as soon as they were through.'

'What time's our appointment with Mrs Amos?'

'Eleven-fifteen.'

'And where does she live?'

'Badger's Close in Bickenden.'

The next village. 'We're in comfortable time, then.' Thanet debated with himself whether or not to ring Mallard, but decided against it. If Mallard had said he would ring as soon as he could, he would. 'Right, Mike. Let's go.'

THIRTEEN

The three impressive modern houses in Badger's Close, Bickenden, had obviously been built in the former grounds of an older house which now looked distinctly forlorn in its truncated garden. They were constructed of traditional building materials – rosy red brick and Kentish peg tiles, their double garages disguised as farm buildings in dark-stained wood. An incongruous touch was that the gardens of each were surrounded by a high brick wall with spiked railings on top, terminating in tall wrought-iron gates with an intercom system built into one of the brick pillars which flanked them. A sign of the times, Thanet supposed.

'Oh yc-c-s!' said Lineham in admiration. 'Now one of those would just suit me down to the ground!'

'Hard luck, Mike. You missed your chance, last year.'

When old Mrs Lineham had been agitating to move in with the young couple, the carrot had been that she and Lineham would both sell their houses and put the money together to buy just such a house as these.

Lineham said nothing but they both knew that it would have been too high a price to pay.

On the gatepost of Mrs Amos's house was a small, neat notice: 'SUSAN A. DESIGNS'.

'What does she design?' said Thanet.

'No idea. But she did say she'd be in her studio, around the back.'

Interesting, thought Thanet. That was one preconception out of the window. He hadn't given much thought to Virginia

137

Mintar's friend, but had nevertheless assumed that she would have enjoyed much the same hedonistic life-style. He certainly hadn't expected her to be a working woman with her own business. How often had he told his men never to make assumptions? The truth was, one made them automatically, without even realising one was doing so. Perhaps there were further surprises in store.

After a brief exchange over the intercom the gates swung slowly open and they followed the path which led around one side of the house. Here there was a single-storey projecting wing similar to that in which old Mrs Mintar lived, but smaller in scale. Thanet guessed that Susan Amos had adapted a granny annexe for her own use.

And yes, the woman who opened the door did not fit his mental picture of her. He had expected someone slim, elegant, well groomed and carefully made up, and Susan Amos was none of these things. Scruffy jeans strained across over-large hips and thighs, her dark hair was an untidy bush as if she had spent the morning running her hands through it and her face was devoid of make-up. Not surprisingly she looked as though she had scarcely slept the last two nights and her manner as she invited them in was subdued. The one striking thing about her was the beautiful knitted jacket she was wearing. Tutored by Joan, who loved such things but could rarely afford them, Thanet recognised that this was no chainstore creation. A knitwear designer, then? He remembered that years ago he had interviewed an actress who utilised her 'resting' periods by knitting picture sweaters, at a time when such things were fashionable. He had bought one for Joan, and still remembered her delight when he had presented it to her.

His first glimpse of Susan Amos's studio confirmed his guess. Around the walls were pinned sketches of sweaters and jackets, with swatches of wool attached, and one whole side of the studio up to shoulder height was taken up by what he guessed was a custom-made fitment of drawers labelled with the names of all the colours of the rainbow. One of the lower drawers stood open, displaying an astounding array of green wool in every hue, tone and texture. Above the unit four samples of her finished work were displayed on a neutral background. They were truly stunning. One jacket in particular caught his eye.

A brilliant kaleidoscope of summer flowers danced across a background of many shades and textures of deep blue, purple, and rich, dark greens. There and then he made up his mind. He would buy it for Joan for Christmas, regardless of the cost. She would absolutely love it!

'Sir?' Lineham was looking at him expectantly.

'Oh, sorry. I was admiring your work, Mrs Amos. It's beautiful.'

She smiled briefly. 'Thank you. Do sit down.' She gestured at a couple of upright chairs and returned to the chair in front of a computer, its screen filled by a screensaver of shooting stars.

'Thank you for agreeing to see us.'

Lineham's mobile rang. He excused himself and went out.

Doc Mallard? Thanet wondered. Best not to start the interview until the sergeant returned, in case they had to break off. Anyway, perched on the edge of her chair with her legs twisted around each other and her hands clasped together so tightly that the knuckles showed white, Mrs Amos looked so tense that she would almost certainly be incapable of talking about Virginia in the way he had hoped. He would spend the time trying to get her to relax.

'We'll just wait, to start, until my sergeant comes back. Meanwhile, I hope you don't mind my asking, but what sort of prices do you charge? That jacket, for instance . . . ?'

Ouch! he thought, as she told him. 'Do you sell direct, or only through retail outlets?'

'No, I sell direct too. Some of my customers come back over and over again.'

'I can imagine.' He hesitated. Would it be unprofessional to broach the subject now? Was it possible that such a request could be construed as an inducement to talk freely? No, surely not. There was absolutely no indication whatsoever that Mrs Amos was involved in Virginia's death. Still, perhaps he ought to wait, come back another time? But then he might risk losing the jacket to another customer. He glanced at it again, wavering. He could just *see* Joan in it. He made up his mind. 'Look, I know this is absolutely nothing to do with the reason for our visit, but would you be willing to sell that one to me? I know my wife would absolutely love it.'

She smiled again, more warmly, this time. 'Of course. I do run a business, after all.'

'We can attend to the details later, then.' Thanet glanced at the door. Lineham was taking longer than he had expected. 'Do you knit your designs yourself?'

'Oh no, I'd never have time. I employ a number of experienced knitters. Most of them love knitting but have run out of people to knit for, so to speak. And I also have a part-time secretary.'

'And you do your designing on the computer?'

'Yes. I took the plunge last year and I must say it's absolutely wonderful. It's so easy to alter and adjust until you get everything exactly right.' She was loosening up perceptibly, relieved perhaps that he hadn't dived straight into talking about Virginia. 'Look, I'll show you.' And she swung her chair around to face the screen.

Thanet got up and went to stand beside her.

'This is the design I'm working on at the moment. The beauty of this software package is that each element of the design is laid on to one transparent sheet, so to speak, and can be positioned wherever I like on the screen.' She was demonstrating as she talked. 'You see? And if I want to remove it, I can sort of peel it off, without affecting the rest of the design. Like this.'

'Amazing!' said Thanet.

'It means I never have to-'

Lineham came back into the room. 'Sorry to interrupt, sir, but could I have a word?'

Thanet excused himself and they went outside, Thanet eager to hear what the sergeant had to say. There was a familiar air of suppressed excitement about Lineham which must denote some interesting new development. Knowing the sergeant so well, however, he guessed that Lineham would keep it until last. He was right.

Apparently Doc Mallard had rung to confirm the opinion given after his initial inspection of Virginia's body: death had been due to asphyxia by drowning and she had probably been unconscious when she hit the water, due to the severe blow to the side of her forehead.

That was a relief, thought Thanet. Ever since Virginia's body had been found he had been haunted by the fear that if only he'd had the well searched on Saturday night, she might have been found alive. But if she had been unconscious when she went in it was more than likely that she was dead even before he first arrived on the scene.

The injury, Lineham was saying, was consistent with her head having struck the stone coping and no doubt blood samples taken at the time would confirm this.

'We hope,' said Thanet. 'Come on, Mike, spit it out, there's something more, isn't there? I can tell.'

'Bruises,' said Lineham with satisfaction. 'On both arms, just above her wrists. Fingermarks, in fact. Doc M. reckons someone grabbed her with force. We couldn't see them when they brought her up out of the well because she was wearing that long-sleeved blouse.'

Thanet had a sudden, vivid mental picture of Virginia at that moment, the wet silk of blouse and pants clinging to every luscious curve of her body.

'And there's another on her right hip,' Lineham was saying. 'The Doc wouldn't commit himself, you know what he's like, but he did agree that it was consistent with her having been shoved against the coping, just before she went over.'

So it was as they thought. Virginia had been attacked, and with some violence, too. It gave Thanet no satisfaction to know this, except insofar as any uncertainty about the manner of her death had now been removed. 'Not much doubt about it then, is there?' he said grimly.

Swiftly he arranged for an application for the warrant to search Digby's house to be made and then they returned to Susan Amos.

She was in exactly the same position as when Thanet had left her and he guessed she had done nothing in the interval except stare blankly at the screen.

She swung slowly back around as they entered and shook her head. 'I simply can't believe that Virginia is dead. I just don't understand how it can have happened.'

'That's what we're determined to find out,' said Thanet.

His new sense of purpose must have shown in his tone of voice because she looked at him sharply. 'What do you mean?'

141

She glanced from him to Lineham. 'Something's happened, hasn't it?'

'It's just been confirmed that Mrs Mintar's death was no accident – that there was a struggle before she was thrown down the well.'

Her eyes widened with shock and her hand flew up to her throat. 'Oh no,' she whispered. 'Oh God, Ginny ... How awful. How terrible ...' She reached blindly into her pocket for a handkerchief as tears suddenly welled up and overflowed, then swung her chair around so that her back was towards them.

Thanet gave her a few minutes and then said, 'Mrs Amos, I can see how upset you are, but we really do need your help. When we arranged this appointment we only suspected what we now know for certain.'

She wiped her eyes, blew her nose and swivelled back to face them, making a visible effort to pull herself together. 'What is it you want from me?'

'We're trying to gather together as much information as possible about Mrs Mintar – we'll call her Virginia too, if you don't mind, to distinguish her from her mother-in-law – and we understand that you and she had been friends for some time.'

She nodded. 'We do go back a long way. We were at school together.'

'So tell us about her,' said Thanet softly.

Susan Amos stared at him, blew her nose once more and put her handkerchief away. Then she raked back her hair in what was clearly an habitual gesture. 'Most people didn't understand her, you know. They just saw what Virginia wanted them to see, the social butterfly who lived for pleasure. But she wasn't like that at all underneath.'

'What was she like?'

Susan hesitated. 'Vulnerable,' she said at last. 'And that was why she put up such a smokescreen. She felt she couldn't afford to let people know that, or they'd hurt her.'

'Why? Had something specific happened, to make her feel that way?'

Susan gave him a long, penetrating look. Clearly she was wondering how much to tell him.

Thanet waited and then, when she did not continue, said, 'I

can see you're wondering how on earth this can be relevant to Virginia's death, but believe me, it might well be.'

But she still held back and he leaned forward and said softly, 'Mrs Amos. Sometime on Saturday night Virginia must have said or done something to precipitate what happened to her. The more we learn about her and the better we get to understand her, the more likely it is that we might work out what that something was. And that might help us to find out who killed her.'

She thought about what he had said for a moment or two and then stood up. 'Right,' she said. 'I'll do whatever I can to help, of course I will. But it's obviously going to take some time. Would you like some coffee? I could do with a cup myself.'

She needed an interval in which to recover from the shock, Thanet realised. 'Thank you,' he said.

In a few minutes she returned with a tray bearing a cafetièr and three mugs.

'Real coffee!' said Thanet, pleased to see that she looked much calmer. 'What a treat.'

She waited until they were all settled and then she sat back, nursing her mug in both hands.

'You asked if anything specific had happened to make her so vulnerable. And the answer is yes, several things. The first, to my knowledge anyway, was when we were fourteen. You have to understand that Virginia absolutely adored her father. He always made a tremendous fuss of her, taking her on outings, buying her presents and so on. He was so good-looking, too, real romantic hero stuff, we all used to swoon over him ... Then suddenly, without warning, he just walked out on them – on Virginia and her mother – and they never saw him again. Virginia was absolutely shattered, I can tell you. She always felt it must have been her fault – children often do in those circumstances, I believe.'

'Why? Had she been giving him a hard time?'

'No worse than most teenagers, I imagine. But she couldn't see it that way.'

'She must have realised her parents weren't getting on, surely?' said Lineham.

'Apparently not. I think half the trouble was that her mother was such a doormat he left out of sheer boredom. And that's why Virginia was so unprepared for it to happen, why it was such a shattering experience for her. I mean, if there had been endless rows it wouldn't have been such a shock, would it?'

'And he said nothing to her about leaving, before he went?' Couldn't face her, probably, thought Thanet. What a coward!

'Not a hint. She just went home one day and found he'd gone, moved out lock, stock and barrel. She couldn't believe what her mother was telling her. Apparently she ran straight upstairs to her parents' bedroom and threw open the doors to his wardrobe. And it was completely empty. "There wasn't even a hanger left!" she said, when she was telling me about it later, and the tears were pouring down her face. "It's almost as though he never existed."'

'Poor kid,' said Lineham. 'What a rotten thing to do.'

'She just went to pieces at school. She was quite bright, you know, there'd even been talk of accelerated O levels, but her work took a nose-dive and never recovered. She just couldn't concentrate, used to spend all her time staring out of the window. And nothing any of the teachers said to her made any difference. To give them credit, they really did try to help her, to make allowances, but it didn't help in the slightest. No, I don't think she ever got over it. And it certainly changed her.'

'In what way?'

'Until then she'd always been a carefree, happy-go-lucky sort of person, very lively and cheerful. After her father left, she was much quieter, more withdrawn. Well, that was understandable, of course. But then a bit later on she changed again. She became, well, rather wild, I suppose. She didn't seem to care whether she got into trouble at school, no matter how many warnings or punishments she was given, and at home she was so rude to her mother I really felt sorry for the poor woman. Eventually the girls at school got fed up with it, started to avoid her and give her the cold shoulder, and one day I said to her, "Look, Ginny, if you go on like this you'll soon have no friends left. I've just about had enough myself." And that did seem to make a difference. But in some respects that attitude never left her.'

'Behaving as if she didn't care what people thought, you mean?'

'Yes.'

'And as if she didn't care how her behaviour affected them?' said Thanet gently. He knew it might be difficult for Susan to admit this, if true.

And indeed, she did hesitate before saying with a sigh, 'I suppose so, yes.'

'And am I right in thinking this especially applied to men?'

Susan gave him one of those long looks. 'I really don't like doing this, you know.'

'Yes, I do know. I'm sure I'd feel exactly the same if it were my closest friend who'd been killed. It's somehow all right to talk about their good points but not to reveal their weaknesses. It's not only that we feel disloyal or as though we're talking about them behind their backs, but also that the dead can't defend themselves. They have no right of reply.'

'That's it, exactly.' She sat in silence for a minute or two and Thanet let her. If Susan was to continue to talk freely it would only be by her own choice. At last she stirred and said, 'I still can't believe she's dead. She was such a . . . vibrant person. It's so sad, to think of all that vitality just . . . snuffed out.' Her tears had started to flow again and she dabbed at them impatiently. 'I'm sorry. This doesn't help, I know. What were you asking me, before we digressed?'

'About Virginia's attitude to men.'

She compressed her lips and shook her head. 'There's no point in pretending she treated them well. She didn't. In fact, I often wondered . . .'

'What?'

'If she was paying out the male sex in general for what her father did to her.'

'Not an unusual thing to happen, I believe.'

'And it was so easy for her, too. You didn't know her, but she had this sort of magnetic attraction. Men couldn't resist her. I've seen it happen over and over again. And she couldn't resist trying to prove her power over them. It's as if she was driven to it. She told me once, she regarded every new man who came along as a challenge. And when she was tired of them, she just dropped them. I think it was almost a matter of principle with her, to be the first one to end the affair. I don't think she ever truly loved any one of them, in fact I'm not sure if she was capable of it. It was so sad, really. She never knew what loving someone was really like. There was something in her which made her hold back – the fear of rejection, I suppose. She told me once that she hoped she never would fall in love because she simply couldn't bear the thought of the pain she would have to endure if he left her.'

And when she was tired of them, she just dropped them. A recipe for disaster if ever there was one, thought Thanet.

'What about her husband?' said Lineham.

'She was fond of Ralph, I'm sure, but her relationship with him was different. She would never have left him, he was her anchor, and she needed him. All the same, it was almost as if . . . How shall I put it? Almost as if she was constantly driven to test him, to see if he, too, would finally give up on her and leave. From little things she said I'm certain she felt guilty about it, but she couldn't seem to stop.'

'And did he ever show any sign of leaving her?'

Susan shook her head. 'No. I think Ralph understood her very well. Also, he's pretty realistic. His job takes him away for months at a time, as I'm sure you know, and he was well aware that Ginny wasn't the sort of girl to sit around twiddling her thumbs while she waited for him to come home. As long as she was still there when he did, that was all that mattered to him.'

'Even so, it couldn't have been easy for him, to sit by while his wife flirted with other men.'

'If you're thinking Ralph could have pushed her down that well, forget it. He'd never have hurt her. Never.'

Thanet could see that there was no point in pursuing that line. 'So, her father's abandonment affected her deeply. But you said there were other things . . .'

'Two, in fact.'

'So what were they?'

FOURTEEN

Susan stood up and stretched, placing her palms as support on the small of her back and leaning backwards. 'Sorry, I get so stiff, sitting,' she said.

Thanet knew how she felt. How many thousands of times had he himself tried to ease an aching back with just that movement? He had suffered from back problems for years and although regular visits to the chiropractor ensured that the pain was never as severe or chronic as it had once been, he could nevertheless sympathise with a fellow sufferer.

'I think I'll stand up for a while,' she said. She walked across to the window and leaned against the sill, facing them. 'If you want to understand Ginny you have to appreciate that although you wouldn't have expected it, from looking at her, she was in fact a very maternal person. Her children mattered to her more than anyone or anything else. And she was a brilliant mother – patient, loving, willing to take endless trouble on their behalf. That was why what happened was so tragic.'

'Caroline's elopement, you mean?' said Lineham.

'That too, later, yes. But you obviously don't know about the baby ...? No? Well, Ginny was only eighteen when she got married. It was January 1976. I remember that because I'd just gone up to university, the previous September. Ginny had failed most of her O levels and left school at sixteen, but somehow we never lost touch. She wasn't qualified for anything, of course, but she did look gorgeous and had a great sense of style, so she got a job in an exclusive little boutique, which seemed to suit her very well. Anyway, to cut a long story short she met Ralph

147

and they got married. His mother wasn't too happy about it. I expect you'll have gathered that she and Ginny didn't exactly hit it off, and of course Ginny was very young. I think what sugared the pill as far as Mrs Mintar senior was concerned was Ralph's suggestion that he and Ginny take over Windmill Court and convert that single-storey wing of outbuildings into a self-contained flat for her. Apparently ever since Ralph's father died she'd been complaining about the inconvenience of maintaining that house, especially as she was away such a lot on her plant-finding expeditions. I suppose she felt she had to keep it ticking over for Ralph's sake.

'Anyway, Ginny became pregnant right away and to my surprise she was delighted about it, told me she felt that at last she'd have someone of her very own to love. But sadly it all went wrong. The baby was born severely handicapped – its brain hadn't developed properly – and it only lived for a few hours. Ginny was devastated.'

Please God that wouldn't happen to Bridget's baby! Once again Thanet was having to force himself to concentrate. The mere mention of babies these days sent his mind scurrying off to that bed in the maternity ward where his daughter was lying, helplessly awaiting developments.

'I was away at university at the time, of course, and didn't see her until Christmas, by which time she was pregnant again – against her doctor's advice, I might add. However, all went well and Caroline was born. Ginny was ecstatic, but I don't think she ever got over losing the first one. She was a girl, too. And of course, that's why she's worked for MENCAP all these years.'

'She worked for MENCAP? We didn't know that.'

'She didn't exactly shout about it but she's been on the committee ever since. She was particularly good at fund-raising. And once a week she'd go along to the Wednesday club – that's a social evening where mentally handicapped adults mix with ordinary people. They have Scottish dancing and play simple games. If you'd seen Ginny there . . . I think she felt that any one of them could have been the baby she lost. And they all adored her.'

So, thought Thanet. Over twenty years of selfless commitment. An entirely new light on Virginia's character.

'But then, of course,' said Susan, leaving the windowsill to return to her chair, 'came the next disaster, Caroline's elopement. You've obviously heard about that. And this time . . . You've seen all the stuff piled up in Ginny's room, I imagine?'

Thanet nodded.

'After Caroline went it was as if . . .' Susan shook her head sorrowfully. 'You know I said Ginny went haywire after her father left? Well this time it was ten times worse, as if she'd finally flipped. She seemed to lose all restraint, take all the brakes off, so that everything she did was over the top. The shopping is a typical example. She'd always loved clothes and enjoyed buying them but now, well, you'll have seen for yourself, it was a compulsion, an obsession, a sickness. She'd always enjoyed going to the Health Club, but now it wasn't just a daily twenty-minute swim it was three-quarters of an hour or an hour – on top of a session in the gym or an hour's tennis. And as for—' Susan broke off.

Thanet guessed what she had been going to say. 'As for men . . . ?'

Susan pressed her lips together as if to forbid herself to elaborate, but it was obvious that Thanet had hit the mark.

'But Caroline's elopement was – how long ago?' said Lineham. 'Four years?'

Susan nodded.

'You'd have thought she'd have begun to get over it by now.'

'Precisely. But that was the trouble. She didn't. If anything she was getting worse.'

'Didn't anyone suggest she tried to get help?' said Thanet.

'Of course! I know Ralph did, because she told me so. And God knows I tried often enough. But she just wouldn't listen, didn't want to know. "Stop fussing, Sue," she'd say. "I'm perfectly all right!"'

'What about Mr Mintar?' said Thanet. 'How did he react to Caroline's elopement?'

'Well, that was half the trouble, of course. Caroline was Ralph's favourite, you see, no doubt about that, so it must have hit him really hard too. But he just isn't one to wear his heart on his sleeve and his way of coping was simply to shut out the memory of her altogether. He said as far as he was concerned she had made her bed and she would have to lie on it. He didn't want to hear her name mentioned again.'

'Impossible, surely!' said Lineham.

'Maybe. But it certainly didn't help Ginny – or Rachel either, for that matter – to have to pretend Caro had never existed. If Ginny and Ralph had been able to, well, grieve together, it would have helped her no end, I'm sure. As it was she just had to bottle it all up most of the time and I think that was why this bizarre behaviour began to build up. I kept hoping that she would gradually adjust, come to terms with the fact that Caroline was gone for good, but she never could. She even employed a private detective to try and track her down at one time, you know, but it was no good. The pair of them seemed to have vanished into thin air. And lately, of course, this business with Rachel hasn't helped. Neither she nor Ralph were happy about Rachel's latest choice of boyfriend. Poor Ginny! Rachel only got back from a year away in Switzerland in June, and Ginny was so looking forward to having her home again. She hadn't wanted her to go away to finishing school in the first place, but Ralph insisted. And then, before she'd been back five minutes, Rachel had taken up with this tennis coach.'

'He's her fiancé now. They apparently got engaged on Saturday night, broke the news to Rachel's parents that evening.'

'Oh no!' Susan breathed. 'Engaged. Oh, my God. How did Ginny and Ralph react, do you know?'

'Opened a bottle of champagne, I gather.'

'They had no choice, I imagine. What else could they do? They wouldn't have dared risk driving Rachel away too. Oh, poor Ginny,' Susan repeated. 'It's unbelievable. Absolutely the last thing she needed.'

Had he known all this before, Thanet thought, he might have been more willing to accept that Virginia had thrown herself down that well in despair. But the conclusion to be drawn from those bruises left little room for doubt.

'Why didn't Virginia like Rachel's boyfriend? Did she say?'

'She thought Rachel was too young for a serious relationship with anyone, but apart from that, she didn't trust him, thought he had an eye to the main chance and probably saw Rachel as a good prospect. He hasn't a penny to his name, I believe. Also, she thought he was too free with his attentions to other young women at the Club. He'd been around for a while before Rachel came home, and Ginny had had plenty of opportunity to observe him.'

'He gave her some coaching, I believe.'

'Did he? That must have been when I was away. Our elder daughter lives in New Zealand and we went over there for an extended trip last winter, didn't get back until April.'

'Wasn't that difficult for your business?'

'It did require a colossal amount of organisation before I went, to keep things ticking over in my absence. But you have to get your priorities right. My daughter was expecting her first baby and there were problems.'

Babies again, thought Thanet. They seemed to crop up all the time. 'Everything was all right, I hope?'

She looked surprised that he had asked. 'Yes. After a few traumas on the way.'

'Good . . . Virginia didn't by any chance hint that there'd been anything between her and Matthew Agon, did she?' If there had been, it would have been to Susan that Virginia would have been most likely to mention it.

She laughed. 'Oh no. He was much too young. She wasn't in favour of toy-boys, as she called them, thought it would be degrading to have everyone pointing and whispering.'

'But she wasn't averse to causing gossip, surely. We understand her affair with Dr Squires is common knowledge at the Health Club.'

'So you know about that. Well, that's different. Matt Agon is young enough to be her son, isn't he? Frankly, I think Howard Squires was absolutely crazy to carry on with a patient like that, but there you are. Some men seem to lose all common sense when they get involved with a woman like Ginny. But that's their affair, isn't it?'

'When did she become involved with him, do you know?'

'Not really. While I was away. It was certainly going strong by the time I got back.'

'Several months ago at least, then. From what you said, about her always liking to be the one to end the affair, it was due to come to an end soon.'

'I agree. And if he does get away with it, he'll be a lucky man. Let's hope he has more common sense in future.'

'She didn't by any chance tell you she was going to break it off with him, did she?' If she had, thought Thanet, what stronger motive could they look for? The prospect of losing her, together with the outrageous way in which she had flirted with her sister's boyfriend on Saturday night, might have been enough to provoke a row in which Squires might have lost his temper.

But Susan was shaking her head. 'But that doesn't mean she didn't. My God, do you think that's what might have happened?' She was looking aghast.

'At the moment we have absolutely no idea. It's all pure speculation. There are a number of possibilities.'

'Well, I hope you get him, whoever he is!' she cried, suddenly passionate. 'I may not always have approved of her behaviour, but she hasn't had an easy time and she certainly didn't deserve this!'

'No,' said Thanet, his tone sombre. 'Of course she didn't.' He rose. 'I think we've taken up enough of your time, Mrs Amos. You've been immensely helpful. Er . . . Before I go . . . ?' And he nodded at the jacket he had chosen.

'Oh, of course.'

The negotiation was swiftly completed. 'Christmas shopping,' Thanet said to Lineham with a somewhat shamefaced grin as they walked back to the car.

'Already? You'll be buying your Christmas cards in the January sales next!'

'Joan'll love it. I didn't want to miss the chance.'

'Just pulling your leg, sir. Bet it was a bit pricey, though.'

'It's good to push the boat out from time to time,' said Thanet, trying not to think just how far he'd pushed it this time. Anyway, he didn't care. He was delighted with his purchase. He glanced at his watch. Twenty past twelve. 'We'll go back to the Dog and Thistle for a bite to eat, before meeting the Super.'

They carried their drinks outside to a table on the wide pavement again. Here beneath the trees they were at least shaded from the fierce heat of the noonday sun. Considering himself briefly off duty, Thanet loosened his tie and undid the top button of his shirt, making a mental note to remember to do it up again. It wouldn't do for the Super to catch him like this. Draco, he was sure, would not allow himself such laxity under any circumstances.

While they waited for the food to arrive they were silent, mulling over the interview with Susan Amos.

'I still can't believe that Mr Mintar was perfectly happy for his wife to carry on like that,' said Lineham eventually.

'Difficult to accept, I agree.'

'And you know what they say about worms turning.' Lineham was warming to his theme. 'Maybe the provocation on Saturday was just too much. Perhaps the pressure had been building up all day. The four of them had been out together earlier, remember, to Sissinghurst. What if she'd been making a play for Mr Prime then, too?'

'Possible, I agree.'

'So Mr Mintar may already have been angry with her, before the dinner party even started. And then on top of all that there was the shock of Rachel's engagement and the strain of having to go through the charade of being pleased . . . Maybe that's it, sir! Maybe he thought that in view of this latest development, they had to act quickly if they were to get rid of Agon before his position became too entrenched. He'd been wanting to pay him off, remember, but his wife was against it. Maybe he grabbed the first opportunity to tackle her about it, while everyone was off changing. We've only his word that he was in his study the whole time. So maybe he went back, had a row with her about it and suddenly it was all too much and he just snapped . . .'

'Could have happened like that, I agree.'

The food arrived and they tucked in. Lineham had chosen the bacon and mushroom baguettes again, while Thanet had opted for home-cooked roast beef with English mustard. It was good, too, the meat thickly sliced and succulent, the mustard freshly made.

'Mmm. I must bring Louise here sometime,' said Lineham. 'Of course,' he went on, 'you could argue that a lot of this applies to Virginia's sister, too. She might have had enough, as well. After all, from what Mr Prime said, it was far from the first time Virginia had had a go at pinching Jane's boyfriends – and had usually succeeded too, by the sound of it, to the degree that she'd put off bringing him here to meet Virginia as long as she possibly could. Not surprising, I suppose. Jane's no oil painting is she?'

'I'll risk a cliché and say you shouldn't judge a book by its cover, Mike.'

'Maybe. But when a woman like Virginia throws herself at you, it must be a big temptation.'

'Obviously one that Prime was strong-minded enough to resist.'

'But Jane wasn't to know that, was she? After all, she's no spring chicken. Maybe she felt Prime was her last chance, and imagined him slipping away from her like others had done in the past. Rachel told Agon that Jane had been really upset, remember, that she'd heard her crying. And Jane and Prime were there for the whole weekend, there was all day Sunday yet to come. Maybe Jane felt she couldn't face it, if Virginia was going to carry on in the same way, and like we said decided to have it out with her. Marilyn Squires was pretty definite about her coming out of the door leading to the kitchen corridor.'

'If she was telling the truth.'

'You think she might not have been?'

'No, I'm inclined to believe her. Anyway, we'll have to interview Jane again, obviously. But it's just occurred to me . . .'

'What?' Lineham stopped chewing.

'Mr Mintar. I wonder how ambitious he is. His father was a High Court judge. What if he aspires to the Bench too?'

'I don't see what you're getting at.'

'Well, it sounds to me as though in that respect Virginia could have been a considerable liability.'

'The way she carried on with men, you mean?'

'Her blatant flirting, yes. Hardly proper behaviour for the wife of a prospective High Court judge, wouldn't you agree?'

'Are you suggesting he might deliberately have set out to kill her on Saturday?'

'No, not at all. But it could have been an underlying reason for him to have been fed up with her, don't you think?' Thanet was keeping an eye on the time. He wanted to be at the Mintars' house ahead of Draco. He did up his top button and tightened his tie. 'Come on, Mike, we'd better go. Mustn't keep the Super waiting, must we? No,' he went on as they walked to the car, 'I think that whoever committed this crime did it on the spur of the moment.'

'I agree,' said Lineham. 'But to change the subject, I wonder how long it'll take to get that search warrant.'

'I expect it'll have come through by the time we've finished at the Mintars'. By the way, I've been thinking, Mike.'

'What?'

'Young Rachel. I feel sorry for her. She's had a rotten time. She's obviously still very upset about losing her sister, you could tell from her behaviour the night before last, and now, on top of that, this terrible thing has happened to her mother.'

'So? We're doing all we can.'

'To find out who was responsible for the murder, yes. But what about Caroline?'

'You want to have another shot at finding her?'

'Why not? It was four years ago, I know, which in one way will make things more difficult, as the trail will be cold. But in another way the lapse of time might help. For one thing she and young Swain might have become more careless as time has gone on, and not be taking as much trouble to cover their tracks. Also, her attitude might have changed, she might not be so hardened against her parents now. And apart from anything else, she has a right to know what has happened to her mother. So yes, I'd say another effort is called for, wouldn't you?'

'Who'll you put on to it?'

'Tanya, I think. It'll give her something to get her teeth into.' Thanet was conscious of time ticking away. It was twenty past one already. Perhaps they had lingered too long over lunch. He had a sudden vision of Draco standing waiting for them in the courtyard, feet planted firmly apart, stopwatch in hand. 'Better put your foot down, Mike. We don't want to be late.'

FIFTEEN

It was twenty-five past one when they pulled up at the Mintars' house.

'No sign of the Super yet,' said Lineham.

'No,' said Thanet with satisfaction. He was watching Digby, who had just emerged from a door at the far end of the coach-house carrying a ball of green twine and a bundle of bamboo canes. At least they'd know where to find him when the search warrant came through.

At 1.30 precisely the car radio crackled into life. There was a message from Superintendent Draco: something had cropped up and he would be unable to keep their appointment. Instead, Inspector Thanet was expected to report to him for an update at five o'clock sharp.

'Bet he never intended to turn up,' said Lineham. 'Just keeping us on our toes, isn't he?'

'I'm not grumbling,' said Thanet, glad of the reprieve. Lineham was probably right.

'So, who first?' said Lineham as they got out of the car.

'Jane Simons, I think,' said Thanet. 'If we can find her, that is. And after that, Mr Mintar.'

The back door stood open but they had to knock twice before Mintar appeared, clutching a white linen napkin and looking even worse than he had yesterday. He was wearing the same clothes and Thanet guessed he had probably slept in them. There were food stains down the front of his shirt and he still hadn't shaved. Those who knew the dapper well-groomed QC only from his courtroom appearances would scarcely have recognised the man.

For a moment or two he stood looking blankly at Thanet as though he'd never seen him before and couldn't imagine what he was doing there. Then came a gleam of recognition. 'Oh, it's you, Thanet,' he said in a lifeless monotone. 'We were just finishing lunch.'

'I'd like another word with you later, sir, if you don't mind. But first, if I could speak to Miss Simons . . . ?'

Mintar seemed to rouse himself. 'I gather you've nothing of moment to tell me?' And suddenly he was his former self, fixing Thanet with that familiar penetrating stare.

'There was one thing, sir.' Thanet had intended waiting to impart this piece of information until the beginning of his interview but Mintar's question had put him on the spot. 'The PM took place this morning—'

'And?' The word shot out like a bullet.

Thanet told him about the bruising, their certainty that Virginia's death had been murder.

Mintar's face was bleak. 'I see,' he said, the words little more than a whisper. He turned away. 'I'll fetch my sister-in-law.'

'Taken a nose-dive hasn't he, sir?' said Lineham softly when he had gone. 'All the same, I wouldn't fancy having to face him in Court.'

'Better keep on the right side of the law then, hadn't you!'

It was a few minutes before Jane Simons appeared and Thanet guessed that Mintar had been breaking the news of the PM results to the others.

'You wanted to see me?' She was looking shaken but was much more composed than the last time they had seen her. The only residual hint of yesterday's tears was a slight puffiness around the eyes.

'Just one or two more questions,' said Thanet. 'I'm glad to see you're feeling a little better,' he added as they all sat down. No need as yet to be too heavy-handed, he decided. In any case, she would have had plenty of time to prepare her story. Prime would almost certainly have told her the gist of his conversation with them on the way into the village yesterday morning, including the fact that he had had to admit that he and Jane had returned separately to the pool. 'We've been talking to everyone who was present at the dinner party on Saturday,' he said, 'getting a

157

clearer picture of the sequence of events that evening. Miss Simons, why did you and Mr Prime give us the impression that you returned to the pool together?'

She caught her lower lip beneath her teeth in an expression of troubled innocence. 'Yes, Arnold told me you'd got the wrong idea about that. I'm sorry. We didn't intend to mislead you.'

'We understand that you had an argument, while you were up in your room, and that you were rather upset.'

'My God,' she said, with a flash of hostility. 'You have been poking about, haven't you?'

'We've had to. Your sister is dead, Miss Simons, and it's our job to try to find out why.'

She compressed her lips. 'I know. I'm sorry.'

Genuinely contrite? Thanet wondered. Or merely politic?

'If you've picked up that much,' she said, 'you've probably gathered what the argument was about. I know you're not supposed to speak ill of the dead but I've always thought that a rather mealy-mouthed attitude. There's good and bad in all of us and my sister was no exception, as I'm sure you're finding out. That doesn't mean to say I wasn't fond of her, I was. She was my sister, after all. But there's no point in trying to deny that she was a terrible flirt. I honestly don't think she could help herself. She simply couldn't resist trying to charm every man who came along. And that, of course, included my boyfriend. I suppose I was taking my resentment of her behaviour out on him, poor man. Very unfair of me, I'd be the first to admit.'

'And you no doubt decided to take her to task about it?'

She lifted her heavy shoulders. She was wearing a sleeveless sundress and Thanet saw the muscles in her upper arms ripple. She could have tipped Virginia into that well with ease, he thought.

'Why deny it?' she said.

'So what did you do?'

'Finished changing, went down to the kitchen. I knew Ginny would still be there.'

Thanet's pulse accelerated. 'And was she?'

'No. I was surprised, I must admit. As I told you yesterday, she was a stickler for getting everything ship-shape. It wasn't like her to leave the clearing away half finished. It was only later, when

158

we realised she was missing, that I began to wonder about it, think that perhaps she had been interrupted.'

'So what did you do?'

'Went on out to the pool, of course. If she wasn't there, too bad. What I had to say to her could wait.'

'You didn't look for her?'

'No. I assumed she'd decided to swim first, finish clearing up later, and had gone up to change. I couldn't be bothered to go back upstairs.'

'Did you look out of the kitchen window?'

'No. Why should I?'

'It didn't occur to you she might have gone outside?'

'It never entered my head! Ralph said he wondered if she might have gone out to finish watering the camellias – apparently Howard and Marilyn arrived before she'd finished, but I'm no gardener, haven't even got a window box, so the idea of going out to water the garden in the middle of entertaining guests? It's just too bizarre! No, I just glanced around, saw she wasn't there, and went out to join the others.'

'Please, would you try to think back . . . When you glanced around, did you see or even glimpse someone, something, anything out of that window? Any movement . . . ?'

'No!' she cried. 'Nothing! If I had, it would have caught my eye and I'd probably have paused to take a better look. But it was pretty dark by then, remember, and I was in a lighted room. I know there are lights in the courtyard but it would still be pretty dim out there, by comparison.' She paused. 'Even so, do you think if I had looked, I might have seen something? Been able to help her? Even perhaps have prevented it?' She gave Thanet a quick, agonised glance, then lowered her eyelids as if to prevent herself from reading an affirmative in his eyes.

Thanet shook his head. 'Impossible to tell, I'm afraid. We don't even know the precise time it happened.'

'I just can't take it in. I mean . . . murders are what happen to other people, aren't they? You read about them in the news-papers, or see them in the news on television. And although you might think oh, how awful, how dreadful, the *reality* of it doesn't come home to you. And then, when it does happen to someone close to you, that sense of unreality persists. I mean, you know it's happening but you still can't believe it. Do you see what I mean?' She paused and then said, 'You will catch him, Inspector, won't you?'

'We'll do our level best, believe me.' Thanet rose. 'Now, I was going to have a word with Mr Mintar.'

'Yes. He said to go along to his study. You know where it is?'

'Thank you. Yes.'

Mintar was sitting behind his desk, his expression grim, the cat on his lap. It turned its head to give them an enigmatic stare as they came in. Mintar waved a hand. 'Do sit down.' He was looking much more alert. No doubt the shock of hearing the post-mortem result had jolted him out of his earlier almost trance-like state.

When they were settled he said, 'So I was right. It was murder. Not that it gives me any satisfaction whatsoever to say so.' His hand was moving in long, regular strokes along the cat's back from the top of its head to the tip of its tail and its purrs were a basso profundo accompaniment to what he was saying. 'And as I also said yesterday, as the husband of the victim I suppose I am, like many an unfortunate wretch before me, the prime suspect.'

'One of them, yes.' Pointless to deny it.

'Since then I have of course begun to think more rationally about the whole business and realised what my wife was doing out there at that time of night. If you remember, I told you she asked me to remind her to finish the watering later. She was obsessive about those camellias.'

Mintar's gaze strayed to the photograph on the desk and briefly his icy self-control faltered: his voice grew husky and the skin of his face seemed to quiver, as if it were having difficulty in containing the emotions threatening to erupt from beneath the surface. He cleared his throat and held up his hand as Thanet opened his mouth to speak. 'No, let me finish. The other thing I wanted to say is that although, yesterday, I told you that I would be open and honest with you, hold nothing back, I was in fact less than frank, out of misplaced loyalty to my wife.'

It was obvious what Mintar was referring to, but he had

nothing to lose by taking the initiative. He must have realised that it wouldn't take Thanet long to put two and two together. 'You're referring to your wife's affair with Dr Squires.' A statement, not a question.

Mintar sighed. 'So you already know. I might have guessed. But I said "misplaced" because I've come to the conclusion that in the circumstances, in some topsy-turvy way I actually owe it to her to speak of it. Whoever killed her has to be found and I vehemently deny that it was I. Not that at this stage I would expect you to believe me, but I wish to make my position quite clear.'

Grammatical even in the grip of emotion, Thanet noted. Habitual precision of speech dies hard.

'Ergo,' Mintar was saying, 'it must have been someone else. The big question is, who?'

'Are you suggesting it might have been Dr Squires?'

'Oh come, Thanet, I'm sure you've already worked out for yourself that if I come top of the list, he must surely come second. And with a woman as beautiful as my wife' – again he glanced at the photograph – 'a *crime passionnel* is bound to be on the cards.'

He gave the cat one final stroke, set it gently down on the floor beside his chair and then leaned forward as if to emphasise the importance of what he was about to say. The cat stood for a moment, its tail twitching angrily, then stalked off and jumped up on to the windowsill where it proceeded to wash itself. Mintar said, 'And that is the point, Thanet. My wife was beautiful, exceptionally so, but beauty can be a burden as well as an asset and brings with it its own special disadvantages. Virginia . . .' His voice grew husky again. '. . . Virginia was like a flame to a moth, men couldn't help being attracted to her nor, unfortunately, she to them.' He cleared his throat, then added briskly, 'I'm sure you must already have asked yourself why I put up with this sort of behaviour, but the fact of the matter is, I would have done anything, put up with anything, to keep her.'

Mintar sat back as if the hardest part of his confession was over. 'My work, as you must be aware, takes me away from home for sometimes months at a time. What was Ginny supposed to

161

do while I was away? Sit at home, knitting? She developed her own interests, of course she did, barristers' wives have to if they are to survive, but unfortunately they were not enough for her. Because what most people didn't realise was that underneath she was very insecure. She needed, absolutely had to have, constant reassurance that she mattered, that she was special. And I simply couldn't give that to her, if I was away for half the year. I understood that and was prepared to turn a blind eye to her affairs with other men, so long as she always came back to me in the end, was always there when I did come home. You see? I really am being absolutely frank with you now. I'd never have dreamt I would say these things to anyone, let alone to strangers. But needs must. I just want you to understand that if you are considering my supposed motive to be jealousy, then you couldn't be more wrong.'

'What about ambition?'

'As a motive? What on earth can you . . . ?' Mintar broke off, but not before Thanet caught the flash of anger. 'Oh, I see! You are suggesting that my wife's behaviour could have compromised my chances? Well, all I can say is that if you offered me a straight choice between a seat in the High Court and Virginia, then there's no doubt in my mind which I would have chosen. One's years on the Bench are brief and I always hoped that as she grew older, Virginia's behaviour would become increasingly moderate. Besides, I would never have contemplated old age without her through choice.' Abruptly he stood up and crossed to look out of the window and Thanet guessed that he was struggling to regain control. They were all three aware that that choice had now been taken away from him, once and for all.

It was time for a change of direction. 'You told us yesterday that your wife never got over Caroline's elopement, and since then we've seen the effects of this for ourselves.'

Mintar swung around, scooping up the cat again as he did so, obviously surprised at the sudden switch. His eyes narrowed. 'What has that got to do with it?'

'I don't know,' Thanet admitted. 'I'm not sure at this stage that it has the least relevance. But it did affect your wife's behaviour and it must have been some aspect of her behaviour that sparked off this attack. At this stage I am simply trying to assimilate as much information as possible and then later perhaps I shall begin to understand what went wrong.'

'So what do you want to know?' Mintar returned to his desk and sat down again.

Thanet had already decided that at this stage he would say nothing about making a further attempt to trace Caroline. He wanted a free hand and suspected that Mintar might object to such a search, as he apparently had in the past. 'You said that Dick Swain's mother was "as unhelpful as she could possibly be" when you tried to find out where the young people had gone. You went to see her as soon as you found out what had happened, I assume?'

'Of course. Immediatcly after finding Caroline's note, next morning. I didn't expect to find them there, naturally, but I did hope she might know where they'd gone. But she wouldn't even let me into the house, slammed the door in my face.'

'You tried again later?'

'Certainly. That same evening, when I thought she might have calmed down. But with no more success. I just got a torrent of abuse. She was blaming Caroline for the whole thing, saying she had turned her son's head and calling her all sorts of filthy names. I might add that the police got no further than I did.'

'What about some time later, when she really might have been more cooperative? Did you ever make another attempt?'

'No. What was the point? There was no reason to think her attitude might have changed. In fact I thought it would be better, less painful, if we tried to put Caroline out of our minds altogether. It didn't work, though. Virginia was inconsolable, it seemed . . . Just a moment . . .' Once again he gave Thanet one of those piercing stares. 'All these questions . . .' He stopped, and his eyes grew distant. Then he shook his head as if to clear it. 'Sorry, go on.'

'What were you going to say, sir?'

'Nothing. It doesn't matter.'

Thanet was suspicious but Mintar obviously wasn't going to tell him. 'I understand Caroline left a note. May I see it?'

Mintar hesitated before depositing the cat on the floor again and taking a key ring from his pocket. Then he bent to unlock one of the bottom drawers of his desk, took out an envelope and handed it to Thanet.

And here, thought Thanet as he took out the letter, was the evidence that however much Mintar had apparently hardened his heart against his favourite daughter, underneath he had grieved as bitterly as his wife. The flimsy piece of paper was virtually disintegrating from much handling and from being folded and refolded countless times over the past four years. Thanet glanced at Mintar and found him watching and as he caught his eye the QC looked away, no doubt aware that Thanet had appreciated the significance of the condition of the piece of paper he was holding. He focused on what Caroline had written.

Sorry, I can't stand this any longer. I'm going away with Dick. Please don't try to find me.

And then, below, smudged with tears:

I do love you all.
Caroline

Handling it very carefully, Thanet laid the letter on the desk, tempted after all to mention his decision to make a further attempt to find her. No, better not to, in case they didn't get anywhere. But he was at least now reasonably sure that should they be successful Caroline would get a warm reception from her father, despite the smokescreen he had put up. 'There's just one other question I want to ask you at present, something that puzzles me. I understand that you were very much in favour of trying to buy Agon off, but—'

'Shh!' Mintar looked at the door and hissed, 'Keep your voice down, for God's sake! If Rachel should hear . . . How the hell you found that out, I can't imagine!'

Thanet lowered his voice. 'Sorry, sir.' And he meant it. The last thing he wanted was to cause further distress to Rachel. 'I wasn't thinking. But as I understand it, your wife was against it. Did she say why?'

Mintar leaned forward, speaking in a near whisper. 'I think

she was afraid – and I must admit she had a point – that he might consider Rachel a greater prize and refuse. And that if he did, he might tell her what we'd done. In which case . . .'

'It might set Rachel against you too. I see. Yes. That makes sense.'

Outside again Thanet said to Lineham, 'You were very quiet in there, Mike. Didn't utter a word.'

'Thought you were doing fine without my help, sir,' said Lineham with a grin.

'Let's check on that search warrant.'

It had been granted and Thanet arranged to meet the team at Digby's house in fifteen minutes.

'Come on, Mike, let's go and pick him up. I think Mr Digby would rather enjoy a ride in a police car, don't you?'

Lineham gave an anticipatory smile. 'This should be interesting.'

Digby was not amused at being dragged away from his work. 'What'll Mr Mintar say? I can't walk out just like that, can I?'

'I'm sure Mr Mintar would have no objection whatsoever.' But he would doubtless have asked plenty of awkward questions, which was why Thanet had no intention of asking his permission.

'Am I being arrested?'

'Certainly not, sir. We just need your help in our inquiries.'

'So I could refuse?'

'You could. But I really don't think that would be a good idea, do you? It might give us the wrong impression, even put ideas into our heads.'

Reluctantly Digby got into the car. 'Where are we going, anyway?'

Lineham grinned. 'You're going to give us a guided tour.'

'Of what?'

'Of your house, of course.'

Digby lunged for the door handle but Lineham had had the foresight to activate the safety locks. 'You have no right, without a search warrant!'

'Got one,' said the sergeant.

'Where is it, then? I demand to see it!'

'All in good time, sir,' said Thanet. 'I assure you, this is all legal and above board. The search will go ahead with or without your cooperation.'

Digby lapsed into a glowering silence which lasted until they pulled up in the lane outside his house. As they drew up four officers got out of a waiting police car.

'Ah, reinforcements,' said Thanet. 'Actually, I don't think you'll all be needed. As you can see, the house is very small, we'd be falling over ourselves.'

The warrant was produced and inspected and Digby capitulated, unlocking the door with an ill grace.

'Now,' said Thanet when they were inside. 'The darkroom is upstairs, I presume?'

'I don't want you mucking about with my equipment!'

'Your equipment will be treated with every respect. In fact, it's not so much your equipment we're interested in, but what you produce with it.'

'You're wasting your time! There's nothing illegal! Nothing pornographic or anything like that!'

'Well, we shall see,' said Thanet. 'But of course, it's not always the material itself that's important, it's the use you make of it.'

'I don't know what you mean. What are you talking about?'

But Digby understood only too well. Thanet could read it in his eyes, could even hear the beginnings of resignation in his tone of voice. Thanet didn't bother to reply, just indicated that Tanya and Lineham should accompany him and set off up the narrow staircase. Digby was left downstairs with Carson.

There were only two bedrooms. As in so many old cottages with limited upstairs accommodation, the bathroom – if there was one – would have been built on downstairs, at the back. Digby's bedroom, furnished in minimal fashion with single bed, a scuffed and battered chest of drawers and a bedside table, overlooked the dreary front garden. A curtain slung across one corner concealed his scanty collection of clothes. No effort whatsoever had been made to render the room attractive.

The room at the back, a state of the art darkroom, was a very different matter. This, obviously, was where Digby's money went. Three tall narrow chests of drawers – custom-made? Thanet wondered – accommodated his prints and negatives. It didn't take long to find what they were looking for. It stood to reason that if Digby stored incriminating material in his darkroom he wasn't going to leave it lying around where a casual search would bring it to light, especially as he had some reputation as a photographer locally and this room would be a prime target for burglars.

They therefore began by removing the drawers and examining them to see if anything had been taped underneath. It was Lineham who struck lucky. 'Sir!' he said.

It was a brown manila envelope and a glance at the first photograph told Thanet that his guess had been right. Digby's net had spread beyond Squires and Virginia.

Digby had been taking a risk. He must have been standing on the terrace just outside the French windows of the drawing room of the Mintars' house – Thanet recognised the furnishings. If either of the two people in the photograph had glanced up they could surely not have failed to catch sight of him, but they were far too engrossed in each other.

They were lying on one of the big sofas, making love. Digby must coolly have waited for a moment when both of their profiles were clearly visible. No one could have mistaken Agon's male-model good looks, that cap of shining blonde hair.

At first Thanet thought the woman was Rachel but then he looked more closely. He glanced up at Lineham, seeking confirmation.

The sergeant nodded, eyes sparkling with the pleasure of suspicion verified. 'Virginia Mintar,' he said.

SIXTEEN

Tanya stopped searching and came to look over Thanet's shoulder as he shuffled through the rest of the photographs in the envelope. They were all more of the same: Matthew Agon and Virginia in compromising positions. The negatives were there too.

'Wonder what Rachel would think if she saw these,' said Lineham.

'Or Mintar, for that matter.'

'From what he's told us, he might not be too surprised,' said Lineham.

'In that case, couldn't they be used as ammunition for him to get rid of the sleaze?' said Tanya. 'No, perhaps not. If he threatened to show them to Rachel, Agon would probably tell him to go ahead, banking on the fact that her father wouldn't want to upset her – or, for that matter, show her mother up in a bad light. But then again, Mr Mintar might feel it would be worth it, to save her from marrying a character like that.'

'Difficult to tell,' said Thanet. He'd have to think about whether or not to show these to Mintar. 'Meanwhile, let's see if we can turn up anything else. The photographs of Squires and Virginia are bound to be somewhere.'

They were, along with several other caches of similar photographs of couples Thanet had never seen before.

'Wonder how many of these he's trying to squeeze money out of,' said Lineham in disgust.

'Well, if this investigation achieves nothing else, it should save a lot of people a great deal of heartache,' said Tanya.

'By the way, talking of heartache, Tanya, I was thinking . . .' said Thanet.

Tanya looked delighted to be given the task of trying to trace Caroline. 'Just up my street, sir,' she said.

'Good. You can get started on it right away, as soon as you've finished here. I'd like you and Carson to stay on, make sure there's nothing we've missed. If Digby is blackmailing any of these people, there should be some kind of evidence somewhere. He may well have destroyed correspondence, if there ever was any, but you might take a look at his bank statements, for instance. He didn't buy all this equipment on a gardener's salary.'

Leaving Tanya to it Thanet and Lineham went downstairs.

The fear in Digby's eyes as he caught sight of the incriminating manila envelopes was plain for all to see.

'Proper little paparazzo, aren't you?' said Lineham, holding them up.

'Where did you get those?' cried Digby. 'I've never seen them in my life before!'

'Don't try to put one over on us!' said Thanet. 'Who else would have taped them to the underside of those drawers?'

'I've been set up!' said Digby. 'You must have planted them yourselves.'

'Who d'you think the Court would believe?' said Lineham. 'You or the three police officers present when they were found?'

'Anyway,' said Digby, 'there's no law against taking photographs, is there?'

'Unless they are obscene,' said Thanet. 'Or blackmail is involved.'

Digby erupted out of his chair and Carson moved quickly to put a hand on his shoulder to restrain him. 'Blackmail! What blackmail? You can't pin that on me!'

'Really?' said Thanet grimly. 'We'll see about that. Tell the others I want him taken in for questioning,' he said to Carson. 'Then you join Tanya upstairs. She'll tell you what we're looking for.'

Ignoring Digby's protests he and Lineham left.

'Let him stew,' said Thanet as they got into the car. 'He can have a taste of his own medicine.'

'He deserves all he gets,' said Lineham. 'Rachel was right, wasn't she? He's a real slimeball.' He glanced at the envelopes. 'Had quite a haul there, didn't we?'

'Certainly did. Tanya's right. This should save a lot of people a great deal of heartache.'

'Will we try to trace them?'

'I doubt it. Where would we start? Unless Tanya and Carson come up with anything, of course. Otherwise it would be too time-consuming and a drain on resources. Anyway, if he is actively engaged in blackmailing any of them, no doubt they'll realise something's happened when the demands stop coming, and there'll be sighs of relief all round.'

'So where now, sir? Agon?'

'Oh I think so, yes.'

This time the receptionist's smile was definitely forced. 'He's coaching again, I'm afraid.' Once again she offered coffee while they waited and once again they refused. As they left she reached for the telephone.

'Looks as though he might be in trouble with the management,' said Lineham. 'Not very good for the Club image, is it, having the police around.'

'Am I supposed to cry?' said Thanet.

This time it was a man Agon was coaching.

'Doesn't look too pleased to see us, does he?' said Lineham, as they sat down on a bench to watch. 'I suppose this is how his affair with Virginia Mintar started.'

'Probably. Almost certainly it was here that she met him.'

'And it must have been going on while Rachel was in Switzerland and Mrs Amos was in New Zealand.'

'Quite.'

Thanet wasn't sure if Agon deliberately kept them waiting but it was a good half an hour before the lesson finished. Thanet didn't mind. There was nothing particularly urgent awaiting his attention and it was good to sit here in the shade, listening to the soothing *thock* of racquet against ball.

Agon finally said goodbye to his client then strolled across, slinging a towel around his neck and wiping his forehead with one end. 'I didn't expect to see you here again, Inspector.'

I bet you didn't, thought Thanet.

170

'I thought I'd answered every question you asked as fully as possible.'

'Let's go and sit at one of the tables,' said Thanet.

'I really have nothing more to add,' Agon insisted.

Thanet said nothing, just led the way.

When they were settled he said, 'You've been less than frank with us, haven't you, Mr Agon?'

'Oh?' Agon's eyes were wary. 'In what respect?'

'Middle-aged, I think you called Mrs Mintar,' said Lineham. 'And, if I recall your exact words, "Why eat mutton when you can have lamb?" Am I right?'

'What are you getting at?'

Agon still looked unruffled. As far as he knew, of course, the only person who could confirm or deny that he and Virginia had an affair was Virginia herself, and she was dead.

Lineham put the manila envelope on the table. 'This,' he said.

Agon's eyes flicked to the envelope then from one face to the other. The calm certainty he must have read there rattled him. 'What is it?'

For reply Lineham took the photographs out of the envelope and, slowly and deliberately, spread them out across the table, in front of Agon and facing him so that he could not possibly misread their contents. Then he sat back and folded his arms.

'My God!' said Agon. He looked aghast. 'Where the hell did you get these? Who took them? I'll have his guts for garters!'

'So, you recognise yourself,' said Lineham. 'And, of course, the lady.'

Agon was silent for a few moments, still studying the photographs. Then, astonishingly, he smiled, a smug, self-satisfied, somewhat prurient smile. 'Actually, you know,' he said, 'they're really rather good.'

'Mr Agon,' said Thanet, intervening for the first time. 'I don't think you quite appreciate the seriousness of your position. Mrs Mintar is dead. Somebody killed her. Now we find that you have lied to us about having an affair with her.'

'Oh no!' said Agon vehemently, leaning forward to emphasise his objection. 'You needn't try and pin that on me! All this was months ago.'

'So why lie to us?' said Lineham, sweeping the photographs together and putting them back in the envelope.

'Well, obviously because I didn't want to seem involved.'

'Implying that you were.'

'No! It was over, done with. I just didn't see the point in bringing it up.'

'Rather a naïve point of view, don't you think?' said Thanet. 'It seems to us much more likely that you didn't want us to know because you hoped we never would find out, especially as no one else seemed to know about it. Incidentally, why was it kept so quiet? We haven't had the impression that Mrs Mintar was exactly secretive about her affairs.'

'She thought people might laugh at her,' Agon said sulkily. 'Because I was so much younger.'

This bore out what Susan Amos had told them.

'Many women would regard it as something of a triumph, to have a younger man in tow,' said Lineham.

'Not Virginia,' said Agon. 'Anyway, I saw no point in telling you, in case you got ideas. And I was right, wasn't I? Though how you think an affair which finished months ago could possibly have made me tip her down a well on Saturday beats me.'

'Unless . . .' said Thanet.

'What?'

'We know of at least one person who is being blackmailed by the character who took these,' said Lineham, tapping the envelope with one fingernail.

'So?'

'What if he was also blackmailing Mrs Mintar?' said Thanet.

'I don't see what you're getting at.'

'Rachel Mintar's a good catch, isn't she?' said Lineham.

'I resent that remark! I love Rachel and she loves me!'

'Resent it or not, it's true. And you admitted to us yourself that her parents weren't exactly over the moon about it.'

'I still don't see—' Agon burst out, and then, as heads at nearby tables turned, in a fierce whisper: 'I still don't see what you're getting at. What have me and Rachel got to do with what happened on Saturday?'

'Possibly quite a lot,' said Thanet. 'Because something else happened on Saturday, didn't it? You and Rachel announced your engagement.'

'So?' said Agon again.

'So maybe this galvanised Mrs Mintar into action.'

'What sort of action?'

Thanet shrugged. 'Just say, for the sake of argument, that whoever took these photographs was blackmailing Virginia Mintar too. Maybe she decided to tell you about it.'

'What would have been the point of that? I mean, what would she have hoped to achieve?'

'She could have threatened to show them to Rachel?'

'You're barking up the wrong tree! I never saw those photographs before in my life! I never even knew they existed until you put them on the table just now.'

'Unfortunately,' said Thanet as they walked away, 'I believed him, didn't you? I'd swear he'd never set eyes on them before.'

'Inspector!' Agon was running after them.

They turned.

'There won't be any need for Rachel to know about this, will there?'

'I'm afraid I can't give you any guarantees,' said Thanet. 'We have no idea as yet what will or will not be considered relevant to our inquiry.'

'But if it isn't relevant?' said Agon eagerly.

'I'm sorry, I just can't commit myself on that, one way or the other.'

'Now look—' said Agon angrily.

'No, sir. You look. This is a murder inquiry and I refuse to have my hands tied by any member of the public wishing to restrict my behaviour for his own convenience.'

'If looks could kill,' said Lineham as they went on their way, 'you'd be dead as a doornail. Though why a doornail should be dead I can't imagine.'

'Brewer would tell you, no doubt.'

'Who's he?'

'It, Mike. Brewer's *Dictionary of Phrase and Fable*. Wait till Richard's on his Os and As, it's amazing what you'll pick up. Anyway, d'you agree with what I was saying, before we were interrupted?'

'That Agon didn't know those photos existed, you mean? Unless he's a brilliant actor, yes, unfortunately. He wouldn't have been so completely confident before we showed them to him, otherwise.'

'Quite.' They were silent for a while, thinking, and it was not until they were in the car that Thanet said, 'I think we might be barking up the wrong tree as far as Agon is concerned, Mike. We must remember that for all we know Virginia was also unaware that those photographs existed. And the problem is, I can't see why else she would have gone out to talk to him in the first place, can you?'

'Perhaps the fact that Rachel had actually gone as far as getting engaged made her reconsider trying to buy Agon off.'

'But her original objection would still have held good, surely, Mike – Agon might have told Rachel her mother had tried to bribe him to leave and turned her against Virginia. No, I don't think she would have risked it.'

'What if she'd threatened to tell Rachel about the affair, then?'

'The same applies, surely. She'd still be running the risk of losing Rachel, if for a different reason. What engaged girl would enjoy being told her mother's been sleeping with her fiancé? The fact is, the poor woman was in a real dilemma as far as Rachel was concerned. Whatever course of action she took to try to get rid of Agon might also have resulted in alienating Rachel, the very thing she wished to avoid.'

'Well, I don't think we ought to give up on Agon,' said Lineham, his mouth setting in stubborn lines. 'If we found his fingerprints on the well cover, for instance . . .'

'Let's hope the lab gets a move on,' said Thanet. 'And no, we certainly won't cross him off our list. But I wouldn't say he's exactly at the top of it, either.'

'So, what now, sir?'

Thanet glanced at his watch. Another hour before he had to report to Draco. But there was no definite lead he wanted to follow up at the moment. On impulse he said to Lineham, 'I think we'll pay a visit to the resident witch.'

'What for?' Lineham grinned. 'Because she intrigues you, I suppose.'

'Well, she is involved, so to speak.'

'Marginally, perhaps.'

'All right, marginally. But involved nevertheless. After all, if her son hadn't eloped with Caroline, who knows? Virginia might still be alive.'

'How d'you work that out?'

'Stop being so logical, Mike, and just drive, will you?'

Lineham drove.

There was no proper driveway to Marah Swain's cottage, just a rough track turning off to the right about half a mile beyond the Mintars' house. Branches of overhanging trees brushed the roof of the car as Lineham drove slowly and carefully along it. The ground was rock hard, the ruts baked solid by the unremitting heat of the past weeks.

'Can't be doing the suspension much good,' the sergeant grumbled.

Thanet suppressed a smile. Lineham was always fussing over his car.

A couple of hundred yards in from the road the track swung to the left and Lineham jammed on his brakes as they rounded the bend. Here the track narrowed to little more than a path and the way ahead was blocked by another car. 'Great!' he muttered. 'We'll have to reverse all the way back, I suppose.'

'Isn't that Mr Mintar's car?' said Thanet.

'So it is!'

The driver's door of the dark green 5 series BMW hung open and the keys still swung in the ignition.

'Begging for trouble, that is!' said Lineham.

Thanet did not reply. The message of urgency conveyed by the open door and the abandoned car had made him recall their last conversation with Mintar. He suddenly realised what it might have been that Mintar had refused to tell him. He snatched the keys out of the ignition and set off up the track at a run. 'Come on, Mike.'

'What?' said Lineham, catching up, bewildered by Thanet's sudden haste.

'I've just – realised – the conclusion – Mintar might have drawn – from the questions – we were asking,' puffed Thanet. He was more out of condition than he thought.

'What?' said Lineham again.

'He said – Marah Swain held Caroline – to blame – for losing her son. Mintar might have thought – we suspected her – of killing his wife.'

'Out of revenge, you mean?'

'Oldest motive – in the world, Mike. If she couldn't – take it out on Caroline – she'd take it out – on her mother instead.'

'Sir! Listen!'

They paused, to do so. Ahead of them there was the sound of banging and shouting. They took off again and a moment or two later came in sight of the house.

Thanet saw at once what Tanya meant. Crouched in the middle of a clearing, solidly built of Kentish ragstone, it had a secretive, almost sinister air. Despite its seclusion grimy net curtains hung at the four tiny windows – all of them, like the front door, firmly shut despite the heat of the day.

'Open – this – bloody door! Open it! Open – this – bloody door!' Mintar's shouts were punctuated by thumps. He was so intent on what he was doing and was making so much noise that he didn't hear them approach and started visibly when Thanet laid a hand on his arm.

'Not much point in that, is there, sir? She's obviously not going to open up.' Now that Mintar had stopped shouting Thanet could hear a radio playing loudly inside the house. Tanya had mentioned this earlier, he remembered.

Mintar stared at him dully, his mind still focused elsewhere. Then, slowly, Thanet felt the tension in the man's arm begin to seep away. Out of the corner of his eye he saw the net at one of the downstairs windows twitch. She was watching, then.

'What were you hoping to achieve, sir?'

Mintar shook his head in despair. 'She knows more than she's telling us. She knows where Caroline is, I'm sure of it. And Caro has a right to be told about her mother! I . . . I . . .' Mintar turned his head away, ashamed no doubt of the tears which threatened to fall.

Thanet saw that he had been wrong. He had misjudged the man. Despair over the death of his wife had loosened the constraints of convention which Mintar normally imposed upon himself, causing this uncharacteristic behaviour. It was not

176

revenge the man sought, but consolation, from the daughter he had lost and mourned in secret. He, Thanet, should have told Mintar of their plans to make a further attempt to trace her. 'What did you propose to do, sir, shake the information out of her? That's not the way to go about it. Besides, I've already put one of my best officers on to trying to find Caroline. I agree with you, she needs to be told about her mother's death. So why don't you let Sergeant Lineham escort you back to the house and let me see what I can do here?'

Mintar nodded meekly and without a word turned away and followed Lineham back across the clearing.

Thanet waited until they were out of sight. Then he knocked loudly at the door and waited.

No response.

He knocked again, and called, 'Police, Miss Swain. I need a word.'

A moment later there was the sound of bolts being drawn back and the door opened a crack. The noise from the radio increased and a whiff of foul air drifted out as an eye appeared, with a wisp of grey hair above. He remembered what Tanya had said about the smell and recalled her description of Marah Swain: '. . . *long grey hair which straggles down over her shoulders and chest . . . dresses like something out of the nineteenth century – shapeless ankle-length black skirt, woollen shawl, thick stockings and old leather boots* . . . He held his identification up to the narrow gap and, raising his voice in case she was deaf as Tanya had suggested, introduced himself. 'I'd like to talk to you.'

'I've got nothing to say.' The voice was rusty, as if rarely used.

'Just a few more questions . . .'

'I told that girl all I know, which is nothing.'

'I just wanted to—'

The door opened a fraction wider, emitting a further gust of throat-gagging odours, and the woman thrust her chin aggressively forward, eyes flashing malevolently. 'I told you, I have nothing to say! Go away! You're trespassing! Get off my property! Go on, get off!' And she slammed the door in his face.

Thanet stared at it for a moment, then turned away, frustrated. It was rare indeed for him to be refused admittance, but there was nothing he could do about it at the moment. He hoped he hadn't made things more difficult for Tanya if she needed to interview Marah Swain again, and wondered how she had managed to get inside the house in the first place. Perhaps the old woman didn't feel as threatened by a female?

Anyway, he consoled himself as he made his way back to Ralph Mintar's car, even five minutes in that cottage would have been too long for comfort, judging by the smell. You'd have to be pretty desperate to enlist Marah Swain's reputed powers as a witch. How could anyone live in such foul air, breathe it in without becoming ill? And what could it be, that could emit that stomach-churning, foetid stench? Thanet's imagination provided him with visions of wisps of steam rising from simmering cauldrons filled with stinking brews.

Poor Mintar. How would any parents feel, if their child proposed such a prospective mother-in-law as that?

Still, feeling sorry for the man did not remove him from the list of suspects.

SEVENTEEN

'Any news?' said Thanet, the moment he arrived home.

Joan was in the kitchen, finishing the preparations for supper. She shook her head. 'No change.'

He kissed her before sitting down heavily on one of the kitchen chairs. It had been a tiring day, culminating in a punishing session with Draco who had wanted chapter and verse of every single interview they had done. Then, of course, there had been a lengthy stint on reports. 'Did Alexander ring?'

'Yes. Unless the situation changes it sounds as though they're planning to go ahead with the induction on Wednesday morning.'

'As we thought, then.'

'Yes.'

So, there'd be another day of waiting and worrying to get through before anything happened, thought Thanet wearily.

'Come on,' said Joan. 'Supper's ready. You look as though you could do with some refuelling.'

They ate in companionable silence for a while and then began to talk about each other's day. Joan told him about a seminar she was running on victim support groups and he brought her up to date on the Mintar case. After he had told her about the interview with Susan Amos (reminding himself that at some point he had to remember to smuggle into the house the jacket he had bought Joan for Christmas), Joan sighed and said, 'How sad. First her father left her, then her baby died, then Caroline eloped and she never saw or heard from her again . . . She probably felt that sooner or later everyone she loved would leave her – and she must have felt she had to walk on eggshells as far as Rachel and this man Agon were concerned, in case she lost her too.'

'I haven't told you the worst of it yet. Virginia and Agon had an affair, back in the spring.'

'Oh, no!'

'I'm afraid so. Rachel was at a finishing school in Switzerland at the time, so wouldn't have known about it, and Susan Amos was in New Zealand. Added to which, it sounds as though they kept it pretty quiet – Susan said Virginia didn't usually go in for younger men because she was afraid of people laughing at her behind her back.'

'She must have been terrified of Rachel finding out and turning against her! What a mess!'

'Quite. So her hands really were tied, as far as getting rid of Agon was concerned.'

'And it was her own fault! How she must have kicked herself, for landing herself in that particular situation. And how she must have hated the idea of him marrying Rachel. Imagine what it must be like, having a son-in-law you'd slept with!'

'Quite. Mind, it didn't surprise me in the least, given that by all accounts Virginia was very fond of men and Agon is a very handsome specimen, if you like the Adonis type. I've seen him in action with one of his pupils and believe me, she was loving every minute of it.'

'Sounds to me as though Virginia was always looking for love but never managed to find it,' said Joan as she began to gather up the dishes.

Thanet rose to help her. 'I'm not so sure. According to Susan, Virginia didn't really ever want to fall in love, for fear of getting hurt if he should leave her. That was why none of her affairs lasted long – she always wanted to get in first, be the one to end them.'

'I'd guess she never forgave her father for abandoning her like that, and has spent her life taking it out on the male sex in general.' Joan set the dishes down beside the sink and began to load the dishwasher.

Thanet put the kettle on. 'That's exactly what Susan said. She also said that Virginia once confessed to her that she couldn't resist trying to prove her power over men, it was as if she was driven to it. She looked on every new man who came along as a challenge. As I said, she even tried it on with her own sister's boyfriend – and not for the first time, either. Apparently Jane had been putting off bringing Arnold Prime to meet Virginia for ages, for fear that once again Virginia would ruin things for her.'

'And she was flirting with this man over dinner, in front of her husband, you say? How on earth did he put up with it?'

'Beats me! Though he does seem remarkably understanding about the way she carried on, says he didn't care as long as she stayed with him, and in view of the fact that he's away for such long stretches of time it would have been unreasonable to expect her to live like a nun.'

'Carrying on while he's away is surely a very different matter from rubbing his nose in it at his own dinner table. I really can't believe he could just sit there and not mind.'

'I agree.'

'Though it does sound typical behaviour for a woman like her, someone who has a low opinion of herself and actually expects that sooner or later everyone she cares about will walk out on her. It's as though they have to push the person they're testing beyond the limits of endurance, just to prove to themselves that they're right, that what they fear will eventually happen. I've seen it over and over again, in my work. And of course, a lot of people just can't take it. Often they do walk out – or snap.'

'You're suggesting this is what might have happened with Mintar?'

Joan shrugged. 'I can't say. I haven't met him, you have. But it's one of the options you're considering, surely.'

'Yes, of course.'

They went on discussing Virginia for some time. Joan's insights were often invaluable to Thanet but this time no new light was shed and he went to bed feeling that there were so many people with just cause for animosity towards Virginia that unless some sound scientific evidence turned up there was little hope of ever discovering who had engaged her in that fatal struggle.

He said so to Lineham, when he arrived at the office next morning.

181

'Not like you to be so pessimistic, sir.'

Thanet sighed. 'One has to be realistic, Mike. Just think about it. Every single one of these people had the opportunity. They all – apart from Mintar, who was supposedly alone in his study – came back to the pool alone. Three of them – Agon and both of the Squires – actually had to pass through the courtyard, and the old lady had ready access to it and indeed was better placed than anyone to choose her moment. And Jane, by her own admission, returned to the pool via the kitchen. As for motive, well, I think we can count Rachel and Arnold Prime out, I can't see any possible reason why either of them should want to get rid of Virginia, can you?'

'I agree with you about Prime. And I'd like to agree with you about Rachel. But it's only just occurred to me . . . What if she'd just found out her mother had had an affair with Agon and they quarrelled about it?'

Thanet shook his head. 'You mean, she found out after the engagement was announced? There's never been any hint that her attitude to her mother was any different from usual during the earlier part of the evening.'

'I suppose if she did find out, yes, it would have to have been later.'

'But how would she have found out? Who would have told her?'

Lineham thought. 'No, you're right. I haven't really thought it through. We've already agreed that Virginia wouldn't have told her and it's hardly likely that Agon would have, is it?' Lineham put on an assumed voice. '"Oh, by the way, darling, did I mention I had an affair with your mother while you were in Switzerland? You don't really mind, do you?" No, I can't really see him owning up in any circumstances unless it was absolutely unavoidable.'

'Quite. So, leaving Rachel and Arnold Prime out of it, if you think about motive . . .'

'They're all in the same boat, aren't they? Mintar and Howard Squires must have been as jealous as hell, ditto Mrs Squires and Jane, and despite what she says the old lady must have been terrified that Virginia would tell Mintar about her illness. And however much Agon pooh-poohs the idea, he must have been afraid that Virginia would tell Rachel about the affair and

Rachel would dump him. Look at what he stood to lose! There's a load of money sloshing around in that household and Agon probably thinks that in view of the fact that Caroline seems to have disappeared off the face of the earth, Rachel stands to scoop the lot when her old man drops off his perch.'

'Mmm. In which case he probably has a nasty shock coming to him.' Thanet had no doubt that like himself Lineham was remembering how distraught Mintar had been, the previous afternoon at Marah Swain's house. 'It's obvious that whatever front Mintar might have put up in the past, Caroline's very much still in the picture as far as he's concerned. But to get back to the point, Mike. The fact remains that unless we get some scientific evidence, there's not much hope of nailing any one of them.'

'Sir, I hate to interrupt your train of thought, but isn't it time you were on your way to the morning meeting?'

Thanet glanced at his watch and shot to his feet. It really would not do to be late this morning and give Draco further cause for complaint. 'Thanks, Mike!'

Once again he made it with seconds to spare.

'This is becoming a habit, Thanet.'

'Sorry, sir. Lot to catch up on.'

'Perhaps you would be so kind as to fill the others in on the progress of the Mintar investigation?'

I will not allow myself to be needled. And there was surely nothing in his subsequent report with which Draco could find fault, he thought as he finished speaking.

He was wrong.

'Any comments?' said Draco, looking from Tody to Boon. They shook their heads.

'Questions?' Draco was tapping his desk impatiently with the end of a Biro. His expression was that of a schoolmaster whose pupils were letting him down.

'Where d'you hope to go from here?' Tody asked Thanet, ever the good boy of the class.

'We were in the process of discussing that when we had to break off for this meeting.'

'Well, it seems to me that there is one glaring omission in what you have been doing,' said Draco. He sat back in his

183

executive-style black leather chair and fixed Thanet with a beady stare.

Thanet's heart sank and he tried not to sound too defensive as he said, 'Oh? What's that, sir?'

'Evidence,' said Draco. 'Or rather, the lack of it.'

Trust Draco to put his finger directly on the weak spot, thought Thanet. 'Yes, sir. We are aware of that.'

'So what are you doing about it?'

Not a lot. 'That was the very point we were discussing, sir.'

'It's not discussion we need, Thanet, it's action. It's all very well being airy-fairy, going around interviewing suspects and hoping to solve the case by making up your mind who did it and then persuading him to confess, but you know as well as I do that confessions can be retracted and that the only hope of getting a conviction is to back up theory with facts, and preferably facts which are incontrovertible and not capable of varying interpretations. So I suggest you give this matter very serious consideration. Evidence, Thanet. Go to it. Evidence.'

Inwardly seething – all the more so because he knew Draco was right – Thanet went upstairs and sat down at his desk.

'Rough time, sir?' said Lineham sympathetically.

'Nothing that wasn't justified, I regret to say.' Thanet relayed Draco's instructions. 'So let's put our minds to it.'

'He can't expect us to manufacture evidence out of thin air!' said Lineham.

They sat in frustrated silence for a few minutes and then Thanet snapped his fingers, making Lineham jump. 'Got it!'

'What?'

'We collect every single item of clothing worn by all the suspects on Saturday night – including swimsuits, towels and bath robes, if used – and send them to the lab to see if there is any crossmatching with what Virginia was wearing, either from her to them or vice versa. And on top of that we chase forensic to see if there was any other evidence found on her – hairs and suchlike, in case we need to collect samples.'

'You can't be serious, sir!'

'Dead serious, Mike.'

'But we can't ask the lab to run tests on all that lot just on the off chance! They'll go spare!'

'Why not? At least the Super won't then be able to say that we're not making an effort.'

'But the cost!'

'Justified, surely, if it helps us solve the case?'

'A bit over the top, though, surely?'

'Certainly not.' Thanet sat back with a glint in his eye and folded his arms as though preparing already to defend himself against criticism. 'We'll say it's upon the Super's direct instructions. After all, if he's not prepared to wait for us to narrow it down to one or perhaps two suspects then he can hardly complain if we do exactly as he says and collect all the evidence we can lay our hands on.'

Lineham raised one eyebrow, but made no further comment. Both of them knew that Draco would complain and complain vociferously – and that Thanet would play the innocent, claiming only to have been following orders to the letter.

'We'll put as many officers as necessary on to it,' said Thanet. 'One per suspect. And who knows? It might work.'

'Whatever you say, sir.'

During the subsequent briefing Thanet noticed that Tanya was missing. 'Where is she?' he demanded.

'Following up something to do with Caroline,' said Carson.

'Oh, I see. Fine. On your way then, everyone.'

There was a general exodus.

'What about us, sir?' said Lineham.

'We wait for inspiration,' said Thanet. 'As soon as all the stuff comes in we brace ourselves for complaints from the lab at the same time as pleading for swift results. Meanwhile, we catch up on some of the backlog of paperwork.'

He had often found that when he was stuck, detaching his mind completely from the case he was working on brought surprising results. But in this particular instance the results came from an unexpected direction. It was late morning when Tanya came knocking at his door.

'Well?' he said eagerly. He could tell from her expression that she had news for him.

'I think I may have traced her, sir.' She was positively glowing with justifiable pride.

'Well done!' said Thanet.

'Brilliant!' said Lineham.

'You said "may",' said Thanet. He waved her to a seat. 'Begin at the beginning, as they say.'

'Well, the first time I went to interview Marah Swain I happened to notice a postcard propped up on the beam over that big old fireplace she's got. It stood out because it was the only piece of paper in the room – there were no books or newspapers or calendars or letters, anything like that. So when you asked me, yesterday, to have another go at tracing Caroline, I thought, what if that card was from her son, and she's not letting on to the Mintars that she knows where they are because she's that sort of person – I mean, I shouldn't think she's the type to care less about saving anyone grief. In fact I'm not sure she wouldn't deliberately hold back the information out of pure spite. So anyway, I thought it might be worth going back and seeing if I could take a closer look at that card.'

'And did she let you in?' said Lineham.

'She wouldn't let us put a toe over the threshold,' said Thanet. 'In fact, I wondered how on earth you'd managed to get in in the first place.'

Tanya looked smug. 'Well, on the first occasion I caught her unawares. The front door was open and when there was no reply to my knock I just walked in. She probably hadn't heard, with that radio blasting out. Anyway, she was in the room at the back and looked very put out to see me, but short of actually manhandling me out there was little she could do about it.'

'I'm surprised she didn't,' said Thanet, 'judging by our reception yesterday.'

'But I did realise there could be a problem today,' said Tanya, 'so I was a bit sneaky, I'm afraid. I said I wasn't there in my official capacity, that I'd come because I'd heard she was good with herbal remedies and I wondered if she could help me.'

'What did you say was wrong with you?' said Lineham.

'Menstrual problems,' said Tanya. 'I thought that might be the sort of thing she could claim to cure.'

'And?' said the sergeant.

'It worked!' said Tanya triumphantly. 'Not that it was exactly what I would call an enjoyable experience. I really think the woman must be deaf because once again the radio was playing

186

far too loudly and I practically had to shout to make myself heard. And on top of that, the smell was worse than ever today.' Tanya wrinkled her nose. 'She'd had all the doors and windows shut and it was truly appalling. I really cannot imagine what it is that stinks like that. I tell you what it reminded me of – some of the disgusting hole-in-the-ground type lavatories I've come across, on really rough holidays abroad, but multiplied a hundred times over and overlaid with stinks from the concoctions she brews up.'

Tanya had a predilection for holidays in primitive, out-of-the-way places.

'You didn't smell it, Mike,' said Thanet. 'It is truly indescribably awful. If you ask me, Tanya, you deserve a medal for going in there a second time.'

'Perhaps that's what it is,' said Lineham. 'A hole-in-the-ground latrine which she hardly ever bothers to empty, in the room at the back.'

'Anyway,' said Tanya, 'I saw right away that the postcard was still there. So I told her what my problem supposedly was, laying it on a bit thick and trying at the same time to get a look at the postcard without seeming to show any interest in it. But it was hopeless – the place is so dark and murky, I shouldn't think the windows have been cleaned in living memory and the walls are a sort of nicotine colour, discoloured I imagine with smoke and accumulated dirt. So I laid on a bit of drama. I hadn't noticed a well outside and there was no tap in the room so I assumed it must be in the scullery place at the back and I pretended to feel faint and asked for a glass of water. I wasn't sure if she'd fall for it but she did and the minute she was out of sight I grabbed the card and managed to see where it was from. There was a message on the back but I didn't dare take the time to read that. I put it back in exactly the same position and was sitting with my head between my knees when she came back a second or two later. She was very quick, I don't think she liked leaving me alone in there even that long.'

'Well done!' said Lineham in admiration.

Tanya pulled a face. 'Of course, I then had to drink from the glass. It was probably crawling with germs so if I go down with a stomach upset you'll know why.'

187

'And where was the card from?' said Thanet.

'Callender, in Scotland. So I rang the police station there and inquired if they knew of a Richard or Dick Swain in the area. It's a smallish town, so I was hoping they might.'

'And did they?'

She shook her head. 'But they said they'd look into it, do their best to help. Anyway, they just rang back to say they'd found his name on the electoral roll. Apparently there's a biggish house not far from the town and he lives in the lodge. I imagine he's the gardener there.'

'Married?'

She nodded, eyes sparkling. 'So they said, yes.'

'Excellent.' This would be good news indeed for Mintar and Rachel. But prudence dictated that something should be checked first. 'Did they actually tell you the Christian name of his wife?'

Tanya looked crestfallen. 'No. I was so excited they'd found him I didn't ask. I should have checked, shouldn't I?'

'It might be a good idea.'

She left in a rush.

'Well,' said Lineham. 'There's a turn-up for the book.'

'Hold your horses, Mike. We're not certain yet. It could be pure coincidence.'

'What, another Richard Swain living in Callender, where the card came from? Some coincidence!'

'Coincidences happen.'

It was a few minutes before Tanya returned. Even before she spoke, her disappointment was evident. 'His wife's name is Fiona,' she said.

There was a brief silence while Thanet and Lineham assimilated this piece of information.

'Then assuming we have the right Dick Swain,' said Lineham slowly, 'whatever happened to Caroline?'

EIGHTEEN

It was Thanet who broke the speculative silence which ensued. 'Let's not jump to conclusions,' he said. 'There are various possibilities.'

'Such as?' said Lineham.

'Well, for a start, as you yourself implied, we could have the wrong Dick Swain.'

'A bit of a coincidence, if it was, surely,' said Tanya.

'That's what I said.' Lineham was nodding agreement.

'Nevertheless, a possibility,' said Thanet. 'And there are others. Caroline might have changed her name to Fiona – she might have felt . . . new life, new identity.'

'Or Fiona might even be her second name,' suggested Tanya.

'True. You'd better check.'

'I suppose it's possible that Caroline started off with Dick Swain but they found it didn't work out and both moved on to pastures new,' said Lineham.

Now Tanya was nodding agreement. 'Yes. Four years is a long time, after all, and living with someone is very different from having a love affair.'

'Especially as they came from such very different backgrounds,' said Thanet.

'And forbidden fruit is often much more attractive than eating it every day,' said Lineham.

Thanet suppressed a grin. It wasn't like Lineham to be so poetic. But he had a point. All in all, it seemed a likely explanation. Caroline's original attachment to Swain may well have been strengthened by the fact that her parents disapproved of it.

189

'But in that case,' said Tanya, 'wouldn't she have returned home?'

Both men thought about that.

'I don't know,' said Lineham. 'She might have felt it would have been too much of a climb-down.'

'To play the prodigal daughter, you mean?' said Thanet. 'Possibly. We don't really know enough about her to be able to judge.'

'If she did take off on her own it'll be like looking for a needle in a haystack,' said Tanya gloomily. 'We wouldn't have a clue where to begin.'

'But, of course,' said Thanet, 'we do also have to accept that something could have happened to her, either before she met Dick Swain that night, or after she started living with him.'

'If it was after, the Callender police would have to be involved in any investigation,' said Tanya.

'Quite. But if it was before . . .'

'Surely,' said Lineham, 'if it happened before she met him that night, if she simply didn't turn up, he'd have come looking for her? And he himself would not have gone at all.'

'I disagree,' said Tanya. 'If he thought she'd changed her mind about eloping he might have been so fed up he took off anyway.'

'Possible,' agreed Thanet. 'Obviously, the first thing we have to do is make sure we've got the right man – get him on the phone and talk to him. I'd like to speak to him myself. Then we'll take it from there. You'd better start trying, Tanya. He might well be out at work, of course, but you'll be bound to get through eventually.'

'Right, sir.'

'D'you think we ought to tell Mr Mintar about this?' said Lineham, when she had gone.

'Not yet. Let's try and find out a bit more, first. I don't see any point in either raising his hopes or frightening him unnecessarily. He's got enough on his plate at the moment.'

'You think she might be dead, sir?'

'What's the point of speculating, Mike? Let's wait and see, shall we?'

But Lineham couldn't leave it alone.

'Because if so, do you think the two murders might be connected, or do you see them as separate issues?'

'How can we possibly tell?' Thanet was becoming exasperated.

'If something did happen to her on her way to meet him, we'd have the devil of a job to find out what it was. The trail would be stone cold.'

'It doesn't take a genius to work that out! Let's hope the eventuality doesn't arise. I said, leave it, Mike! Obviously it's a potentially serious situation but we can't say more than that at the moment. In any case, I'd better go down and give the Super an update or he'll be complaining about being kept in the dark again.'

Draco listened with his usual concentration. 'You're right,' he said when Thanet had finished. 'Talk to Swain first then take it from there. I agree that the most likely explanation is that she found him too much to stomach at close quarters and moved on to pastures new. Let's hope so, anyway. Keep me posted – and meanwhile, don't forget you're conducting a murder investigation. Done anything about evidence yet?'

'Well in hand, sir.' Thanet had difficulty in keeping a straight face and on the way back upstairs allowed himself the luxury of a broad grin.

'You're looking more cheerful, sir,' said Lineham.

'Not really. I'm afraid we've got a frustrating time ahead.'

He was right. They did. He had set things in motion and now they had to sit back and wait. Very early on in their careers policemen learn to cultivate patience but Thanet always found it especially frustrating to be entirely dependent upon the activities of others to provide him with further impetus in an investigation. There was invariably work to do, of course, dangling ends of other cases to be tied up, but today he found it virtually impossible to concentrate. He felt in limbo, as if everything were on hold. He saw little point in further interviews with any of the suspects in the Mintar case until he had some material evidence, if only the merest scrap, to guide him in one direction or another. And it was equally pointless to speculate on Caroline's fate or discuss how best to proceed in finding out what had happened to her until they were certain that she was in fact missing. He wondered how Mintar would react if this proved to be the case. According to other witnesses, the QC had for the last four years been behaving as though Caroline were dead and gone, but that episode at Marah Swain's house yesterday had convinced Thanet that this was just a front, a mechanism by which Mintar had attempted to cut himself off from the pain of believing that she might still be alive and had not cared enough about her family to get in touch. If she really were dead, had been dead all along . . . It didn't bear thinking about. To lose, in effect, wife and daughter within the space of a few days and on top of that to be suspected of killing one of them . . . Tentatively, Thanet tried to imagine what it would be like, but in view of Bridget's current vulnerability it was too painful and he gave up; he tried to immerse himself in routine, failed once more, and found his thoughts going round and round in the same vicious circle yet again.

It would have helped to find relief in activity but he dared not go out in case Tanya managed to get through to Dick Swain. Swain might well be out at work but if her guess was right and the fact that he lived in the lodge of a big house meant that he was employed to work on the estate, he might well drop in from time to time or hear the telephone ring as he was passing by. And the truth was that as time went on and Thanet had more and more time to brood he was becoming increasingly concerned that something had indeed happened to Caroline on the night she eloped. It was, after all, surely unlikely that she would have allowed four whole years to go by without so much as a phone call to her parents, to let them know that she was all right and give them the opportunity to heal the breach between them. By all accounts she had been a much loved daughter, on good terms with them until she fell for Swain. Staring at the phone, willing the call to come through, Thanet compared himself with wry amusement to a love-sick teenager to whom the ringing of the telephone was the most longed-for sound in the world.

The occasional interruption was a welcome relief. At one point Tanya put her head around the door to tell him that Caroline's second name had been Anne. So that was one possibility out of the window. And as he had predicted, the laboratory manager was kicking up a fuss over the amount of stuff Thanet's team was bringing in for examination. Lineham had to field more than one irate phone call and eventually Thanet said, 'Let me speak to her.' He was, he realised, spoiling for a fight, ready to do anything, in fact, to relieve the tension that was steadily building up in him. Careful now, he told himself. It would be pointless and counter-productive to antagonise her.

'Hullo, Veronica. Luke Thanet here. Look, I really must apologise about this. I do appreciate how fed up you must be to have this avalanche descend upon you, but as DS Lineham says, the Super is insisting that we concentrate on finding some useful scientific evidence and I can't see any other way to get it. Unless . . .' He allowed a thoughtful pause.

'What?' The voice at the other end was understandably eager.

Faced with that mountain of time-consuming work, who could blame her? thought Thanet. 'I understand the fingerprint comparisons with those on the well cover aren't ready yet?'

'Not yet, no. Yours isn't the only case we're dealing with, you know, Luke. We do have other matters to attend to – in fact we're absolutely snowed under at the moment. Which is why—'

'There wouldn't be any way of hurrying them up, would there?'

'Why, specifically?'

'It's just occurred to me . . . If one of them gave us a definite lead, you might not have to bother with most of the stuff that's been coming in today.'

'I see what you mean. Yes.' A long-suffering sigh. 'Well, I suppose I could try to expedite matters a little on that front . . .'

'If you could, that would be great!'

'But I hope you realise that this puts me in a very difficult position. You're not the only one breathing down my neck, you know.'

'I appreciate that, Veronica. But this way—'

'Oh God. Here's another load of stuff arriving. Look, I can't promise anything, but I'll see what we can do.'

And the connection was cut.

'Very neat,' said Lineham, grinning.

'Had to hurry them up somehow, didn't we?'

But the small glow of satisfaction soon faded and it was back to waiting again.

It was five o'clock when Tanya again put her head around the door. 'I've got through at last,' she said. 'To Mrs Swain. Her husband's not there. D'you want to talk to her?'

Thanet nodded and picked up the phone. 'Mrs Swain?'

'Yes.'

Even in that single monosyllable Thanet detected a Scottish accent and his heart sank.

'Mrs Richard Swain?'

'Yes. What is it? What's wrong?'

'Nothing. Please don't be alarmed. I don't know if DC Phillips explained, but we're trying to trace a Mr Richard Swain in the hope that he might be able to give us some information in connection with an investigation we're conducting. I wonder if we could just check that we have the right Mr Swain. Is your husband normally called Dick?'

'Yes, he is.'

'Do you happen to know how long he has been living in Callender?'

'About four years, I think. Something like that, anyway. We met three years ago, and he'd been here a wee while before that. If there's nothing wrong, why are you asking all these questions? Is he in trouble?'

'No, not at all. It's just something we need to clarify, that's all. If you could just bear with me a little longer . . . Could you tell me if he originally came from Kent?'

'Yes, he did. He was raised in a village called Paxton. Why can't you tell me what all this is about?'

So they did have the right man. Good. 'I'm sorry, I can't do that. No doubt your husband will explain, when I've spoken to him. What time will he be back, do you know?'

'Not until sometime tomorrow. He's away to the Midlands overnight visiting nurseries, choosing plants to order in the autumn for Mr McNeil.'

His employer, Thanet presumed. 'Can I get in touch with him?'

'I'm afraid not. I don't know where he'll be staying. He said he'd find a bed and breakfast place. He's travelling around, you see.'

'Will he be ringing you tonight?'

194

'I don't think so, no. It's only the one night he's away.'

'Well, if he does, would you ask him to ring me? And if not, could you get him to ring the minute he gets back tomorrow?' Thanet dictated his office and home numbers and rang off.

Then he gave up and went home.

But for once he did not find his usual consolation there. Both he and Joan were too on edge about Bridget to be able to relax and it was a relief finally to go to bed, switch off the light and know that tomorrow should bring an end to the waiting and answers to the interminable questions which tormented them: *Would Bridget be all right? Would the baby be all right? Would it be healthy, perfectly formed? Would its internal organs be properly developed? What would be its chances of survival? How would Bridget react if anything went wrong?*

But nothing would go wrong, Thanet told himself fiercely. It was a good hospital and she was in expert hands. Because of the complications they were keeping a close eye on her. Everything would be all right.

Joan too was finding it difficult to get to sleep. Normally they slept back to back but tonight, needing her proximity, Thanet turned on to his left side and curled himself around her. She responded at once, snuggling in close to him, but whereas the natural consequence of such a manoeuvre would normally have been that they made love, this time neither of them had the heart for it. With their daughter in such a potentially dangerous situation it just wouldn't have felt right, that's all.

Thanet's arm tightened around Joan's waist. 'She's in good hands,' he whispered. 'She'll be fine.'

'I know.'

But the fact that they couldn't be certain continued to torment them through the night.

Next morning Thanet was shaving when the telephone rang. He jumped and nicked himself. 'Damn,' he whispered, dabbing at the drop of blood which oozed out and reaching for the styptic stick. Joan had answered the phone in the hall downstairs and he went to the top of the staircase. 'What?' he said, almost afraid to ask.

'Alexander,' she said, putting the phone down. 'Just confirming that they're going ahead with the induction this morning.'

'Good.' It was a relief to be certain that one way or the other the matter should be resolved before too long. Thanet felt he couldn't have faced another day like yesterday. As it was today promised to be action-packed. Dick Swain should be ringing back and with any luck Veronica might come up with some useful information on the fingerprint comparisons.

One look at Lineham's face when he got in was enough to tell him something important had come up.

'What's up?' he said.

'Good morning to you too, sir.'

'Mike! Come on, what have we got?'

'Veronica Day has been on the phone. She'll be sending the paperwork over later, but she thought we'd want to know. They've come up with a match.'

'Any use?'

'Pretty significant, in the circumstances. If you remember, there's a metal handle at each side of the well cover to pick it up by and no doubt that's how both Mrs Mintar and Digby would have lifted it off and replaced it. But whoever put it back that night wasn't used to handling it and no doubt they were in a hurry too. So they didn't use the handles, simply grabbed it by the edges. I'm sure you'll agree that there's only one way two full sets of four fingerprints could have been found on the under edges of the well cover, with thumb-prints in the appropriate positions on the top—'

'Get on with it, Mike. So, whose?'

But Lineham was enjoying keeping him in suspense. 'According to Veronica Day, although some of the prints are blurred several of them are clear enough to make the match conclusive . . .'

'Mike! Whose?'

Lineham told him.

NINETEEN

'Right,' said Thanet. 'As soon as the morning meeting's over we'll be on our way. I don't suppose Dick Swain's rung in yet?'

Lineham shook his head. 'I thought his wife said he wouldn't be home until later on this morning.'

'She did. We'll probably be back by then. It's just that I don't want to take this particular call on my mobile – it could be at an inconvenient moment and there may be too many distractions. Tell Tanya if he calls while we're out I'll ring him back as soon as I can.'

Before going downstairs to the meeting Thanet rang Veronica Day to thank her for expediting the matter of the fingerprints and to request that the lab now focus on one particular set of clothes. 'I'm hoping to bring the suspect in this morning and if you could find anything which indicates contact with the victim, that would be an enormous help.'

A resigned sigh. 'I'll see what we can do.'

Thanet's news about the fingerprints at once restored him to Draco's good books. 'Excellent, Thanet, excellent. I knew things would start to move once you really focused your mind on getting some evidence.'

Thanet forbore to point out that they had been waiting for these particular results for days.

'You'll be anxious to get on with it, then. Well, I won't delay you. Well done.'

'We haven't got a confession yet, sir.'

Draco smiled benignly. 'You will, I'm sure, Thanet. You will.'

197

I hope, thought Thanet as he hurried back upstairs. You could never count on it. Already he was working out tactics. Perhaps it would be better to send someone to bring the suspect in? But no, he didn't see why he should deny himself the pleasure of seeing that self-assured façade crumble when it became apparent that this time an arrest was being made.

Lineham jumped up eagerly as Thanet entered the room.

'Right, Mike, let's go. Did you check his whereabouts?'

'Not expected at work till ten, sir.'

'Good. We'll pay him a little home visit, then. Where does he live?'

'Palmerston Row.'

'Does he, now. That brings back memories. Remember the Julie Holmes case?'

This was one of the first murder investigations Thanet and Lineham had worked on together.

'I remember them all, sir.'

He probably did, too, thought Thanet indulgently. Lineham's enthusiasm for his work had never waned. Although he himself had not returned to the area for more years than he cared to count, he found that it was little changed. The mean little back-to-back Victorian terraced houses still looked seedy, furtive almost, despite the attempts to smarten them up with inappropriate replacement windows and mass-produced front doors from DIY stores. Number twenty-nine displayed no such signs of proud ownership. Peeling paintwork, grimy windows and the row of bells beside the front door indicated that it was probably divided up into bedsitters by a parsimonious landlord.

Lineham rang the appropriate bell and they waited.

No response.

'Probably still in bed,' said the sergeant, putting his finger back on the bell and leaving it there.

A minute or two later there were sounds from inside and the door opened a crack. 'For God's sake stop making that filthy row!' A double-take. 'Oh, it's you, Inspector.'

'Yes, it's us. May we come in?'

A reluctant step backwards. 'If you must.'

Lineham was right. Agon had obviously just got out of bed.

He was naked except for a pair of boxer shorts patterned all over with hearts. A present from Rachel? Thanet wondered. Or from her mother?

Agon padded up the stairs ahead of them, his bare feet soundless on the threadbare carpet. No daylight filtered into the narrow hall and staircase and the light from the unshaded low-wattage bulb at the top was obviously on a timer; as he reached the top it went off. He cursed and switched it on again before turning right.

His bedsitter was at the front, overlooking the road, probably one of the largest rooms in the house. It was furnished with the bare essentials: single bed, sagging armchair, cheap deal wardrobe and a rudimentary kitchen area – table, plastic washing-up bowl and gas ring. The microwave and television set, no doubt his own, stood out by virtue of their newness and only his clothes, visible through the open door of the wardrobe, showed any degree of care – presumably because they were important to his image. Otherwise, the place was littered with the detritus of careless living: there were used mugs everywhere and empty takeaway cartons on the floor beside the chair, forks and spoons still in them. There was a stale, frowsty smell in the air which Thanet thought probably emanated not only from the residue of food in the cartons but from what looked like a pile of dirty washing on the floor in one corner. A glance at Lineham's face told Thanet what the sergeant was thinking. *What a slob!* Thanet wondered if Agon had ever brought Rachel here. He doubted it.

Agon thrust his arms into a striped towelling dressing gown, kicked a pair of dirty socks into the pile and scooped up the cartons before dropping them into a waste bin. 'Wasn't expecting visitors,' he said.

'So I see. A bit of a contrast to your fiancée's house, isn't it?'

'I don't see what business that is of yours.' Agon folded his arms defiantly.

'Oh, but it is very much our business, sir.' Thanet nodded at Lineham.

'Matthew Agon, I am arresting you on suspicion of the murder of Virginia Mintar ...' Lineham went on to deliver the caution.

199

Agon raked a hand through his hair and his mouth dropped open. 'On suspicion of murder? I don't believe it! On what grounds?'

At this point Thanet knew he had a choice. He could either proceed with the interview here or take Agon back to Headquarters for questioning. Agon was no fool and if Thanet took him in the tennis coach would probably insist on a solicitor being present. Here, this might not occur to him.

'Why don't we all sit down and discuss it?' he said.

'Oh no, you don't,' said Agon. 'I know my rights. If I'm being arrested, I'm not saying another word without a solicitor present.'

Thanet caught a rueful glance from Lineham. *Nice try, sir.* 'Very well. That's up to you. So if you wouldn't mind getting dressed . . .'

Agon ran a hand over his chin. 'I haven't even had a chance to shave yet.'

'We don't mind, do we, Sergeant?'

'No, not at all.'

'Well I bloody well do!'

'You use an electric razor, sir?'

'So what?'

'Then you can bring it with you. We wouldn't like you to feel uncomfortable, would we, Sergeant.'

'And if you don't mind I'd like to pee as well.'

'I think we might accommodate you there, sir. Sergeant Lineham will go with you.'

Agon scowled but seemed to accept that he had no choice.

Back at Headquarters they put him in an interview room and left him to organise his legal representation.

'We'll let him sweat for a while,' said Thanet. 'Let's go and see if Dick Swain has rung.' He glanced at his watch. Ten-fifteen. He wondered how Bridget was getting on. It would be some time before they heard anything, he supposed.

'Not yet,' said Tanya, in response to their inquiry about Swain, so they settled down to wait. Half an hour later they were still discussing tactics for the forthcoming interview with Agon when the call came through.

'Mr Swain?' Thanet indicated that Lineham should listen

in to the conversation and then introduced himself before quickly establishing that this was indeed the Dick Swain they were looking for.

'What the hell is all this about? You ring up out of the blue, frightening my wife out of her wits . . .'

'I'm sorry if she was alarmed. I did tell her that there was no reason to be.'

'Well, she was. Is. So what's the story?'

'You remember Caroline Mintar?'

'Yeah.' At once his tone was wary.

Thanet cursed the fact that this conversation was being conducted by phone. You could learn so much from looking at a witness while speaking to him. Facial expressions, gestures, movements of hands and feet were all signals, unspoken indications of what the person being interviewed was thinking and feeling. Over the phone you had to rely on tone of voice alone and subtleties were usually lost. 'We are trying to trace her. I'm afraid her mother has died and we're sure Caroline would want to know.'

'So what's it got to do with me?'

'The last time her family had any communication from Caroline was when she left home four years ago, leaving a note to say that you and she had gone away together.'

Silence, so prolonged that Thanet said, 'Mr Swain? Are you still there?'

'Yes.' Swain sounded shaken, the belligerence gone. 'I'm just trying to take in what you're saying.'

'What do you mean?'

'Let me get this straight. For the last four years her family has believed that Caroline was with me?'

'Yes.' It was obvious what was coming.

'Well, she isn't. She never has been. That night . . .'

'What?'

'She never turned up. I waited and waited, but when she didn't come I thought she'd changed her mind. Her family was dead against me. And I was all packed up and ready to go, so I thought, what the hell, I'm not staying around here. I'm off to make a fresh start somewhere else.'

'So why Scotland?'

'Paid for the tickets, hadn't I? We were going to Gretna Green. Big romantic stuff.' Even four years later and presumably happily married to someone else, the residual bitterness could still be heard in his voice.

'You never tried to get in touch with her?'

'Nah. What would have been the point? We had our chance and she blew it. That was that, as far as I was concerned . . . But look here, if she did leave that night, where the hell did she go? You say her family hasn't heard a word from her since?'

'No. As far as they were concerned she had gone off with you and that was all they knew. They tried to trace you both in the interim but without success. They had no idea where to start looking.'

'So what happened to her?'

'That's what we're beginning to worry about.'

'I mean, if she came away, leaving a note . . . But like I said, I waited and waited . . .'

'I suspect she didn't turn up because her grandmother unexpectedly returned home that evening a day early from a long trip abroad, and traditionally they always have a family celebration on those occasions. I imagine Caroline wouldn't have been able to get away as early as she intended without arousing suspicion. Her grandmother says she was like a cat on hot bricks all through dinner. Where were you supposed to meet?'

'In the lane, at the entrance to her drive. I had an old van . . . I even had her bag in the back, she'd given it to me ahead of time so no one would see her leaving with it that night.'

'With her clothes in, you mean.'

'Yeah.'

'What did you do with it? The bag?'

'Chucked it in the river when I got to London.'

'Bit drastic, wasn't it?'

'I was bloody well pissed off, wasn't I. The train got in to Charing Cross and—'

'Just a minute,' Thanet cut in. 'You said you were driving your van.'

'I was. To begin with. Broke down, didn't I, just after Dartford. I tell you, it wasn't exactly the best night of my life. So I hitched a lift to the nearest station. And don't ask me why I didn't just leave her bag in the back of the van because I couldn't tell you. I think at that point I must still have been hoping she'd somehow catch up with me. But by the time I got to London I'd seen how stupid that was, and it's only a few steps from Charing Cross down to the river so I thought, what the hell? It was sort of a . . .' Swain groped for the word, and found it triumphantly, '. . . a symbolic gesture, you might say.'

'Yes, I see.' And Thanet did.

'Look, I'm sorry I can't help you. I would if I could, honest. You will try and find her? Let me know, if you do? I feel sort of . . . responsible, even if I'm not, if you see what I mean.'

'Yes, of course. I'm afraid we shall have to request that your local police verify your wife's identity.'

A brief silence, then, 'Yeah, I see. Sure. That'll be OK.'

'Good.' Thanet thanked him and rang off.

He and Lineham looked at each other.

'Doesn't look too good, does it, sir.'

'I'm afraid not.'

The telephone rang and Lineham answered it. He covered the receiver. 'Mr Agon's brief is here and complaining about being kept waiting, sir.'

'Tell him we'll be right down. That was quick!' said Thanet as they went downstairs.

'Double quick time!' agreed Lineham.

The 'him' was in fact a 'her', they discovered. Thanet had come across her in Court, an attractive young woman in her early thirties and a recent arrival in the firm of Wylie, Bassett and Protheroe, a leading firm of solicitors in the town. Thanet had had dealings with Oliver Bassett, the senior partner, on several occasions. He was surprised to see Barbara Summers here, though. Her normal field was juveniles and family matters. Since when had Agon been her client? Thanet wondered. Then, catching the smug, almost possessive glance which Agon cast at her while Thanet was greeting her, realised that in all probability their relationship until now had been that of coach and pupil. Faced with the urgent necessity of summoning legal representation, what more natural than that Agon should have thought of a solicitor he knew? This would also explain why he had been able to get hold of her so quickly. He would be used to snapping his fingers and have his female clients come running. A glance at her left hand told Thanet that Ms Summers was unmarried and no doubt as susceptible to Agon's charms as any other member of her sex.

Barbara Summers caught Thanet's sudden look of comprehension and her lips tightened. 'Let's not waste time, Inspector.'

'As you wish.'

Lineham started the recording and began the interview by repeating the caution. Thanet was careful to play by the book and wanted it on tape. *You do not have to say anything. But it may harm your defence if you do not mention when questioned something which you later rely on in court. Anything you do say may be given in evidence.*

'Now then, Mr Agon,' said Thanet. 'You must understand that you are in a very serious position.'

'My client is well aware of that and so am I,' said Barbara Summers coldly. 'We wish to know the grounds upon which you have made this preposterous arrest.'

'All in good time, Ms Summers. These things can't be rushed. I don't know how *au fait* you are with the situation ... ?'

'Mr Agon has explained it to me.'

'Good. Then you will know that prior to his engagement to Miss Rachel Mintar, he had an affair with her mother, Mrs Virginia Mintar, in connection with whose murder he has now been arrested. I'm sure he has also told you that we have photographic evidence of this affair.'

'Yes, Mr Agon has given me a very full and frank account of all this. And he wishes it to be put on record that Mrs Mintar was the initiator of that affair. She, in effect, seduced him.'

Looking at Agon leaning back with apparent nonchalance in his chair, legs stretched out in front of him, genitals bulging in his tight jeans, Thanet wondered what a jury would make of this claim. The man couldn't help but exude sexuality and it was difficult to imagine him playing a passive role in any love affair. 'I see,' he said drily.

'And he also wishes to point out that he has absolutely no motive for committing this crime.'

'Perhaps one will emerge,' said Thanet. 'As you yourself were not present that night, Ms Summers, it might be helpful for me to set the scene for you.'

'Helpful to whom?'

'To you.'

'I'm not here to listen to stories, Inspector, simply to reiterate that these charges against my client have no foundation and should be dropped forthwith.'

'In that case, hearing what I have to say should merely strengthen your conviction of his innocence. From his point of view, would that not be a constructive course of action?' Thanet was rather enjoying this sparring. Both of them knew that he wasn't going to leave this room until he had said what he wanted to say and that she would continue to go through the motions of putting obstacles in his path. It was all part of the process, in some ways almost a kind of bizarre foreplay to the real action to come.

She gave a long-suffering sigh. 'Very well, then. If we must.'

Thanet gave a brief account of the dinner party, of Rachel's and Agon's arrival with the announcement of their engagement, and of the so-called celebration which followed.

Barbara Summers was becoming increasingly restless. 'Really, Inspector, is all this relevant?'

Thanet was terse. 'Highly.' He waited a moment for a further objection but none came, so he continued his summary of events. When he got to the point where the table was cleared and everyone dispersed, he stopped. 'And this, of course, is where we get to the interesting part. Perhaps I should explain that the kitchen courtyard was Virginia Mintar's pride and joy. She took particular care of four large camellias in tubs, to the extent that she always insisted that they were watered with water from the well, tap water being too hard for them. Except at weekends it was the gardener's job to do so, but this was a Saturday and she was actually engaged in this somewhat laborious task when Dr and Mrs Squires arrived. Naturally she stopped what she was doing and went to greet them, putting her watering can down beside the well wall with the intention of finishing the job later. In fact, she asked her husband to remind her to do so. Consequently, and with tragic consequences for her, she did not at that time replace the well cover, which was normally secured in position by a padlock and chain. Mrs Squires confirms that the cover was left off.'

Thanet had been watching Agon closely. The tennis coach had been feigning boredom, turning his head from time to time to gaze out of the window and examining his fingernails, one of which seemed to engage his attention. But now, for the first time, Thanet got a reaction: Agon seemed to freeze – so briefly that Thanet could almost have thought he had imagined it. But he hadn't, he was certain. Had Agon suddenly realised where this might be leading?

'Later, soon after they realised that Mrs Mintar was missing and started looking for her, Mr Squires is pretty certain that the cover was back in its usual position. We think that whoever replaced it pushed Mrs Mintar down the well before doing so but was obviously not familiar with the arrangements for securing it. Next morning, when the gardener noticed that the watering had not been finished, the padlock and chain were not in position.' Thanet paused to give weight to his next words.

'To fetch your swimming costume from the car, you, sir, had to walk right past that well.'

As yet Agon had not said a single word throughout but as Thanet had hoped this stung him into speech. He sat up with a jerk and gave a derisory laugh. 'And that's why I've been arrested? Just because I walked past the bloody well? Anyone could have replaced that cover! Anyone! For all you know Virginia might have thought it was dangerous to leave it uncovered and put the cover back herself, intending to fix the padlock and chain later. The same goes for old Mrs Mintar – her front door is only a few yards away and it's quite likely she noticed the well was uncovered when she went back after dinner. And Dr Squires and his wife had to walk past it too, both of them – twice, in fact. Once on the way home to change into their swimming things and once on the way back. What's more, they actually knew the cover had been left off – you said so yourself.'

Thanet again allowed a telling pause before saying quietly, 'But their fingerprints are not on the well cover, Mr Agon. Yours are, where you picked it up. A full set from each hand. Thumb-prints on top, fingerprints underneath.'

TWENTY

Almost before the words were out of his mouth realisation hit
Thanet with a jolt which caused his heartbeat to accelerate and
the blood to pound in his ears. How could he have been so
stupid, so incredibly short-sighted? The truth was, he had been
so delighted to have something positive to go on at last that he
hadn't thought the matter through sufficiently. It gave him little
comfort to think that both Lineham and Draco had fallen into
the same trap. For it was suddenly obvious to him what Agon's
response would be and he, Thanet, would be defenceless against
it. What should he do? Get out of here fast and think again was
the answer, before Agon had time to respond.

He was on the point of getting up and Agon was opening
his mouth to speak when help came from an unexpected
quarter.

Barbara Summers laid a restraining hand on Agon's arm and
shook her head to silence him. 'I should like to confer with my
client,' she said.

'Very well,' said Thanet, on a rush of relief. He nodded
at Lineham who terminated the interview and switched the
recorder off.

'Talk about being saved by the bell!' he said, the moment
they were out of the room. He headed up the stairs two at a
time and Lineham raced after him.

'What do you mean, sir? What's the hurry?'

'I've got to speak to Veronica. Let's pray she'll come up with
something. If not, we'll just have to try and find an excuse for not
carrying on with the interview until she does.' Already Thanet

was dialling. 'And what if she doesn't? What a fiasco! I could kick myself, I really could.'

'Sir—'

'You still haven't seen it, have you, Mike? Not that I can blame you. It only just hit me, down there, the moment I told him about his fingerprints being on the well cover . . . Honestly, you really would think that after all these years I'd have seen this coming!'

'What? I still don't know what you're talking about!' Lineham's face betrayed his frustration.

'Oh, sorry, Mike, it's just that – Hullo? Veronica Day, please . . . Veronica? Luke Thanet here. Look, I don't suppose by any chance you've – You were? You have? What?' Thanet sank down on to his chair, the receiver pressed to his ear, listening intently. 'That's terrific!' he said at last. 'Really tremendous. I can't tell you how grateful I am. Thank you, I owe you one. You really have saved my bacon.' *Or stopped me making a fool of myself, anyway.* 'What a relief!' he said to Lineham as he put the phone down.

The sergeant folded his arms and gave Thanet an accusing stare. 'If you wouldn't mind telling me what all that was about . . .' he said.

'Mike, I'm sorry, I really am. As I was saying, it was when I was telling Agon about his prints being on the well cover that I suddenly realised he could come up with a perfectly simple explanation . . . All he had to say was that when he went to get his swimming things he'd noticed the cover was still off, thought it looked dangerous, especially as it was beginning to get dark by then, and put it back on for safety's sake. And there'd be no way of proving that Virginia wasn't already down there when he did so, or even that someone didn't come along later and remove it again.'

'Unlikely, surely.'

'Oh come on, a good defence counsel would make mincemeat of us and you know it. The truth is, I did what I'm always telling you lot not to do – i.e. rush ahead without stopping to think things through. That was why I was so anxious to speak to Veronica just now. As you know, I asked her earlier to give the clothes Agon was wearing that night priority and guess what?'

'They found something? What?'

Thanet told him.

A broad grin spread across Lineham's face. 'Let's see him wriggle out of that one.'

'Yes, but let's not rush into it this time. Let's think of ways he might.'

Twenty minutes later the interview was resumed. Agon was looking smug and confident again, Thanet noted.

'My client wishes to make a statement,' said Barbara Summers.

Here we go, thought Thanet.

And indeed, Agon's explanation was just as he had predicted. 'So,' he said when Agon had finished, 'you're saying in effect that your conscience wouldn't allow you to leave the well uncovered in case there was an accident.'

'That's right.' Agon was positively glowing with self-righteousness.

'So why didn't that same conscience tell you to own up to having handled it until now, when you've been forced to do so?'

'That is perfectly obvious, surely,' said Barbara Summers. 'In the circumstances my client was afraid that such an admission would place him under suspicion. As he had acted from the highest of motives he felt that this would be unfair and unreasonable, and he was not inclined to risk it. Of course he now regrets that he didn't give you a full and frank account in the first place, and wishes to apologise for misleading you.'

'A full and frank account . . .' said Thanet. 'I'm afraid I'm not convinced of that.'

'What do you mean?' she said.

'That shirt you were wearing on Saturday night, Mr Agon. Pale mauve, as I recall, and very stylish . . .'

Agon looked surprised at the sudden change of subject but couldn't resist the appeal to his vanity.

'Ralph Lauren,' he said.

'Pretty new, too, I'd guess. When, exactly, did you buy it?'

Agon glanced uneasily at his solicitor.

'Why do you want to know?' she said.

'It's a simple question,' said Thanet. 'If your client is innocent, as he claims, he should have no problem in supplying the answer – though I should warn him that it would be unwise to try to mislead us. These things can be checked, as I'm sure you are aware.'

'Saturday morning,' said Agon.

'And where?'

'Maidstone. At a shop in the High Street. But I don't see—'

'Let's be quite clear about this. You are saying that you bought the shirt you were wearing on Saturday night, the night Virginia Mintar was murdered, that same morning, in Maidstone?'

Barbara Summers broke in. 'Look, what is the point of all this, Inspector?'

'The point is this, Ms Summers. In view of the fact that Mr Agon admits to having had an affair with Virginia Mintar, I wanted to be quite certain that he could not claim to have worn that shirt on any occasion when he was engaged in intimate contact with her. You see, while you were conferring with your client just now, I was in my office speaking to the manager of our laboratory.' He looked at Agon. 'If you remember, yesterday you were asked to hand over the clothes you were wearing on Saturday night to one of our officers, for examination.'

Agon had guessed what Thanet might be leading up to. He was now looking apprehensive and the colour was draining from his face, his healthy tan taking on a yellowish, jaundiced hue.

'She has just told me that two of Virginia's hairs were caught up in the cuff button on the left-hand sleeve of your shirt, Mr Agon. Perhaps you wouldn't mind explaining how they got there?'

Agon stared at Thanet and then glanced at Barbara Summers. She was watching him, eyes narrowed and lips pressed together in a hard, unforgiving line. '*We're waiting.*'

'I've no idea what you're talking about,' he said, summoning up a degree of bravado.

'You'll have to do better than that, I'm afraid,' said Thanet.

'If it's true, then it must have happened by accident.'

'Oh? When?'

A shrug.

'And how?'

Still no response. Agon was looking sullen, frustrated.

'Come now, it's unlikely you would have forgotten, surely? A woman's hair gets caught in your cuff button and you don't even remember the incident? Presumably you would have had to release it – and in front of half a dozen other people, too.' Thanet turned to Lineham. 'Make a note, Sergeant. We must check with the others.' And, to Agon, 'You must have been sitting next to Virginia Mintar, of course.'

Again, no response.

'Were you? Again, we can easily check.'

Thanet waited a moment and then said, 'You may choose not to answer these questions now, Mr Agon, but I'm afraid you won't get away with remaining silent in Court. Sooner or later the truth will come out.' He paused to allow what he had said to sink in, then went on, 'I'm aware, of course, that there might have been mitigating circumstances – provocation, even. You've told me yourself that the Mintars didn't approve of your relationship with Rachel and had been upset by the announcement of your engagement – as I recall you even said that it was surprising it wasn't you who had ended up at the bottom of the well. Sergeant Lineham here asked if you weren't perhaps exaggerating and you said, and I quote, "You weren't there, Sergeant. I was."'

'So?' The word was forced out of him reluctantly.

'So I'm simply saying that it wouldn't have been surprising if, seeing you cross the courtyard to your car, Virginia Mintar had seized the opportunity to try and get you to back out of it.' He paused again. 'She offered you money, didn't she?'

A flicker in Agon's eyes told Thanet he was right. 'How much?' he said. 'Twenty thousand? Thirty thousand? No? Fifty thousand, then? Even more? My word, Mr Agon, don't tell me you passed up the opportunity to be a rich man? How very noble of you!' Thanet leaned forward. 'So how did she react, when you refused? She must have been desperate. What happened? She came at you, didn't she? And you grabbed her by the wrists, to fend her off—'

'I had to!' Agon burst out. 'It was self-defence!'

There was a brief, charged silence as they all absorbed what was tantamount to a confession. Thanet couldn't resist a brief, exultant glance at Lineham. *We did it!*

Then Agon turned to Barbara Summers, sitting as if turned to stone beside him. 'It wasn't my fault,' he said, his eyes begging her to believe him. 'She came at me like a madwoman. I had to stop her!'

'Tell us exactly what happened,' Thanet said. 'From the beginning.'

Agon squeezed his eyes shut, massaged his right temple and shook his head as if to clear it of emotional turmoil. Then, picking his words with care, he began to talk.

It had all happened very much in the way Thanet had described. Virginia had called out to Agon as he was taking his sports bag out of the car. They had walked towards each other across the courtyard, meeting in the middle, beside the well.

Listening intently to Agon's account of the subsequent conversation Thanet imagined it had gone something like this:

'I wanted a word in private.'

'What about?'

'Don't play the innocent, Matt! You must have realised that little charade back there was all for Rachel's sake.'

'I do appreciate that I wouldn't exactly be your first choice of son-in-law. In the circumstances.'

'Exactly. So we – Ralph and I – were wondering if anything might make you reconsider, break off the engagement?'

'Such as?'

'Shall we say, a substantial financial inducement?'

'What did you have in mind?'

'Say, fifty thousand pounds?'

'No way.'

'Seventy-five, then? No? A hundred?'

'Look, you can stop right there, Ginny. You'll just have to come to terms with the fact that I love Rachel and Rachel loves me. She's over eighteen and she can make up her own mind about who she's going to marry. Afterwards, well, then you and Ralph can continue to keep her – us – in the style to which she is accustomed.'

'You needn't think you'd get a penny from us!'

'Oh come on, Ginny, I can't believe that. Be realistic. Ralph

wouldn't like to see his only daughter living in squalor in a bedsitter or going hungry, for that matter, and neither would you.'

'But just think what you could do with that kind of money, Matt! You could go anywhere you liked, stay in the best hotels . . .'

'But for how long? Sooner or later the cash would run out and I'd be back to square one. No, I really think it's time to settle down. I rather fancy myself as a family man.'

'Family man? You? Never in a thousand years!'

'Just wait and see.'

'Not on your life! Can't you get it into your head that there's no way we're going to let this happen?'

'And how, precisely, do you propose to prevent it?'

'By telling Rachel about the affair you had with me, of course. I didn't want to, naturally, if there was any way of avoiding it—'

'I bet you didn't! Mummy wouldn't want her little girl to think she's been a big bad mummy, would she?'

'But if I have to, I will. That's just a risk I'd have to take.'

'Then I shall deny it. Who d'you think she's going to believe? Who d'you think she's going to want to believe? After all, there's something pretty disgusting about a woman of your age shagging a young lad like me, isn't there? Especially if she happens to be your mother . . .'

'Then I told her a few home truths,' said Agon, finishing his account of the conversation. 'And that was when she came at me.'

Thanet could imagine how cruelly provocative those 'home truths' had been – must have been, to make Virginia react as she had, if Agon's account was to be believed.

'She was like a wildcat, hissing and spitting, fingers hooked like claws . . .'

Propelled by pent-up fury, frustration and fear, Thanet imagined.

'She was going for my face and I grabbed her wrists, to hold her off.'

Ah yes, thought Thanet. So that was it. Agon had had at all costs to protect his one priceless asset, his incredible good looks. Damage them and much of his power over women, the charm upon which he relied so heavily, would be lost.

'But she was like an eel, twisting and turning, and all the time trying to reach my face with those disgustingly long fingernails of hers. I thought, if I could just manage to turn her away from me and pin her against the well wall while I secured her hands behind her back . . . But it all went wrong. I gave her one almighty twist and before I knew it, she was gone . . .'

His imagination supplied Thanet with an echo of the splash as Virginia's body hit the water. 'And then?' he said grimly.

'And then, what? That was it.'

'I see. You had no idea whether she was alive or dead but you simply replaced the cover and walked away, went back and enjoyed the swimming party. The jury's going to love that.'

Agon looked from Thanet's face to Lineham's and then, finally, to Barbara Summers's, reading the same expression of condemnation in each. His jaw set and he said doggedly, 'It was self-defence, I tell you.'

Thanet nodded at Lineham. 'Charge him,' he said, in disgust.

TWENTY-ONE

'Agon? And Virginia? That's incredible!' Mintar's mouth twisted in revulsion and he buried his face in his hands, shaking his head in disbelief. 'How could she?' he groaned.

Thanet wasn't sure that Mintar had even taken in properly the fact that Agon had been charged with Virginia's murder. Thanet had tried to be tactful but nothing could disguise the sordid nature of the whole affair and Mintar had obviously focused on the fact that his wife had slept with the man his daughter was engaged to – a man whom Mintar abhorred and who was moreover young enough to be Virginia's son. And there was of course more bad news yet to impart. How was Mintar going to react to the news of Caroline's disappearance? Now that they knew the barrister was innocent Thanet's sympathy for him was unbounded. By now he would have expected the man to have begun to pull himself together just a little, but so far there was no sign of this. Increasingly haggard, careworn and unkempt with every day that passed, Thanet thought that Mintar's colleagues would scarcely have recognised him if they saw him in the street, and he had to admit he was both surprised and puzzled; he would have expected Mintar to have more steel in him.

'I'm sorry to bring such bad news, sir. This must be an awful blow to you.'

'And Rachel!' Mintar raised his head. 'How is she going to take all this?'

How indeed? thought Thanet.

There was silence for a few moments and then Mintar said

with a weary sigh, 'Well, I suppose the only good thing that can come out of all this is that she will at last see what Agon is really like, and that will be the end of it.'

Thanet sincerely hoped Mintar was right. In affairs of the heart young girls frequently failed to follow the dictates of reason. Still, Rachel had obviously loved her mother and been very distressed by her disappearance, so perhaps he, Thanet, was being unduly pessimistic. In any case, there was no doubt about it, both she and her father were going to have a very bad time when all this came out in Court. Meanwhile . . .

'Let's hope so,' he said. 'Meanwhile, I'm afraid there's more bad news.'

'What?' Mintar's tone was flat, his eyes dull. He obviously felt that after what he had just been told, no news could possibly be of interest to him.

Someone tapped at the door and opened it: Rachel.

Thanet cast a warning glance at Mintar. *Don't tell her about Agon yet.* That was one conversation which needed to be conducted in privacy. 'Ah, Rachel,' he said, pre-empting any questions she might ask, 'just the person I wanted to talk to. You might be able to help.'

'Me? How?'

She was, Thanet was glad to see, looking much better. Just as well, in the circumstances. She was going to need all the resilience she possessed today. 'I was just going to tell your father—'

'Bad news, Rach, he said.' Mintar put out a hand to her and she crossed to stand beside him. Still seated, he put his arm around her waist and pulled her to him. *We'll face this together.*

'About Mummy?' she said fearfully.

'About your sister.' Thanet looked at Mintar. 'You remember I told you yesterday that we were making another attempt to find Caroline?'

Mintar and Rachel exchanged apprehensive glances. 'What do you mean, bad news?' said Mintar.

'We have finally managed to trace Dick Swain.'

They both looked stunned for a moment and then Rachel burst out, 'But that's marvellous! Brilliant! Where are they?'

Her father said warily, 'Why should that be bad news, Inspector?'

'Because Caroline is not with him. He is living in Scotland and I spoke to him myself this morning. He tells me that on the night they were supposed to have eloped she never turned up and he was so fed up about it he decided to take off by himself, leave without her.'

They both stared at Thanet in silent disbelief. Thanet found it impossible to read Mintar's reaction, so complex were the emotions which chased each other across his face: incredulity, obviously, and then – what? Relief? Excitement? Perhaps. And finally, as the implications dawned, anxiety and finally fear.

'But that's not possible!' Mintar said at last. He released Rachel and stood up. He began to pace about in agitation and it was obvious he was thinking furiously. Finally he stopped and said vehemently, 'The man's lying, he must be!'

'He's been married for the last three years to someone else – I've spoken to her, too, a very nice young Scotswoman.'

'Then where's Caroline? What's he done to her? If any harm has come to her . . . You're not letting the matter rest, I hope?'

'Of course not! If necessary we shall ask the police where he is living to investigate at that end. But the obvious thing to do is begin here.'

Rachel hadn't said a word, was still standing frozen with shock. Now she whispered, 'But if she isn't there, where is she?' She turned to her father. 'Dad, where is she? *Where is she?*' Her fragile composure was fast disintegrating again and her father put his arms around her and held her close.

'Shh,' he said, soothing her, stroking her back, her hair. 'Shh. This isn't going to help Caroline, is it?'

She took a deep breath, straightened her shoulders and pulled away from him a little. 'No,' she said, 'it isn't.' She looked at Thanet. 'What did you mean, I might be able to help?'

'Perhaps we could try to talk about this calmly,' said Thanet. 'If you would both sit down?'

Without being asked, Lineham fetched an upright chair and set it down beside Mintar's. When father and daughter were both settled, he said in response to Thanet's nod, 'We just wanted to ask a few questions about the night she left, miss.'

'I don't understand any of this. She said in her note she was going away with Dick.'

'We know that,' said Thanet. 'There doesn't seem to be any doubt about what she intended to do that night. But on the face of it, it seems that she didn't do it.'

'And we think we might know what went wrong,' said Lineham. 'If you remember, that same evening your grandmother arrived home unexpectedly, a day early, from one of her expeditions. She tells us that on such occasions it is usual to have a family celebration and that that night was no exception.'

'That's true,' said Mintar. 'But what's that got to do with Caroline's disappearance?'

'We think that in all probability this meant that Caroline wasn't able to get away as early as she intended and that when she therefore did not show up Dick Swain simply thought she had changed her mind and, as he was all packed up and ready to leave, he decided to do so anyway.'

'And he never tried to contact her again?'

'He says not,' said Thanet, 'that he decided to put the whole affair behind him. I had the impression, though he didn't actually say so, that with hindsight he suspected it wouldn't have worked anyway.'

Rachel had been listening intently and now she suddenly said, 'You're right! I remember now . . .'

Everyone looked at her. 'What?' they all said, together.

'Normally Caroline was pleased when Gran came home. We both were. It's such fun. Gran is always full of stories and usually brings us all really exciting presents. I'd forgotten until just now, but that night Caroline was really put out, said she'd made other plans. She even said she thought she'd give dinner a miss, but I told her she couldn't possibly do that, Gran would be too upset. So she stayed . . .' Rachel stared at Thanet with an expression of dawning horror. 'So this is all my fault, isn't it? If I hadn't persuaded her to change her mind, she'd have gone off with Dick and she'd still be living with him. But now, we haven't got a clue what happened to her. If he didn't wait for her, she'd surely have just come home again, wouldn't she?'

219

'Or have gone to his house to look for him.' Mintar was looking grim and now he stood up again, as if propelled by an invisible force. 'This time I'm going to get the truth out of that bloody woman if I have to knock the door down!'

'You'll do no such thing, sir!' Thanet was on his feet too. 'It wouldn't help Rachel to get yourself into trouble, would it? Besides, we're ahead of you in your thinking. Our first move will obviously be to interview Dick Swain's mother and, as she has been so uncooperative in the past, we have even taken the trouble to obtain a search warrant and bring reinforcements with us in case we need to make a forcible entry. I just wanted to put you in the picture first.'

'Good!' said Mintar. 'Then I'm coming with you! I want to hear what she has to say for herself the minute she says it!'

Thanet hesitated. He should have foreseen this, he realised. In Mintar's position he would feel exactly the same. And judging by the mulish expression on Mintar's face, nothing short of physical restraint would stop him.

'Very well,' he said with a sigh. 'But I must insist that you give me your word not to interfere in any way.'

'I promise.'

Rachel jumped up. 'I'm coming too.'

'No!' said Thanet and Mintar together.

'Why not?' she cried.

'It wouldn't be appropriate,' said her father.

An argument ensued, resulting in Rachel's departure in tears, slamming the door behind her.

'Perhaps I should have agreed,' said Mintar, looking after her. 'I hate to see her upset like that. God knows, she has enough to put up with at the moment. And we haven't even told her Agon has been arrested yet! I shudder to think how she's going to take that.'

'I know. I'm afraid she's in for a very tough time. But it's better for her to stay here at the moment. It could get ugly, judging by Miss Swain's past behaviour.'

The courtyard seemed full of police cars, though there were in fact only two beside Lineham's. In view of the fact that it was only one solitary woman they wanted to question, Thanet had debated with Lineham whether even two would be one too many, but in the end he had opted for the former. He was devoutly hoping that the show of force would be sufficient to ensure that no actual force would be necessary. Now, as the little procession set off down the drive and turned right for the short journey, the doubts reared up again: was he taking a sledgehammer to crack a nut? No, crack that nut he must. It really was absolutely essential to interview Marah Swain and find out whether or not she had seen Caroline that night and it was quite on the cards that once again she would flatly refuse to talk to them. Much as he disliked the idea, it seemed to him that if she wouldn't cooperate this time the only solution was to try to frighten her into doing so and hope that should he succeed he would be able to tell whether or not she was lying.

As pre-arranged, they all left their cars on the road and walked up the narrow track, Thanet equipped with loud-hailer and some of the officers carrying the heavy metal cylinder with side handles which is the contemporary version of the battering-ram. They had instructions to make sure that it and they were visible from the cottage windows, but to keep well back until called to action. *Please God, let me not be making a fool of myself.*

Even beneath the trees it was hot and still, the silence broken only by the shuffle of their feet in the leaves which, parched and crisped by the unremitting heat, were already falling prematurely from trees starved of moisture.

When they reached the clearing they stopped. With door and windows still shut fast the cottage continued to exude that air of brooding menace which had so affected Thanet yesterday. It looked impregnable, a symbol of the intractable mystery which surrounded Caroline's disappearance. Well, he was soon going to change all that, thought Thanet grimly, his jaw setting in a determined line. He nodded, and his men fanned out around that section of the perimeter facing the cottage, with the steel enforcer in a prominent position. Mintar hung back as requested; Thanet didn't want the sight of him to encourage Marah Swain to refuse them entry. Then, adrenalin beginning to pump through his system, he and Lineham crossed the clearing and knocked at the door. Once again there was that tell-tale twitch of the curtain at one of the downstairs windows and now that they were close to the house he could again hear the radio playing. Did she ever switch it off, he wondered?

Lineham knocked again. 'Police. Open up.'

No reaction.

Further knocking produced no result and Thanet walked halfway back across the clearing and spoke through the loud-hailer. 'Open the door, Miss Swain. We know you're in there.'

Still no reaction.

Thanet gestured to the men carrying the enforcer and they moved forward a few steps. Then he tried again. 'Look out of your window, Miss Swain. As you see, we have the means to make a forcible entry, and the warrant to justify its use, if you continue to refuse to let us in. You don't really want us to break your door down, do you? Because that's what's going to happen, in just a few minutes from now.'

He paused, to give her time to absorb this. *Come* on, *open up! Open up!*

But still she refused to cooperate. Ah well, he told himself, I've given her plenty of opportunity. . . He raised the loud-hailer again. 'Right,' he said. 'I'm going to count to ten, then we are coming in. One, two . . .' He waved the men forward and they advanced as he counted. '. . . seven, eight, nine . . .'

Relief gushed through him as at last the door swung slowly open. Essential as it may have been to gain entry he knew that if they had had to break in his self-respect would have been badly dented. He handed the hailer to one of his men and then he and Lineham stepped inside.

So intent had he been on getting access, Thanet had temporarily forgotten about the smell. Sour, rank and stomach-turning, it almost stopped him in his tracks. He saw Lineham falter beside him before they both moved on.

Marah Swain was standing squarely in the middle of the room, defiance in every line of her stance, legs planted slightly apart, arms folded across her chest, head slightly down as if about to charge. Her long grey hair probably hadn't been cut in years and straggled in greasy wisps down to her breasts and halfway down her back. It was the first time Thanet had seen her properly and she was wearing the ankle-length black skirt, woollen shawl and old cracked-leather boots described by Tanya. He wondered if she ever changed her clothes and was reminded of a book he had once read in which it was described how in remoter country districts in the nineteenth century children used to be greased all over before being sown into their underclothes for the duration of the winter. For that matter, the whole room seemed to exist in a time-warp. Tanya had not exaggerated: *It's like something out of the Middle Ages . . . doesn't look as though it's been cleaned for about a hundred years, with bunches of dried herbs and stuff hanging from nails all along the beams in the ceiling and every windowsill crammed with jamjars full of things I wouldn't like to examine too closely.* In the background a Radio Kent announcer launched incongruously into the lunchtime news.

'What's all the fuss about, then?' she said.

'It's you who has caused all the fuss, as you put it,' said Thanet. 'If you'd let us in quietly in the first place none of this would have been necessary.'

'Why should I let in any old Tom, Dick and Harry just because they ask to? It's my house, I've got every right to refuse.'

'Not in this case,' said Lineham, producing the search warrant. He held it out to her but she refused to budge and he was forced to advance and hold it out for her inspection.

She gave it only the most cursory of glances, then shrugged. 'Go ahead,' she said. 'Search all you like.'

'Before we do, there are one or two questions we want to ask,' said Thanet. Normally at this point in an interview he would attempt to make it less confrontational by suggesting they sit down but a brief glance around the room convinced him he would prefer to remain standing. Both the cushion on the only armchair and the stained and filthy cover on the sofa repelled rather than invited relaxation. Besides, Marah Swain gave the impression that she would in any case have refused to budge. Her solid bulk looked as though it had almost taken root in the spot where she was standing.

'About Caroline Mintar,' he said.

'Oh, her,' she said, and spat on the floor.

The gobbet landed near Lineham's foot and Thanet awarded him full marks for self-restraint; the sergeant didn't even flinch.

The light pouring in through the doorway was briefly blotted out and Thanet glanced back over his shoulder to see what was going on. Mintar was now standing just inside the room. Obviously his need to know what was happening had got the better of him. Thanet hoped he was going to keep his promise and stay out of the proceedings. 'Yes, her,' he said, turning back to face the old woman.

'The bitch!' she said.

'It has always been understood that she and your son went away together, but we've now spoken to him—'

'To Dick?' For the first time, her expression altered. It was avid with curiosity. 'You talked to Dick?'

'Yes, this morning. And he tells us—'

'How is he? Is he all right?'

'All in good time, Miss Swain. He told me that Caroline never turned up that night and he went away without her. We know that she was delayed, but that she left home as intended. We assume that when she didn't find him at their prearranged meeting place, she would have come here looking for him.'

'Well, you assume wrong! And even if she had, I'd have sent her packing!'

Thanet's heart sank. The woman was lying, he was certain of it. This wasn't looking good for Caroline.

Marah Swain was still speaking. 'If it hadn't been for her, my Dick would never have gone away and left me.' She stopped suddenly and looked at Mintar, and an expression of extreme malevolence narrowed her eyes and twisted her mouth. 'Your Dick too, eh, *lover*?'

It took a few moments for the implications to sink in.

Mintar, Dick Swain's father?

A glance at Mintar's stricken face confirmed the truth of it and Thanet looked in disbelief from the QC now avoiding his eye to the woman standing triumphantly with arms akimbo. Impossible to imagine a coupling between these two, but then there was no telling what Marah had looked like all those years ago. Difficult as it might be to believe, perhaps in her youth she had simply been a buxom country girl, as fresh as a daisy and with all that flower's innocent charm.

But of course the worst of it was that this meant Dick and Caroline were brother and sister. Which explained so much – why Mintar had been so dead against Caroline's association with Swain, why he had been so devastated by her elopement, why he had refused to take more than the most cursory steps to find her, why he had preferred to try to pretend she had never existed rather than confess the truth to his family and face up to the fact that it was he who was really responsible for the disastrous consequences of that liaison long ago.

Thanet's sympathy for the man dissolved like snow in summer. The truth was that loss of face had been more important to Mintar than his daughter's welfare and Thanet found that unforgivable. If the QC had only had the courage to tell Caroline the truth as soon as she started to show a serious interest in Swain, then none of this would have happened. She would never have left home and Virginia would have been saved from the worst of her excesses and might even still be alive.

Thanet stared at Mintar in horrified disbelief. *How could you have allowed this to happen?*

After one shamefaced glance at Thanet Mintar rallied and retaliated, evidently feeling that there was now nothing to be gained by keeping his promise not to interfere. 'You're lying about Caroline, Marah,' he said harshly. 'Tell us what really happened that night.'

'I did. I have. I never saw hide nor hair of her. Believe me or not, as you choose.'

'We choose not to,' said Thanet grimly. And then, to Lineham. 'Get four more officers in here, Sergeant. We're going to take this place apart.'

'Carry on!' she said, folding her arms again and shifting slightly to firm up her stance, as if to indicate that nothing was going to make her budge, physically or mentally. 'Search away! I don't know what you think you're going to find!'

'That remains to be seen,' said Thanet as the officers, three men and a woman, came in. He wasn't sure himself what he was looking for. Just some indication that Caroline had been here that night, he supposed, though how realistic an expectation that was after the passage of four years, he had no idea. He only knew that the woman standing there like an immovable obstacle was not going to defeat him if he could possibly help it. 'And turn that wretched radio off!' he said to Lineham, as the presenter launched into an interview with a local celebrity. 'I can't hear myself think!'

'Now,' he said into the ensuing silence. And paused. Surely he had heard something? What? He cocked his head, listening intently.

The others looked at each other, puzzled, and Lineham opened his mouth to speak.

Thanet put up his hand. 'Shh!'

But there was nothing, only a tense, expectant silence as they all waited for they knew not what. Thanet relaxed, shook his head and was about to go on speaking when the sound came again, just the faintest metallic chink. Glancing around, he saw that this time they had heard it too.

And then, in a flash, he remembered. Understood.

He looked at Marah Swain, standing as if carved in stone in the centre of the room and she read the knowledge in his eyes, raised her head slightly and gave him a defiant stare. His gaze moved down to her feet, squarely planted on a thick, multicoloured rag rug of the type once common in poorer country households. He advanced upon her. 'Move aside,' he said.

She stood her ground and he gestured to his men, who seized her by the arms. She went limp and they were forced to drag her back, a dead weight, her heels rucking up the rag mat. Now they could all see what he had suspected: there was a trapdoor beneath it.

Thanet went down on his knees and shoved the rug aside. He seized the iron ring folded down into a recess at one side of the door and lifted, swung it back and almost gagged as an even more powerful, suffocating stench gushed up to meet him, filling his nose, his mouth, his lungs. Wooden steps fell away into the darkness. 'A torch,' he gasped, looking up at Lineham. 'I need a torch!'

'A torch,' repeated the sergeant, looking at Marah Swain, but she simply turned her head away, refusing to answer. A quick glance around failed to reveal one and on a bright summer's day like this no one had thought to bring one along. An officer was dispatched to fetch as many as he could muster from the cars on the road but Thanet couldn't wait for his return. Tying his handkerchief over nose and mouth he automatically dug into a pocket for the matchbox which of course wasn't there. Since he had stopped smoking he never bothered to carry one. 'Anyone got a match?'

One of the men fumbled in his pocket and produced a lighter.

Thanet snatched it from him and then, taking a deep breath of the relatively fresh air in the room, he descended half a dozen steps before lighting it. Holding it at arm's length he peered into the blackness surrounding him.

The hairs at the back of his neck prickled as in the far corner of the cellar, where the darkness was most profound, something moved. There was that sound again, but louder this time and now he could identify it: the clink of metal on stone.

Then, so faintly as to be almost inaudible, there came a whisper. 'Please, help me,' it said.

TWENTY-TWO

'You ought to have seen the state she was in ...' Thanet shuddered, remembering.

It was late that same evening and he and Joan were sitting in the garden, enjoying the cool of the day. Thanet was savouring the pleasure of a case brought to a satisfactory conclusion and the opportunity to relax without feeling the unremitting pressure of a serious investigation hanging over his head. If it weren't for the anxiety over Bridget his happiness would have been unalloyed, but she was now well advanced in labour and the portable telephone lay to hand on the table between their coffee cups, a constant reminder of the all-important event that was taking place some sixty miles away.

Over supper Thanet had been telling Joan about the events of the day and had just reached their dramatic conclusion. Now he shook his head in pity at the memory of Caroline's plight. 'Honestly, Joan, she was barely recognisable as a human being. She was chained to the wall like a criminal in a medieval dungeon, lying on this disgustingly filthy mattress. I shouldn't think she'd seen soap and water since the day she left home, and her clothes were in tatters – I imagine they were the same ones she was wearing that evening. Her hair was so matted I should think it will probably all have to be cut off, and when I picked her up she was so thin it felt as though she might just fall apart in my arms. It was like lifting a bundle of bones. We've all seen photographs of the survivors of the Nazi prison camps but believe me, when you are faced by the reality . . . And that smell . . . I don't think I shall ever forget it.' Even now, despite the fact

228

that the minute he got home he had stripped off, consigned his clothes to the dustbin and taken as hot a shower as he could bear, that cloying, noxious odour still seemed to clog his nostrils, obstruct his breathing and surround him like a miasma.

'The chain was long enough to enable her to move a few feet away from the mattress but no further, and she was surrounded by piles of excrement. Everywhere you moved, you stepped in it, and she was caked in it – she was too weak to stand up so if she got out of bed I imagine she had to crawl.'

Joan had been listening in horrified fascination. 'I've come across some pretty awful behaviour in my clients, but nothing quite as horrendous as this. How can anyone treat another human being like that? It's beyond belief!'

'But sadly, this kind of thing does occasionally happen. Over the years I've read of such cases from time to time and presumably there are many more that never come to light.'

'But why do people do it?'

Thanet shrugged. 'For various reasons, apparently. I remember reading of two separate instances in the United States when women had been locked up for years in bomb shelters because jealous husbands convinced them that there had been a nuclear war. And there have been some pretty dreadful cases in remote country areas when people – men as well as women – have been locked away for as long as thirty or forty years.'

'You're right, I'd forgotten. It's coming back to me now. I remember reading ages ago about the case of an Italian woman in her sixties who had been kept locked up by her relations since she was a young woman because, they said, she was "different" after an illness and they had decided to keep her hidden – to preserve "family dignity and honour", was the way they put it, as I recall!'

'It's virtually impossible to understand the mentality of people like that, isn't it, especially when there's collusion and more than one person is involved.'

'But in this case it was just Marah Swain.'

'Yes. She's such a strange woman. In many ways she's a relic of a past age, a throw-back, if you like, and as such quite outside the normal parameters of acceptable behaviour today.'

'But that's no excuse, surely!'

'Of course not. There *is* no excuse for treating another human being like that. Reasons, perhaps; excuses, no.'

'Her reason being that she blamed Caroline for leading her son astray and ultimately driving him away?'

'Partly, yes. But I did wonder, from something she said . . . Though I don't know, perhaps I'm attributing too civilised a motive to her.'

'Civilised? I'd have thought that was the last word you'd ever apply to her, from what you've been saying. What can you mean?'

'Well, after we found Caroline, Marah said very little, in fact. But as Mintar carried the girl out she did call after him, "They had to be stopped, see. Not natural, was it?"'

'Oh, I see. You're talking about the incest. Though we don't actually know that there ever was any, do we?'

Thanet shook his head. 'Not *know*. Suspect, perhaps.'

'Still, you think she might have felt she couldn't allow it either to go on or to happen, whichever the case may be?'

Another shrug. 'I can't think what else she meant.'

'But she needn't have *kept* Caroline locked up, surely?'

'I don't know. You think about it. When would she have let her go? There would never have been a right time. Besides, I think her desire for revenge was and still is just as strong a reason for keeping Caroline there, if not stronger. She showed absolutely no shame or remorse for what she had done, or pity for Caroline's condition. Just imagine what that poor girl must have gone through! It takes a pretty tough person to survive intact four years of straightforward solitary confinement, let alone under the conditions of filth, near-starvation and total darkness that Caroline had to put up with . . .'

Joan shivered. 'It doesn't bear thinking about. I suppose it's too early to have any idea how well she'll recover?'

'Physically, do you mean? Or mentally?'

'Both, I suppose.'

'I was talking to Doc Mallard about that this afternoon. He heard what had happened and called in at the hospital to see how Caroline was. According to him the human body has an amazing ability to adapt to food deprivation and survive, which is why, during the war, so many prisoners of war did just that. After initial loss of weight the metabolism stabilises, apparently.'

'But aren't there possible long-term effects – like infertility, for instance?'

'Sadly, yes.'

Reminded of Bridget they both glanced at the telephone. When would it ring?

'Doc Mallard mentioned that, but he didn't go into it. I suppose in Caroline's case they'll just have to wait and see. But he does think her eyes will gradually get back to normal.'

'I suppose she couldn't stand the light, after so long in darkness.'

'She couldn't bear to open them at all. We had to cover them, to protect them.'

'Poor girl. What a dreadful, dreadful ordeal.'

'At least she's in good hands now.' Caroline had been taken straight off to hospital. 'I'm sure her father will make certain she gets every care. But as for her mental state, well, who can tell? In any case, it's bound to take time.'

'I can't imagine how she could ever forget an experience like that. And her father was there when you brought her up, you say? How did he react, when he saw the state she was in?'

'He was absolutely shattered, as you can imagine.' Thanet could remember only too vividly the shock, horror, disbelief in Mintar's face as he looked at the stinking, filthy, skeletal figure lying limply in Thanet's arms and whispered his daughter's name. 'Caroline?' He remembered too the way Mintar had without hesitation or repugnance taken her from him and after one piercing glance of accusation and reproach at Marah Swain, borne his pathetic burden tenderly away. He had sat down to wait for the ambulance in the shade of the trees at the far side of the clearing, cradling his daughter with the gentleness of a mother nursing her newborn baby.

'But what made you guess, about Caroline being in the cellar?'

Thanet considered, shrugged. 'Pure luck, really.'

'Oh come on, Luke! You're being modest again.'

'No, really. Marah Swain had the radio on, you see, and it was getting on my nerves so I asked Mike to turn it off. If I hadn't . . . Well, I don't know. Perhaps one of us would have remembered a cellar being mentioned, eventually. Tanya heard about it during routine questioning of someone in the village whose husband had been friendly with Dick Swain as a boy.

'Anyway, when the radio was turned off I thought I heard something. No one else had, but we all listened. Then it came again and this time they all heard it. And then I did remember the cellar, and suddenly realised why it was that Marah had planted herself bang in the middle of the room and hadn't budged ever since we came in.'

'And that had struck you as odd?'

'Yes, it had. Everything about her body language said, whatever happens you are not going to make me move from this particular spot. She was standing on one of those thick rag mats people used to make out of old clothes.'

'I know the sort you mean. They were made with a fat metal hook, from strips of material. I saw someone demonstrating how to make them once at a country fair.'

'Anyway, it was there to cover the trapdoor, of course, and, together with the radio which was invariably playing, it would have been pretty effective at muffling sounds from below. Poor Caroline's voice is so weak now that she would never have been able to make herself heard anyway and I imagine in the early days Marah would have had no compunction about gagging her if anyone came. I should think that apart from those who want to buy one of Marah's home-made remedies very few visitors ever go to that house. In any case, we actually had to manhandle her, to drag her away from that trapdoor.'

They were both silent for a while, thinking, then Thanet said, 'You know, before we found Caroline, when it dawned on me what Marah was saying, that Mintar was Dick's father, I couldn't feel any sympathy for the man, but when I saw the way he looked at Caroline, the tenderness with which he took and handled her despite that terrible smell . . .'

'Imagine how he must have felt, seeing his daughter in that state!'

Once again they both looked at the telephone lying on the table before them, willing it to bring an end to the interminable waiting.

'So what did you mean, you couldn't feel any sympathy for him?'

'It's obvious, surely. If you think about it, he was the one who was really responsible for the whole disastrous sequence of events.'

'By seducing Marah in the first place, you mean?'

'Partly that, yes. Though looking at her now, I must confess I find it virtually impossible to imagine them as lovers.'

'He didn't deny it, though?'

'Oh no, not at all.'

'Well, there was nothing very unusual about what he did. I'm not condoning it, of course, but throughout the ages young men have sown their wild oats and usually done their best to avoid the consequences. What I don't understand is why it didn't come out in the first place – and why it's remained a secret all these years.'

'Ah, well, I can answer that. Lineham and I followed the ambulance to the hospital.' Thanet was recalling now the horrified expressions on the faces of the nurses when they had seen the state Caroline was in. Caroline herself had uttered not a single word since the moment of her discovery; indeed, but for the tears which oozed from beneath her closed eyelids, had appeared incapable of showing any emotion either. Her father had remained equally silent and it wasn't until she had been delivered into expert hands that Mintar had finally collapsed on to a chair in the relatives' room and, burying his head in his hands, had groaned, 'It's all my fault, Thanet, isn't it? Oh God, I can't bear it . . . Caroline . . .' And then, his defences eroded by distress, fear and guilt and driven, evidently, by the need to tell someone, anyone, the true facts of the story which he had kept bottled up for more than twenty-five years, he had poured out the whole sorry tale.

Thanet realised that Joan was patiently waiting for him to go on. 'I had a long talk with Mintar while Caroline was being examined and those were two of the questions I asked him. Apparently this affair with Marah – if it could be called that – took place just after he had passed his bar finals. He blames his euphoric mood for what happened. He'd been sharing a flat in London while he was studying and had come down to spend a

233

few weeks at home before taking up his pupillage in Chambers in the Middle Temple. I suspect that after keeping his nose to the grindstone for so long he was ready for a bit of fun before launching into the next stage of his career. I'm surprised he didn't take off and do some travelling, but of course it wasn't as much the done thing then as it is now. And apparently his mother was just back from a trip and had indicated she expected him to spend some time with her. Anyway, the fact of the matter was that entertainment was a little thin on the ground in Paxton, so he spent a lot of time walking. So, apparently, did Marah. She inherited her interest in herbs from her mother. She and Marah used to scour the fields and hedgerows most days for the ones she wanted and after she died Marah continued the habit. Mintar had known Marah for years, her father was the Mintars' gardener, and now one thing led to another. I imagine the truth is he was bored and she was just, well, available, I suppose. He doesn't try to excuse his behaviour.

'Soon afterwards he went back to London to start his pupillage. He was nearing the end of it and was hoping shortly to be invited to become a full member of Chambers when, on a visit home for a weekend, he ran into Marah and she told him she was pregnant. It was far too late for an abortion by then. I don't know if she was rather naïvely hoping he might marry her but in any case, when he made it clear that this was definitely not on the cards, she demanded some sort of compensation and threatened to tell his father and even to visit his "office", as she called it, if it wasn't forthcoming.'

'I get the picture,' said Joan. 'Daddy was a High Court judge, so there would be hell to pay if he heard his son had fathered a child with the gardener's daughter, especially one as unprepossessing as Marah. And Mintar's Chambers wouldn't be exactly happy about it either, to put it mildly. The bar's a pretty stuffy profession when it comes to that sort of thing, I imagine.'

'And as you say, especially when the girl is someone like Marah. Imagining her turning up in Chambers was a nightmare scenario. Mintar suspected he would lose his chance of a place and was afraid he'd become a laughing-stock and wouldn't get one elsewhere either if the news got around. All in all, he saw the prospect of his career being blighted before it ever got off the ground. His problem was that he didn't really have much to offer her as an inducement to keep quiet. He had a small allowance from his father, enough just to keep him ticking over until he started to earn some money, but his prospects for the foreseeable future were pretty slim. In those days young barristers invariably had a hard time of it waiting for work to trickle down to them and when it did the fees were not very high. It's not like nowadays when if you're lucky enough to get into a good set of Chambers you'll probably be offered a pupillage award to smooth your path. So he racked his brains desperately to try to think of a bribe that would keep her quiet.'

'Quite a problem!'

'Exactly. But in the end he did come up with a solution. Marah has lived in that cottage for so long everyone assumes it belongs to her, but it doesn't, it's actually part of the Windmill Court property. He promised her that if she remained quiet about his being the father of her child, he would not only pay her a small weekly allowance but would give her the right to live in the cottage rent free for the rest of her life.'

'But he had no right to promise her any such thing, surely? The cottage may be his now but at that time it would have belonged to his father. And even if his father died, it could then have been passed on to his mother.'

'True. But in the event, that didn't happen. Perhaps he already knew of some family trust or arrangement whereby the property would go straight to him on his father's death. I don't know any more than I've told you. Anyway, he admits he banked on the fact that Marah was too unsophisticated to question his right to dispose of the cottage as he wished and he was right. She seemed perfectly satisfied with his offer and the legal-looking document he drew up and presented to her. After all, a roof over your head for life is not to be sniffed at.'

'But what if *her* father had died before Mintar inherited? Wouldn't the cottage have been required for his successor as gardener? How would Mintar have persuaded his father to let her stay on by herself?'

Thanet shrugged. 'No idea. I suppose he thought he'd cross that hurdle if he came to it. In the event, presumably he was lucky and it never happened. The arrangement seems to have worked perfectly all these years until now.'

'But why was she satisfied with the promise of living in the house rent-free? After all, she had him over a barrel, didn't she? Why didn't she stick out for ownership?'

'I asked him that. He thought it might simply have been that it never entered her head. It wasn't as though it was her idea to use the house as a bargaining position, it was his proposal in the first place and he said she was very taken with the suggestion. He was still very nervous that she might think of demanding ownership, of course, and that would have put him in an impossible position. For one thing, as you so rightly pointed out, the cottage wasn't his to dispose of, and for another, even if it had been, it would have been a disastrous move to make. Once it was hers she could have broadcast the truth of Dick's parentage whenever she liked and there would have been nothing he could do about it. This way, they were on equal terms and each had a hold over the other. If she spilled the beans he could turn her out and if he reneged on the agreement she could make sure he paid for it.'

'So why did she suddenly decide to go back on the arrangement this afternoon?'

'I think she realised the game was up and she had nothing to lose by telling us. When inquiries were made about Caroline in the past she'd always managed to fob people off, but this time she could see how determined we were to find out what had happened to the girl. She must have realised that when we did, it was more than likely that the secret of Dick's parentage would come to light. Also, I think that, as I said, even after all this time she was still burning with rage against Caroline and she needed to lash out one last time and vent her anger on someone. Mintar was the perfect target and she couldn't resist the temptation of humiliating him in front of witnesses.'

Joan pulled a face. 'Charming!'

'Quite. And I must say, I think he deserved it. Because what I find unforgivable as far as he's concerned is the fact that if only he'd had the guts to own up to being Dick's father when Caroline and Dick started going out together, none of this need have happened. There'd certainly have been no elopement, Caroline would never have had to endure that terrible incarceration and – who knows? – perhaps Virginia might still be alive.'

They both started as the phone rang.

Joan snatched it up. 'Alexander?' She nodded vigorously at Thanet then listened intently. 'A girl? That's wonderful! And everything's all right? Oh, what a relief! And how's Bridget? Oh? An emergency caesarian? Oh dear! So how is she now? Oh, good. Excellent. Yes, I see. Oh . . . Oh . . . Good . . . Yes . . . I see . . . We'll have to keep our fingers crossed then. Yes. Well, we'll ring the hospital in the morning and come up to see them both tomorrow evening, if all is well. Give her our love, won't you. 'Bye.' Joan put down the receiver and turned to Thanet, eyes filled with tears. 'You heard all that?'

Thanet nodded speechlessly, having himself run the gamut of emotions from elation and relief to fear and back again to relief throughout the brief call.

Joan filled in the details for him. 'The baby is one and a half kilos – that's about three pounds, five ounces, and an excellent weight for thirty-three weeks, apparently. She's been examined by a paediatrician and he says she's in very good shape. She's had to go to the Special Care Baby Unit, but that's routine with premature babies and no cause for alarm.'

When she had finished, Thanet jumped up. 'Just wait there,' he said. A few minutes later he returned with glasses and a bottle of champagne in a cooler. 'I put this on ice earlier,' he said, with a grin stretching from ear to ear. 'As an act of faith. But before I open it . . .' He disappeared into the house again and came back with a parcel. 'I bought this for Christmas,' he said, 'but I just can't wait that long to give it to you. And now seems as appropriate a moment as any.'

'Oh Luke, how exciting! I love unexpected presents!'

He watched indulgently as she unwrapped the jacket and it tumbled out on to her lap, a kaleidoscope of sumptuous colour.

'Oh!' she breathed, holding it up to admire it. Then she looked at him and again there were tears in her eyes. 'It's absolutely beautiful! Wherever did you find it?'

'That's a secret.'

She put her arms around his neck and kissed him. 'I love it, I really do. Thank you, darling!'

'Thought you would,' he said, smugly. 'And now . . .' The cork popped, the foam spilled out in the time-honoured way, and they raised brimming glasses in a toast.

'To the next generation!' he said.

TWENTY-THREE

In the aftermath of the case there was a mountain of paperwork to deal with and Thanet and Lineham spent much of the following day glued to their desks. By 4.30 Thanet had had enough. 'I'm going to look in at the hospital, see how Caroline's doing.'

Lineham nodded, grinned, and said, 'OK, Grandad.'

Thanet had been swamped with congratulations once the news got around and took the teasing in good part. 'That's enough of that, Mike!'

'Are you going up to see Bridget tonight, sir?'

'Try and stop me!'

Lineham opened a drawer in his desk and took out a gaily wrapped parcel. 'Would you give her this, with love from us both?'

'Of course,' said Thanet, touched. 'But how did you manage to produce it so quickly?'

'Had it in the drawer for a week or more,' confessed Lineham with an uncharacteristically shy smile. 'Louise said she'd played safe and chosen yellow.'

'I'm sure Bridget will be delighted. Thank you, Mike. And tell Louise we really appreciate it.'

'Louise went through much the same performance as Bridget herself, with Richard.'

'I remember. I must say, it's such a relief it's all over.'

'I know just how you feel.'

Thanet drove to Sturrenden General and before leaving the car locked the parcel in the boot. The trouble with being a

239

policeman was that you saw thieves and villains lurking behind every bush.

The Sister recognised Thanet immediately. She had been on duty yesterday when Caroline was brought in.

'How is she?' he said.

She pulled a face. 'Put it this way: she'll survive, no question of that, but as to whether she'll ever completely recover . . . But it's early days yet. We'll just have to wait and see how she goes on. At the moment we're trying to get some nourishment into her, but we have to be very careful, take it very slowly.'

'Yes, of course.'

'Her father was talking about moving her to a private hospital or taking her home and hiring nurses to look after her, but we advised against it, for the moment anyway, and he seems to have given up the idea.'

'Is she talking at all?'

'Just a few words. Most of the time she just lies there, staring into space.'

'Has her sister seen her yet?'

'Yes. She's with her now, as a matter of fact. She's been here all day, she and her father. We did try to prepare her, but she was terribly upset when she first saw Caroline, as you can imagine.'

'Yes, I can.' Thanet's tone was grim. Rachel had a great deal to be upset about at the moment and he wondered how she was bearing up.

'And that was *after* we'd cleaned her up. Honestly, Inspector, in all my years in the nursing profession I've never seen anything like the state she was in. I don't think I shall ever forget it.'

'I know. I don't think any of us will.'

'Anyway, as I say, she's in no danger now and we're doing all we can for her.' The Sister's eyes were straying to the paperwork awaiting her attention.

Thanet took the hint. 'I'm sure. May I see her?'

'Of course.' A nurse was called to take him to Caroline's room. She was the only patient in a little side ward with two beds in it. She was lying flat on her back and Thanet suspected that she was asleep, as she didn't move a muscle as he came in. He couldn't be sure, though, as she was wearing dark glasses.

Rachel and Mintar were sitting one on either side of her, holding her hands. They glanced up and smiled briefly at him as he came in. Thanet went to stand beside the bed and take a closer look at the patient.

At least today Caroline was recognisable as a human being, he thought, even though she did look as though she were in the final stages of anorexia. She was so thin that her body scarcely mounded the bedclothes and the shape of her skull was clearly discernible. Her skin was unnaturally pale, with a greyish hue, and still pitted with dirt despite the cleansing processes to which she must have been subjected. Although they had not shaved her head as Thanet had feared they might, only scanty wisps of hair remained and alopecia, caused no doubt by prolonged malnutrition, disfigured her scalp. She was a truly pathetic figure and Thanet's heart went out to her for the suffering she had undergone and the long, slow difficult road ahead of her, back to anything resembling normality.

He sensed that Mintar was watching him but when he glanced up the barrister's eyes fell away. Thanet guessed that he was still overwhelmed with remorse.

Caroline must have woken up because her head turned slightly on the pillow. Her father leaned forward and said softly, 'This is Inspector Thanet, Caro. He was the one who found you.'

Her lips moved and they all strained to hear. 'I know,' she whispered. She released Rachel's hand and opened hers to Thanet, raising one finger to beckon him closer.

He clasped the little bundle of bones, conscious of their fragility, and leaned forward in response to the slight pressure he felt. When her fingers relaxed, he stopped, now close enough to see her eyes through the dark lenses. She was gazing up at him as if trying to memorise his features. Then her lips moved again and he turned his head slightly the better to hear what she was about to say.

'Thank you,' she whispered. And her fingers tightened again upon his. 'Thank you.'

He smiled warmly at her, squeezed her hand and said, 'Just get well again quickly.'

He saw that slow tears had begun to slide down the sides

of her cheeks and he released her hand, straightened up and glanced at Rachel, who reached for a tissue and dabbed them gently away.

Although Rachel looked pale and strained, with dark circles beneath her eyes, she seemed to be coping well, Thanet thought. It was obvious that her concern for her adored sister was engaging all her emotional energy at present and perhaps having Caroline restored to her was at least in some measure consoling her for having in effect lost both mother and fiancé within the space of a few days.

Mintar had risen. 'We can never thank you enough,' he said. His eyes, too, were full of tears.

'No,' said Rachel, chiming in.

Thanet shook his head. He hadn't come here for this. 'I must go,' he said. 'I just wanted to check on her progress.' And he escaped, to avoid further embarrassment.

Later, on the way to London, loaded with gifts for Bridget and the baby, he told Joan about this little scene and said, 'I'm not sure he'll be quite so grateful when he fully realises the consequences of all this.'

'When it's all made public, you mean?'

'Yes. Well, it'll all have to come out in Court, won't it? There'll be two cases, not one, remember. Agon will be standing trial too. As for Marah . . . I can just imagine Mintar's colleagues looking at her in the dock and thinking, how *could* he? It'll all be a tremendous scandal in legal circles and I should think he can forget about a seat on the Bench, in the High or any other kind of Court.'

'What will she be charged with?'

'False imprisonment, almost certainly.'

'And what sort of sentence will she get?'

'Years, I imagine.'

They were silent for a while and then Thanet said, 'No, I'm being unjust. He'll always be thankful we found her, no doubt about that. And who knows? Perhaps the fact that at last he is going to have to pay in personal terms for his lack of courage will alleviate just a little the shame and guilt which at the moment is eating him up. I think he'd got to the point where he couldn't live with his conscience any longer. Remember how Mike and I found him trying to batter Marah's door down in an attempt to discover what had happened to Caroline?'

'Yes. You said all along you couldn't understand why he hadn't persisted in his efforts to trace her.'

'I know. But once we learned Dick was his son, of course . . . Well, obviously, if he had managed to find her he'd have had to own up, not only to Caroline but to her mother, too. And I imagine that apart from anything else he just couldn't face the possibility of losing Virginia.'

'And he lost her in the end anyway. I was thinking, what you said last night . . . You really think she might still be alive if he'd had the guts to admit that Dick was his son when Caroline first started going out with him?'

'I think it more than likely, yes.' They had left the M20 for the M23 and were now approaching the link with the M25. Thanet fell silent as he fed into the stream of traffic in the nearside lane and it was a few minutes before he went on. 'Everyone seems to agree that it was Caroline's elopement that seemed to push Virginia over the edge. It was if she just cast aside those internal restraints we all live by. She'd always enjoyed shopping, for example, but now it became an obsession. Ditto with her exercising. She'd always been attractive to men and had affairs but according to what her sister told Arnold Prime, she now "couldn't keep her hands off anything in trousers", was the way Jane apparently put it. She even eventually broke one of her own last taboos and had an affair with a much younger man. And it was this, finally, that was her undoing.'

Ever since his confession and against his solicitor's advice, Matt Agon hadn't stopped trying to justify himself. Apparently Virginia's spell had bound him fast and for the first time in his life he had proposed marriage, begging her to leave her husband. She had simply laughed at him and, consistent in this respect at least, had at once broken off their relationship.

Thanet was pretty certain – though of course Agon hadn't said so – that the tennis coach had seen ensnaring Rachel as the perfect revenge for this humiliating rejection. Thanet suspected too that it was partly Agon's residual anger with Virginia that had caused him to react so violently when she attacked him.

'You're probably right,' said Joan, when Thanet had finished telling her all this. 'A man like that, used to making easy conquests, would take it pretty hard when the one woman he's ever really fallen for laughs in his face when he proposes to her.'

'My mistake was in more or less dismissing Agon as a suspect,' said Thanet. 'And that was because I seriously underestimated Virginia's love for Rachel.'

'Her one remaining child.'

'Exactly. I thought, you see, that she wouldn't have dared offer to buy Agon off in case he told Rachel about it and Rachel turned against her. And I should think that initially that was true. But when it came to the crunch, when Agon actually proposed to Rachel and was accepted, Virginia was prepared to go to any lengths to get rid of him, regardless of the cost to herself.'

Briefly he imagined the scene the night of Virginia's death: Virginia clearing up in the kitchen, glancing out of the window and seeing Agon crossing the courtyard to his car, calling out to him on impulse, anxious to do something, anything, to get her daughter out of his clutches. 'When Agon turned down the very substantial bribe she offered she played her last remaining card and threatened to tell Rachel of her own affair with him. She must have known that if she did it would almost certainly alienate Rachel but by then she was desperate. He said he would flatly deny it had ever happened, that Rachel would certainly take his word against hers, especially in view of the fact that Virginia was so old. He ended up by telling her what he called "a few home truths". I imagine they were pretty cruel, and I think it was these insults, combined with sheer frustration that Virginia had just seen her last hope of saving Rachel fly out of the window, that made her go for him.'

'And having thrown her down the well he just put the cover back on and walked off, not knowing if she was alive or dead!'

'Precisely. It's not too difficult to believe. I should think Agon has spent his life looking after number one. If he'd gone for help, he'd have had to explain how the accident – if you could call it that – had happened in the first place. Far easier to pretend it never had.'

They were now approaching the A3 turn-off and Thanet signalled and eased into the inner lane.

Joan waited until he had negotiated the complicated round-about at the top of the slip road before saying, 'You've some-times said that in domestic murders like this it is often in the character of the victim that the seeds of his own destruction lie. Would you say that was true in this instance?'

'Partly, I suppose. But I also think that in Virginia's case circumstances conspired against her. I know that on the surface she seemed to have everything any woman could want – plenty of money, a lovely house and luxurious life-style, – but it wasn't material satisfaction she was looking for. One after another all the people she loved most were taken away from her and every time it happened she slipped a little more out of control.'

'Except her husband.'

'True. But although she always came back to him, needed him as a sort of anchor, I don't think she could have cared very deeply for him or she surely wouldn't have treated him the way she did. No, it was her children she truly loved and ultimately it was that love which was her undoing. So I suppose it was her emotional make-up and her husband's moral cowardice that proved the fatal combination.'

Joan sighed. 'And it's their children who are going to have to pay for it.'

'I'm afraid so. Poor Caroline was doomed from the moment she fell for Dick. Even if the elopement hadn't gone so drastically wrong, she'd still have spent years in an incestuous relationship and if they'd had children—'

'I simply cannot understand how her father was prepared to bury his head in the sand and just let that happen!'

But Thanet was still thinking of Caroline. 'It never ceases to amaze me how sometimes the most trivial of events can have such far-reaching consequences.'

'What do you mean?'

'Well, you wouldn't think that the fact that a grandmother returned one day early from a trip abroad would trigger off a tragic mistiming worthy of a Hardy novel, would you?'

'If you put it like that, no.'

'Hang on a minute.' They had just turned off the A3 into Roehampton Lane. 'Did Alexander give you directions to the hospital?'

'Yes.' Joan was rummaging in her handbag. 'Here they are.'

'We'd better concentrate, then.' Thanet never felt more of a country bumpkin than when driving in London.

Twenty minutes later he was turning into a hospital car park for the second time that day, but on this occasion his heart was light and full of joyous anticipation.

Laden with champagne, gifts for Bridget and the baby and the biggest teddy bear Thanet had ever seen they navigated the corridors of the hospital to the maternity ward, where they found Bridget in a little room of her own – a privilege accorded to those who had undergone a caesarian, apparently. And there was a cot beside the bed! The baby must be making good progress, then.

Thanet was also glad to see that now all the anxiety was over, although she still looked rather pale Bridget's natural ebullience had surfaced once more. Both she and Alexander were understandably glowing with pride and delight. He and Joan tiptoed across to peer into the rather unusual cot, a kind of perspex box.

'They call it a bassinet,' said Bridget. 'It's used for premature babies, to keep their temperature up.'

'She's got your mouth,' Joan said to Bridget.

Bridget laughed, then winced, clutching her abdomen. 'Oh, don't make me laugh, whatever else you do! Alexander's mum says she's got Alexander's!'

'Have you decided what to call her yet?'

'Margaret Anna.'

Joan flushed with pleasure. Margaret was her mother's name. 'Your grandmother will be thrilled.'

'But we shall call her Meg. Would you like to pick her up?'

'Oh, is that allowed?'

'Of course. Just for a few minutes anyway.'

Alexander, Thanet saw, had produced a video camera and now filmed the scene as Joan carefully lifted up the feather weight bundle and cradled her for a few minutes before handing her to Thanet.

He laid his cheek against the soft down of the baby's head and inhaled the distinctive, milky scent of new life, admired the perfection of her tiny features. He glanced at Joan and as their

246

eyes met he knew that she too was remembering the moments when they had held their own first-born, now a mother herself. Suddenly he saw himself in a new light, as a link in the chain which joined one generation to another, stretching back into the obscurity of past ages and ahead into the unknown future.

As he laid his new granddaughter back in the cot he said a brief prayer for her health and safety, then turned to watch, smiling, as Bridget began to unwrap her parcels.

At this moment, he thought, there was nowhere on earth that he would rather be.

ABOUT THE AUTHOR

Dorothy Simpson is a former French teacher who lives in Kent, England, with her husband. Their three children are all married. This is her fifteenth Luke Thanet novel. Her fifth, *Last Seen Alive*, won Britain's prestigious Silver Dagger Award. Her most recent Thanet novels are *No Laughing Matter*, *Wake the Dead*, and *Once Too Often*.